Love and LANDSCAPE

rockland falls book three

BESTSELLING AUTHOR
LACEY BLACK

Enjoy the view!

♡ Lacey
Black

Lacey Black

Love and Landscape

Rockland Falls Book 3

Lacey Black

Index

Also by Lacey Black

Rivers Edge series
Trust Me, Rivers Edge book 1 (Maddox and Avery) – FREE at
all retailers
> ~ *#1 Bestseller in Contemporary Romance*

Fight Me, Rivers Edge book 2 (Jake and Erin)
Expect Me, Rivers Edge book 3 (Travis and Josselyn)
Promise Me: A Novella, Rivers Edge book 3.5 (Jase and Holly)
Protect Me, Rivers Edge book 4 (Nate and Lia)
Boss Me, Rivers Edge book 5 (Will and Carmen)
Trust Us: A Rivers Edge Christmas Novella (Maddox and
Avery)
> ~ *This novella was originally part of the Christmas*
> *Miracles Anthology*

BOX SET – contains all 5 novels, 2 novellas, and a BONUS
short story

Bound Together series
Submerged, Bound Together book 1 (Blake and Carly)
> ~ *An International Bestseller*

Profited, Bound Together book 2 (Reid and Dani)
> ~*A Bestseller, reaching Top 100 on 2 e-retailers*

Entwined, Bound Together book 3 (Luke and Sidney)

Summer Sisters series
My Kinda Kisses, Summer Sisters book 1 (Jaime and Ryan)
> ~*A Bestseller, reaching Top 100 on 2 e-retailers*

My Kinda Night, Summer Sisters book 2 (Payton and Dean)
My Kinda Song, Summer Sisters book 3 (Abby and Levi)
My Kinda Mess, Summer Sisters book 4 (Lexi and Linkin)
My Kinda Player, Summer Sisters book 5 (AJ and Sawyer)
My Kinda Player, Summer Sisters book 6 (Meghan and Nick)
My Kinda Wedding, A Summer Sisters Novella book 7
(Meghan and Nick)

Rockland Falls series
Love and Pancakes, Rockland Falls book 1
Love and Lingerie, Rockland Falls book 2
Love and Landscape, Rockland Falls book 3

Standalone
Music Notes, a sexy contemporary romance standalone
A Place To Call Home, a Memorial Day novella
Exes and Ho Ho Ho's, a sexy contemporary romance
standalone novella

Co-Written with *NYT Bestselling* Author, Kaylee Ryan
It's Not Over

*Coming Soon from Lacey Black
With Me, a Rivers Edge Christmas Novella
Love and Neckties, Book 4 in the Rockland Falls series
Just Getting Started, Book 2 with Kaylee Ryan

Lacey Black

Chapter One

Jensen

I yawn for the fourth time in under five minutes.

Last night was rough. Ashley called three times with some sort of *issue* regarding our four-year-old son, Max. First, he wouldn't eat his dinner. An hour later, he didn't want to take a bath. Then finally, he refused to go to sleep. It was all bullshit.

By the time the third call came through just after nine, I was already shoving my tired feet into my worn work boots and was grabbing my keys. The drive to my ex-wife's house was short, considering I intentionally rented a house in the same neighborhood once I realized our marriage wasn't going to be saved. I wanted to be close to Max. I wanted as much time with him as possible. I wanted to give him a slice of normalcy, no matter what that ended up being.

Unfortunately, it ended up being two parents who still argue and fight (albeit outside of his earshot) over stupid shit we have no business fighting over. Divorce is hard, that's for damn sure. It's not how I saw my life going; definitely not what I pictured would happen before I even hit my thirties.

Now, here I am: thirty years old, co-parenting with a woman who teeters the line between hating me and wanting me back (not happening, by the way), and working myself into an early grave.

But I wouldn't trade it for anything.

Well, maybe less of the guilt trips from the ex, but everything else is on point and keeping my ass extremely busy.

Case in point: I'm driving to meet an attorney on behalf of a new client. A new client who just so happens to have purchased the biggest house in Rockland Falls. A house that has a lot of history. My history.

But I'm not getting into that now. I have too much shit to do on this gorgeous, sunny August afternoon than to take a painfully uncomfortable trip down memory lane. Right now, I have to get myself in business mode and present new landscape design plans to a man from New York. It's the first time I'm laying eyes on the entire property in more than a decade, but I know it like the back of my hand. I know it hasn't been touched since the previous owners moved out, leaving their million-dollar mansion for a new place in the Hamptons, leaving everything behind without batting an eye. That means I'll be dealing with out of control weeds and shrubbery, and probably a little damage to the foundation. No, I'm not talking the house foundation, but the ground. The dirt. The ornate stonework. The sprinkler system. It'll be a mess, but I'm up to the job.

When I approach the large gate, I find it already open. I turn my big truck onto the concrete drive and slowly make my way up to the house. Overgrown isn't exactly the word I'd use right now. The place looks like absolute shit. The shrubs hang over the drive and the grass is completely overtaken by weeds, and that's just the initial assessment from the gate. As I continue up the path, the house finally comes into view.

The Elliott mansion, or House on the Coast, as it was called when featured in *Unique Homes* magazine.

The older home stands before me, looking a little worse for wear. The drapes are all pulled shut, giving the house a dark, empty feel. The paint is chipping on the ground-to-roof pillars. The large fountain on the front lawn is full of leaves and a tree branch. There's an odd smell that tells me something has crawled off somewhere to die, possibly a raccoon or an opossum. The property looks like a war zone and has definitely seen better days.

I park my truck next to a fancy Mercedes with New York plates. A man wearing a suit more expensive than my truck payment steps out of the house and greets me in front of our vehicles. "Mr. Grayson, so wonderful to finally meet you," he says, extending his hand and offering a firm handshake.

"Likewise, Mr. Paige. And please, call me Jensen."

"David," he instructs, offering me a friendly smile. "As you can see, the property is requiring a little work. The owner has instructed me to hire a local landscaper to do whatever necessary to get the property back in tip-top shape. Most of the shrubbery needs to go, if not all of it. That's your call," he says, walking toward the fountain. "The owner would like to try to salvage the fountain, if possible, but wants to add more flower gardens, primarily here in the front," he adds, waving his hand to the grassy area around the ornate fountain, "and along the deck area in back."

I jot down notes in my book, keep pace with the attorney as we tour the front of the property. Eventually, we head toward the back and my heart starts to pound in my chest. Memories flash through my mind in a rapid-fire sequence. Much of my youth was spent here, right alongside the first girl I loved.

Pushing those thoughts away, I scan the expansive property. The pool is still there, empty except for leaves, sand, and what looks like rodent hotels made from sticks and mud. That'll be a bitch to clean. The hand-stamped, hand-laid pavers wrap around the in-ground pool, leading to the area once covered with deck chairs. Those chairs are still there, but are dirty and broken, most likely from the decade's worth of weather and sun.

"The owner wants to keep the pool, and gave specific instructions about the pool house," David says, pulling my attention away from the current state of the pool area and glancing toward the small structure just off to the side.

Lacey Black

My heart gallops in my chest as I look at the building I had been avoiding to glance at thus far. The memories come fast and hard. Shared kisses, stolen nights, and an awkward first time all entombed within those four walls. It holds my past, and being here again is like a dagger to the heart. It's a reminder of plans made and then thrown out the window. It's a shrine to the girl who stole my heart and then trampled it into the sand beneath our feet. Being here is much more painful than I had anticipated, like being surrounded by ghosts.

I don't speak as he goes through the instructions, detailing what the new owner would like done to the backyard. It'll be a massive job, a huge undertaking, and that's without the fountain, pool, and pool house work.

But I'm going to do it.

I'm taking this job in hopes of eradicating those ghosts, those memories. It's time to move on. I thought I had once, but that wasn't what I did. I put a Band-Aid over gaping wounds in hopes of fixing the problem. It didn't. The only thing that helped with the healing was Max. Even when everything with Ashley went to shit, he was the balm that helped heal my aching heart. Those scars are still very much a part of me, but having my son has given me something else to focus on.

Something greater to live for.

At the end of the meeting, I shake David's hand, promising to get him my designs by the end of the week. Since I'm the only landscape architect they've inquired about, the job is already mine. I can start as soon as the designs are complete, and then I can move on with my life and my business. Upward and onward, as my mom would say. It's time to leave the past where it belongs.

In the past.

And as soon as I complete this job, I'll be able to do just that.

* * *

Come Thursday, I pull my truck up to the home I helped purchase a few years back. The small three-bedroom ranch sits on a corner lot and features a large backyard, perfect for our young son. At the time, I thought this house was what we needed to fix our problems. Turns out, purchasing a house only comes with a whole slew of new problems. Bills to pay, upkeep to maintain, and space to fill with things. Ashley was all about the last one, going shopping as often as possible to fill our new home with crap. Often, she'd use Max as her excuse to spend every last penny we had in the checking account, but the truth is, she is materialistic as hell. Keeping up with the Joneses is one of Ashley's favorite pastimes.

I head up the walk, noting the disarray of the landscaping. Part of me wants to offer to fix it, but it's not my problem now. If Ashley doesn't want to trim the shrubs or pull the weeds from the beds I spent so much time building and maintaining, well, that's not for me to worry about anymore. She wanted the house in the divorce, and with that comes the yard work.

Knocking on the door, I smile instantly when I hear running feet on the hardwood. The door flies open and I'm greeted by my son's big toothy grin. "Daddy!" he hollers moments before throwing himself in my arms.

"Hey, Buddy, are you ready to go?" I ask, setting him down and stepping inside the front entry.

"His bag is on the table," Ashley states, walking around the corner. She's dressed to the nines in designer clothes with her dark hair curled just right and her makeup flawless. It's a little extreme for a Thursday night at home, which tells me either she's going out or she's trying to make me jealous. She's notorious for both and often combines the two. One time when she called me to come help with Max, she answered the door in a little nightgown I bought her when my older sister, Harper, opened her lingerie shop. I'm not sure what result she was looking for, but I'm pretty sure me practically ignoring her wasn't it.

The frigid bitch welcome I received the next few weeks was enough to make my balls shrivel up.

"Thanks," I reply in way of greeting, reaching for my son's bag of goodies. I have enough of everything he needs at my place, but he's four, and like most four-year-olds, he has a handful of his favorite toys that go everywhere with him.

Including his Sawyer Randall autographed baseball.

I can feel her eyes on me as I help Max get his shoes on. I know she's expecting me to say something, give her a compliment. Ashley was never shy on fishing for them, and that sure as shit hasn't changed even after the divorce. I should just grab Max's hand and head out the door, but I know that'll make it worse in the long run. She'll call all weekend and want to talk to Max or she'll text me at all hours of the night to discuss arrangements for something that could be made during normal human waking hours.

Deciding the compliment is the lesser of the two evils right now, I say, "Your hair looks nice."

There.

Simple.

Basic.

Nothing in that statement says 'I love you, let's get back together.'

"Thanks!" she coos, twirling her hair around her finger. "I just got it cut and highlighted for my date tonight."

Oh, I see where this is going.

Do not engage.

Do not engage.

"Well, we better get going. Have a good evening," I add, turning and pushing open the screen door.

"I'm sure I will! Jefferson Riley is picking me up in thirty minutes," she says, her eyes dancing with delight, but I have a feeling it's more for show than anything else. She's trying to get a rise out of me, especially when she throws out the name Jefferson Riley.

Jefferson owns Riley Landscape, the new landscaper in town. I've had a small list of clients jump over to him this past summer, considering the first thing he did was come in and undercut my prices. My loyal customers have remained steadfast, though. What gives me the leg up in the business is my Bachelor of Science in Landscape Architecture, while Jefferson carries an associate's degree in horticulture. Basically, I can do more shit than he can, primarily in the design field. I also carry an additional three years' worth of schooling debt to boot.

Fortunately, Max has already hightailed it to my truck and didn't hear about her date. Not that I'm trying to keep anything from him, but when it comes to adult shit, like the demise of our marriage and dating, I try to keep his little ears away from it. Unfortunately, his mom doesn't hold that same sense of respect. Often, she's used him with petty disagreements, filling his little ears with things she knows he'll relay to me, just to get a rise out of me.

Works every time, too.

"See you Sunday night," I holler, without so much as a backward glance. I'm sure she'll start blowing up my phone in about three minutes, considering I didn't give her the attention she was shooting for.

As soon as Max is buckled in his car seat, I hop in my truck and head the few blocks over to my place. He's chatting a mile a minute about starting preschool next week. I can't believe he's starting his second year of preschool and getting ready to turn five in a few weeks. In the past year since the divorce, he's grown leaps and bounds, becoming quite the little man. Max likes to be outside in the

dirt, like me, and has a new love for baseball. He played his first
summer of tee-ball, which basically just involved standing at the tee
and swinging until he connected.

"Are we having pizza?" he asks as I pull into the driveway.

"Maybe," I answer, drawing out the word.

"Yay!" he bellows as he unbuckles the belt. Max and I have a
standing pizza date on the night I pick him up from his mom's.

Ashley and I share joint custody of Max. It was one of the
stipulations I had upfront when it came to the divorce. She balked, at
first, crying about how she'd miss him when he was away. Well,
tough shit, lady. He's my son too! It took mediation before we were
able to come up with a joint agreement. We settled on four days her,
three days me, and vice versa the next week. Sure, that means I have
him most weekends, but I don't mind. If I have to work, and usually
I do during the heat of summer, my mom or one of my sisters helps
me out. Max loves my family and readily goes with any one of them.

My mom owns Grayson Bed and Breakfast, where I spent part
of my childhood. Originally, both of parents purchased the old,
rundown home to bring Mom's dream of turning it into a bed and
breakfast to fruition. Unfortunately, Dad couldn't keep his dick in his
pants and screwed around. They split up not too long after the B&B
took off, leaving Mom to run it solo, while raising four kids. The good
part was that we were still at home and were able to help
tremendously.

Marissa, the youngest, was the first to show real interest in the
business. She lived and breathed the B&B, even as a young child, so
it was no surprise when she returned from college and joined Mom.
Marissa does a lot of the cooking, which is her favorite part, and most
of the day-to-day dealings. Her boyfriend, Rhenn, moved in with her
recently, and together, they share the tiny cottage behind the house.

I'm not sure where their relationship is headed, but I'm pretty sure it's toward happily ever after.

Samuel is the oldest Grayson sibling. When our father left with someone half his age, Samuel stepped right up into that fatherly role. I hated it, to be honest. I was a teenager who didn't want to listen to my older brother. Samuel is blunt, a tad boring, and as anal as they come. He's completely by the rules and a total black or white guy, with no areas of gray anywhere to be seen. That's probably why he's perfect as a mortician at an area funeral home.

My sister, Harper, is two years older than me, and second in line. She's the wild child, choosing to run off and model after high school before eventually returning home to our small North Carolina town. Of course, she was completely bored working nine-to-five in an office somewhere, which is probably why she made the total leap of faith a few years back and opened her own shop. A lingerie store, to be exact. She sells all kinds of bras and panties to the old biddies of Rockland Falls, and that totally suits her personality.

Last weekend, I helped her boyfriend, Latham, move into her small house. They went to school together and have always gotten along like fire and gasoline. Completely combustible, explosive when mixed. He owns the hardware store next to her panty place. They were actually bidding against each other for the small store nestled between their respective buildings, which Latham ended up winning. In the end, though, they both won when he made a big gesture for her heart and won that too.

That leaves me, third in line of the four Grayson siblings in Rockland Falls, a town built around a small waterfall just off the coast of the Atlantic Ocean. I've always loved our quaint little town, with its town square that hosts multiple celebrations each year and friendly neighbors who'll always jump in and help if you're ever in a pinch. It's where I grew up and where I always saw myself raising a family.

Lacey Black

That picture might have blurred over the years, but I still see myself growing old here, building my business and working in the dirt, and maybe even, someday, settling down again.

Not that I'm looking, mind you, but I do like the idea of finding someone to spend the rest of my life with, helping me raise my son, and maybe even giving him a few siblings along the way.

Of course, that person's going to have to be tough as nails to deal with my ex-wife for the next fifty years. Hell, she's probably not even out there. Who would willingly jump into a relationship with a man whose ex-wife tries to drive him crazy every hour of every day? Who likes to play games where only she knows the rules and isn't about to share? Who uses people and throws them away at the drop of a hat?

Yeah, that's what I thought.

Chapter Two

Kathryn

The sun sits high in the August sky, but there's no warmth as I walk through the house for the first time. I have no clue what I was thinking, coming back here. Too many memories, both good and bad, invade my thoughts as I move from room to room, surveying what was left behind by our hasty retreat. The furniture is covered with cloth and everything else is covered in a thick layer of dust. This place will be a major undertaking to get cleaned, but I'm up for the challenge.

At least I think I am.

My attorney, David, tried to convince me to hire it out. The cleaning of such a large house is sure to take forever, but I didn't want someone else here, underfoot and going through everything. This is my house.

My memories.

The phone in my pocket vibrates again, but I ignore it. I already know it's one of two people, and frankly, I'm just not ready to deal with either of them. I came here to get away from all the chaos they've created, and hopefully, rediscover the girl I use to be. Before New York City, business dealings, and fake smiles. Before my life became about what the bottom line was and how much profit the firm made.

Back when all I cared about was painting.

Jensen.

The future.

But all of that was stolen from me, like a thief in the night.

Lacey Black

Now, here I am, at the place it all began. I try to push all thoughts of what could have been from my mind, but my heart doesn't seem to get the memo. Being here is harder than anticipated. The memories are too strong, too raw, too painful.

I hold my purse against my side and make a dash down the grand staircase. I don't even stop to reminisce about how many times I slid down the banister. Even as a teenager, I found joy in that simple act, but right now, I just need air that isn't stale and stuffy from years of being closed up and hidden from the outside world.

The moment I step outside, I can finally take a deep breath, but it's hard. The familiar panic is there, right along with the tears, as I inhale through my nose and exhale through my mouth, just like my doctor told me so many years ago. I'm all too accustomed to the rapidly beating heart, the uncontrollable shaking, and the inability to catch a breath as the panic attack sets in. They've never really been horrible, but enough to scare the crap out of me and usually anyone around me when it sets in. I've had them since I was eighteen. Since the night we left. Since I was forced to start my life over, without so much as a look back.

It takes a few minutes, but eventually, my breathing starts to even out and the pressure in my chest eases. I hate having an attack, but it's something I've learned to live with for the last twelve years. The usual trigger is a new situation in which I feel uncomfortable and uneasy, much like this. I knew this would be a trigger. I knew it would be hard. But I'm going to fight through this.

I'm super sweaty, and it isn't completely due to the August heat. Unfortunately, it's one of the side effects of my panic attacks. I hate it—no one likes someone with sweaty pits and who freaks out when she is alone in an unfamiliar location, especially in the real estate business world. It just goes to show you how much I wasn't made for corporate America.

20

When I feel like I can walk on sturdy legs, I force myself to head around to the back of the house. I step over fallen branches and can't believe how overgrown everything is. My attorney had arranged for a landscape architect to come up with a new design for the property, which was delivered to me before I got in my car and made the drive down the coast to Rockland Falls. It's going to be perfect. The company, New View Landscape and Design, incorporated the few things I had asked, while adding in a lot I hadn't. Really, I gave them free reign to redesign the entire property and grounds, utilizing their expertise and creativity.

Everything but the pool house.

As I round the corner, the expansive backyard comes into full view. The pool is in rough shape, but mostly cosmetic, at least according to the pool company that came over yesterday and inspected it. I glance down in the gaping hole as I make my way to the wooden structure in the yard. I push open the door, noticing instantly the lack of panic setting in. Instead, I feel the rush of familiarity and calm wash over me as I glance around the mostly-empty building. It's definitely in need of a little TLC, but for the most part, the building is fairing pretty well, all things considering. The building inspector said the house itself and the outbuildings were all sound, though needing some cosmetic repairs. This structure will need a new roof, which will begin next week, with many of the other repairs around the house.

All in all, this home will receive a new facelift, including a new roof, kitchen, carpeting and tile, and two new windows on the lower floor that were broken by a tree branch. All of those tasks, with the addition of a complete exterior repaint, will be completed by a contractor. An electrician will begin going through the wiring and updating a few fixtures, while a plumber makes sure everything is in proper working order with the pipes.

Everything else is on me. At first, I almost caved to David's suggestion to hire the work out, but at the end of the day, I'm looking forward to getting my hands dirty cleaning the house. Even more so, I'm excited at the thought of painting. I can practically smell the fumes and feel the splatter on my skin right now. Most people would look at an eight thousand square foot home in need of fresh paint as some sort of torture task, but not me. Personally, I can't wait to dip the brush and give the entire place a whole new appearance.

A fresh start.

I spend the next hour walking around and exploring, making a mental note of everything I need to do, and just enjoying the sound of the waves crashing against the shore. This home has always had a spectacular view of the Atlantic Ocean and is just down the road from the infamous Rockland Falls waterfall that the town was named after.

By the time the sun starts to set, I make sure the house is secure and head out to my car. It's a new cherry-red BMW that I hate, but Mother insisted I have a car to represent the family business and myself. Honestly, give me an old truck on a dirt road and I'd be happier than a bedbug in a hotel. *But Elliotts don't drive Chevrolets, Kathryn,* I hear her voice in my head for the thousandth time.

I head down the paved driveway and engage the security gate before turning on the highway and heading toward town. I'm staying in a bed and breakfast, one that isn't too far from where I grew up. I got very lucky when I called and the Clawsons had a cancellation in their reservations. Otherwise, I'm not sure I would have been able to stay at one of the many B&B's in Rockland Falls. Actually, the probability of having to pitch a tent in the backyard was very high. Thankfully, they were able to accommodate me for three nights. That gives me three whole days to get a bedroom and bathroom ready for me to use, as well as the temporary kitchen that the contractor is setting up for me.

The drive to the bed and breakfast is familiar, yet so foreign at the same time. Houses are the same but the landscape has changed. New families have taken up residence, different businesses occupy the storefronts, and unknown people loiter the sidewalks and city park. I feel like an outsider in the place I spent eighteen years of my life, and that leaves a hollow pit deep in my gut.

As I pull alongside the road in front of the Clawsons', I can't help but dread this moment. If they recognize me, I'll be bombarded with a million questions I'm not prepared to answer, and it'll be around town before the dinner dishes are cleared. Sure, I knew coming back to Rockland Falls wouldn't mean I was anonymous, but I was hoping to keep it hidden for a few days anyway. A week would be pushing it.

The woman I remember as Janice Clawson appears on the porch, waving. Whether I'm ready or not, I slide from my car and grab my bag before making my way up the stairs. "You must be Kathryn. It's lovely to have you stay with us, honey."

She pushes open the door and steps back for me to enter. Inside, the place has a formal feel to it. Floral curtains and wingback chairs, antique pieces, and a formal dining room. Nothing like the Grayson Bed and Breakfast. Of course, it's been more than a decade since I was inside it, but the Grayson home had a friendly, cozy feel to it. This one reminds me of my childhood, actually, and makes me worried I'll wrinkle the linens just by looking at them.

"Here's a pamphlet with all of the details for your stay," Janice says, handing me a brochure. "Are you new to the area?" she asks casually while running my credit card.

Her innocent statement is confirmation that she doesn't remember who I am. It probably helps my last name has changed since I was in Rockland Falls last. Plus, no one would expect Kathryn

Elliott-Dunnington to stay at a bed and breakfast when she owns the largest home in the county.

"New enough," I reply with a smile, not really wanting to tip her off.

"Well, if you have any questions, please don't hesitate to ask. There are several local shops and touristy places to visit while you're in town, and I always recommend taking a trip out to the falls. Our town was named after it, you know," she says with a warm, grandmotherly grin as she completes our transaction.

Janice continues to talk about the history of the bed and breakfast as she leads me up the stairs and toward my room. Each one is named after a president and boasts a large four-poster bed and private bathroom. My room has a small sitting area by the window, something I'm sure I'll take full advantage of.

When she leaves me to my own accord, I place my satchel bag on the small table and remove the contents. Everything the lawyer gathered before my trip, as well as all the legal papers I've reviewed a million times in the last six months. Yet, here I am, pulling them out and scanning them again. First, the will. Then, divorce papers.

Those have yet to be signed.

My phone rings again, a reminder of *why* those papers haven't been autographed by both parties. The urge to hit ignore again is strong, but I know he'll just keep calling. When those calls go unanswered, he'll find another way to get what he wants, and having Charles Dunnington III show up in Rockland Falls is exactly what I *don't* want to happen. This is my new, fresh start, and nowhere in that picture is the man I'm trying to detach myself from.

Sighing audibly, I grab the phone and click accept.

"Finally! I've been trying to reach you for two days. I was about to send the dogs out for you," Charles exhales dramatically, making me roll my eyes.

"Well, good evening to you too. No need to send the dogs. As you can tell, I'm alive and well, and also not any of your concern any longer," I remind for the thousandth time.

Charles huffs another exaggerated breath. "Don't be like that, Kathryn. Sarcasm and attitude are beneath you."

"See, that's where you're wrong, Charles. It's exactly where I am."

Again, a sigh. "I made a mistake, Kathryn. You've made your point, now come home."

My blood starts to boil. "A mistake? A mistake?" I ask, my voice elevating with each word. "A mistake is forgetting to pick up the dry cleaning. Screwing your secretary on your desk isn't a mistake, Charles."

I'm greeted with silence.

"You and I both know the love ran out a long time ago," I whisper, hating how those words still affect me.

"It was never about love, and you know it. We're a perfect match, darling."

"On paper."

"Many couples have this type of marriage, Kathryn," he says, reminding me of all of the marriages of convenience in our circle of friends.

"And they all screw their secretaries every chance they get," I state boldly, knowing my words are a billion times true. Most of our friends are accustomed to this lifestyle, where the husband runs around with someone half his age and the wife screws the pool boy. He comes home and gives her a bigger diamond than the previous one, and they all forget no one is happy and they drink their wrongdoings away with hundred-year-old scotch.

The difference was I thought it was love. But the truth is, I just *wanted* it to be love. I wanted Charles to replace the memories that kept me up at night. I *wanted* him to prove to me that he was different than all of the other rich assholes out there. Unfortunately, what I wanted and what I got were two totally different things. Charles ended up being exactly like everyone else, including the screwing his secretary bit.

"Listen, I'm tired. I've been on the road all day and I'm ready to turn in. We tried, Charles, but it didn't work. I don't want that lifestyle anymore. I deserve better," I whisper, hating I've resorted to begging to finalize our divorce. We've gone round and round for the last few months, but each time, Charles halts the process with some bullshit filing or delay.

"For the record, I don't want this," he says quietly, the resolve evident in his word.

"Well, I do."

He exhales and I can practically picture him sitting at his desk, running his hand through his hair in frustration. "What am I going to tell everyone?" he says softly, almost absently.

What I want to say is, "Tell them you were caught fucking your secretary and your wife didn't accept your peace offering." That she felt relief mixed with her anger the moment she heard the fake moans of pleasure from the bottle-blonde bent over his desk. Fake, I would know. I've faked for the last eight years.

Instead, I say, "I don't care what you tell them. Blame me for all I care. Just sign the papers, Charles. I've already given you the company. This is the final step."

It's true. I gave him the company I worked for since graduating college. My dad specialized in high-end real estate and his company grew leaps and bounds when we relocated to New York City. He was always based out of there, but we lived in Rockland Falls. Daddy flew back and forth my entire childhood, until one night, it all ended. We moved.

After my college graduation, I took my position beside him in the company. He had several agents beneath him, including Charles Dunnington III. To my father, he was the son he never had. Smart, driven, and wooing his young daughter. My father nudged me in his direction every chance he got until finally, I caved. Dating Charles was like dating any rich asshole. Gifts out the ass and fancy dinners that cost more than some people's used cars. But deep in my heart, I knew it wasn't what I wanted. I knew Charles wasn't the man for me. Yet, I refused to listen. He was a balm, a salve to cover the gaping hole in the chest I received when I left Rockland Falls.

Now, I'm looking to right my wrong.

I'm ready to start over.

I'm ready to live my life on my terms, no one else's.

"I've already signed, Kathryn. They were filed last week. I was just hoping you'd give me one final chance, but it looks like it's not going to happen."

The relief and joy mixing in my chest brings tears to my eyes. "Thank you," I choke out, trying to keep the emotions at bay.

"Just know you can't come back now. I'm not taking you back in, Kathryn. This is your decision and it's final," he says sternly.

I roll my eyes, wishing he could see it. He always hated when I'd do that, especially in public. "I'm not worried about ever having the urge to crawl back to you, Charles."

"There's no reason to be snippy. You want this divorce, fine. I have granted you this one last wish."

Again, an eye roll. "Whatever." It's not like I've ever asked him for anything other than the divorce. Well, and maybe faithfulness, but hey, you can't win them all, right?

"I'm sure your attorney will send you the final papers soon," he says as he hangs up without saying goodbye.

"Finally," I breathe a sigh of relief, firing off a quick text message to my attorney to be on the lookout for the signed documents. I may have to fly back to New York one final time, but that's fine. As long as it happens, that's all I'm asking for. It'll be worth the trip back.

For now, I can breathe a little easier.

I set the copy of the divorce papers aside and grab the landscaping designs for the property. They're stunning and I find myself staring at the simple lines and stark beauty in the colors. My mind is transported back to a time when Jensen would be digging in the earth, up to his elbows in dirt and mud.

I wonder what ever happened to him and his dream. Did he go to school and start his own company? Did he get married and have kids? The painful pang in my chest hits hard. I rarely allow myself to think of that. Of him.

But being home isn't helping. Being in Rockland Falls only reminds me what I used to have and what was thrown away in the middle of the night. It was never my decision, but I was the one to live with the consequences and the damage done.

I was alone.

Chapter Three

Jensen

Come Monday morning, the jobsite's booming. My full-time employee, Jonas, is meeting me here, along with my new hire, Wes. Today's his first day, and I'm anxious to see what he can do. We have a big undertaking here, but on top of that, we have dozens of other customers to maintain. My after-school kid, Brody, will continue to help with the small mowing jobs, with Jonas' help, which will leave a big chunk of the heavy lifting here to the newbie and me.

I park my truck amongst the mix of other contractors. There's a local plumbing operation on-site, as well as a family-owned construction business whose job is the massive kitchen overhaul. Even my sister's boyfriend, Rhenn, is here with the electrical company he works for. It's definitely all hands on deck for such a massive a project at the Elliott mansion.

What I don't see yet is the mini excavator I rented to help dig up some of the overgrown small trees and shrubs. The plan for this week is to clear out a lot of the old landscaping and start fresh. Most of the large trees will remain, though pruned back to be more appealing. The use of the mini is on my schedule for tomorrow and Wednesday, and even though I rented it for forty-eight hours, the company I get it from is good about delivering the machine the day prior.

With my coffee mug in hand, I slide out of my truck and head to the tailgate. I pull my plans and clipboard out and set them down on my makeshift desk, ready to get this huge project started. I ignore the pull I feel to look at the house. There's nothing there for me anymore, and no reason to torture myself with the memories that house holds.

"Hey, Jensen," I hear over my shoulder and find Jonas and Wes heading my way.

"Hey, guys," I reply, sticking out my hand for my new hire.

Wes is a hair shorter than my six foot two inch height and a few pounds heavier. He comes highly recommended by the horse farmer outside of town, where he worked as a part-time hired hand for the last few years. With my business expanding in Rockland Falls and the surrounding areas, I've been in desperate need of more help for a while, but haven't bothered to sit down and actually take the time to hire someone. Instead, I've been working myself into an early grave doing most of it alone. Now, with Max in preschool and approaching kindergarten next fall, I want to be able to attend his school functions without falling asleep where I stand.

"Ready to get started," Wes says, placing his hand in mine and giving it a firm shake.

"We have a large project here. It's not going to be an easy job to cut your teeth on, Wes, but I think you'll learn a lot from this one job alone," I tell him, taking a sip of my coffee from my mug. I practically live on caffeine.

"I'm excited," he responds with a decisive nod.

"Yeah, it won't be long at all before you learn Jensen's favorite phrase is 'What in the living fuck?'" Jonas laughs.

I sigh, knowing he speaks the truth. When shit starts to go down on the jobsite (and it always does), my reply is always the same. Unfortunately, it's been a hard habit to break when I'm around Max. I've had my ass chapped several times by Ashley when our son comes home and repeats the phrase.

"Let's hope Wes doesn't hear that for at least the first few days," I reply with a smirk.

Jonas blows out an exaggerated gasp. "Try a few minutes," he teases, making me smile at his goodhearted joshing.

"Whatever," I reply. Straightening up, I turn to my two full-timers. "We have a massive project. Heavy machinery will be here sometime today, and our first task is going to be to clear the site of everything we're replacing. There's some dirt work too, reshaping beds and building a new retaining wall around the entire front," I say, falling easily into work-mode.

Wes and Jonas listen intently as I go through the plan, detailing the new areas we're building and what needs to be removed. Jonas will help where he can, but his job this week will be to maintain our current clientele. Sure, there's a lot of simple mowing jobs, but when you're spread out over the entire county and everyone has a different schedule, based on their needs, it's a juggle to keep it all straight.

"Jonas, I'm going to have you help me mark everything with Wes's help. Then you can head out and we'll start clearing," I add, finishing off my coffee and setting the mug in the cupholder in my truck cab. With my clipboard in hand and colored paint ready to go, the three of us head out to start marking.

It takes us just over an hour to walk the property and mark everything out. One of my professors in college suggested the colored paint technique and I couldn't have been more pleased. It's a hell of a lot better than trying to decipher codes or markings. The basis of it is I use a few different colors of paint to put an X on the tree or shrub. Red means remove completely, blue means trim, and purple means relocate, and green means leave untouched. It's a simple system that has never failed when I've been off working somewhere else. Jonas knows what needs to be done based on the colored markings.

When it comes time for Jonas to head out, Wes and I throw on our work gloves and get ready to start clearing. I'm in a zone, moving easily in the thick, overgrown weeds and mountains of decaying leaves. This is probably the worst part of any job, but once you get past the physical aspect, I love it. The removal of the old means I'm making way for the new. That's what I look forward to the most. Getting my hands in the dirt and giving space a new life.

It's about noon when my phone rings. I almost ignore it, but as the business owner, I rarely afford myself the luxury. I spot Jonas' name on the screen, drop my gloves, and answer the phone.

"Hey, bossman, we have a problem. Mr. Rhodes showed me some concerning markings on his walnut tree in back. I think you need to take a look at this," Jonas says, the concern evident in his voice.

"What in the living fuck?" I mutter to myself, rubbing my hand over my forehead. I can already tell this phone call is an issue. No, not the call itself, but the reasoning behind it. That's never good when Jonas calls me about the health of a tree.

There are several active tree watches in North Carolina right now that are cause for concern, but the fact that it's a walnut tree tells me it's bad. The walnut twig beetle is a killer with no pesticides available. If this tree is infected, that means the tree is coming down.

Trying not to get ahead of myself just yet, I reply, "I'm on my way. I'll leave Wes here clearing. If it looks like we may be a while at the Rhodes place, I'll send you back here to help him."

"Sounds good, bossman. Sorry to pull you away from the job," he says before signing off.

"Shit," I mumble, sliding my phone back into the clip at my hip.

"Problems?" Wes asks, taking a drink of water and breathing deeply. Clearing is hard work, as Wes is learning real quickly.

"Yeah, there's something going on with one of the big old trees at one of our clients' houses. Jonas is concerned. I need to head over and check it out. If I'm going to be long, I'll send Jonas back over to help you," I tell my newbie.

This is a good test for him. Even though I hate leaving him alone on his first day, the work doesn't require supervision. It's basic clearing of the old shit. Even though he'll be alone, I know about how long it should take him on this task. Jonas will know too, so if we get back and it's not to where we need it to be, then I know he didn't work hard enough while alone.

"Keep going on these front beds, and if you get this all cleared before one of us gets back, you can head to the back. Start with the ones along the back terrace first. Since I have to take my truck, make a pile over by those hedges. We'll load it all in the back of my truck when we return," I tell him, shoving my gloves into my back pocket and heading toward my truck. "Oh, and take a thirty-minute lunch break. We usually stay on-site, but if you need to leave, just shoot me a message. Sign in and out on the timesheet on the clipboard," I add.

"I brought a lunch, so I'll just chill under the shade of the trees," he says, waving me off.

I hope Wes works out. I'm definitely in need of good help, but admittedly, trusting someone with my business doesn't come easily. In fact, it's fucking difficult as hell. I built my business for three years before I hired Jonas, which ended up being the best thing that happened to me. Yet, here I am, still struggling to keep up with the job, as well as being there for Max. Sharing custody with Ashley was the only option for me, but I knew my job would take a hit. I'm managing, but it's hell on the sleep schedule, you know? Especially when Ashley's as high maintenance as ever.

Not my problem anymore, yet it is.

She's Max's mom, and we share the parenting obligations, but that doesn't mean it's easy. Hell, most days, I'd rather drop her off in the desert and tell her "good luck." But I can't do that. I won't do that.

Lacey Black

Max needs her. So, I'm stuck dealing with her drama and her constant nagging. At least until he's eighteen…

Heading down the driveway, I can't help but glance back at the house in the rearview. Years ago, my life was completely entangled with this house. I had always envisioned it going one way, but that dream changed overnight. Instead, I had to pick myself up off the ground and start over. That's where Ashley came into play. No, our relationship wasn't always bad, but it was happy, at least for a while.

As I pull onto the highway, I meet a fancy car getting ready to turn into the homestead. My heart starts to pound in my chest when I spy the long, blonde hair pulled back in a ponytail. Part of her face is covered by sunglasses, but my gut still clenches. It's probably just because of the hair. It's because I'm here, at the Elliott mansion. It's the only reason I feel the pull. It's memories.

The new owner is here.

Not Kate.

* * *

Yep, the tree has to come down. The walnut twig beetles have already penetrated the bark and cankers are forming. The result is an early case of thousand canker disease, and yes, the entire tree must come down, eventually. Right now, with the help of our county pest management agency, we've set traps on the tree and surrounding ones that'll remain for six weeks. Once that's complete, we will have to remove the tree, since there is no treatment for this type of beetle. The local agency is handling the survey of surrounding trees, but so far, we've been lucky and haven't found anything. The important thing is not to move the wood. When the tree comes down, we'll either grind or burn the entire thing on-site.

This job took longer than anticipated, considering the phone calls I had to make, so Jonas went back to the Elliott mansion to work with Wes. All of his afternoon jobs were pushed back, though my part-time after-school employee, Brody, was able to jump in and complete some of the mowing jobs.

By the time I'm finally heading back to the jobsite, it's nearing five. My entire day was shot at the Rhodes' place, dealing with their infested tree. Now, I'm more than ready to kick off my boots, pop the top on a cold beer, and relax watching mindless television, but I have to check the big site first.

The first thing I notice when I pull in is that the mini excavator was delivered. That means I'll definitely spend my day tomorrow pulling the shrubs and digging up the old beds. That'll keep Wes and me busy for a while. My blood starts to pump as I think about getting in the seat of that machine. I love digging in the dirt, whether it's with my own hands or a bucket on an excavator.

I hop out of my truck and spy Jonas and Wes heading my way. They're both smiling, thankfully, and I'll take that as a good sign. "Hey, bossman," Jonas hollers as he approaches.

"Well, how'd it go?" I ask, grabbing the clipboard and checking today's progress. When I glance up, surprised to see how much clearing they accomplished, I encounter matching grins.

"Not too shabby, huh?" Jonas boasts.

"Great job," I tell them both, proud of the two of them for getting the majority of our handwork accomplished today. "Tomorrow, Jonas, you'll work on your list," I add, pulling a printed sheet out of my clipboard. "Wes, you'll be back here with me."

"Sounds good," Wes replies, reaching over and offering me a hand.

Placing my hand in his, I say, "You did well today."

"Thanks. I'm happy to be here. See you tomorrow," he says, throwing a wave and heading toward his truck.

When he pulls away, I finally speak to my right hand. "Everything went well?"

Jonas blows out a breath with his chuckle. "Man, that guy is a machine. I had to practically force him to take breaks. I don't know if he was just trying to make a good impression, but he worked hard. I hope he works out. He seems like a good dude, and I enjoyed trying to keep pace with a young guy."

I blow out an exasperated breath. "You're like six years older than he is," I remind my employee and friend. Jonas just turned thirty-two earlier this year and has been with me for four years. He's a single father of two who went through his divorce about a year before I did. It was nice to have someone to talk to, who had been through what I was going through. Between him and my buddy, Garrett, they made sure I tipped back a few beers and always had a ride home when necessary.

"Yeah, well, he's got a lot more energy than I do," Jonas states, taking a cold bottle of water from the cooler I keep in my truck bed.

"He's not chasing two kids around at night."

"Good point," he laughs, finishing off the bottle.

"How'd everything else go today?" I ask, nodding toward the house.

"Carpenters headed out about thirty minutes ago. They got the kitchen gutted and hauled away. Rhenn came out earlier and told me to tell you hi. He was hoping to catch you, but promised to give you shit tomorrow," Jonas adds with a grin.

Rhenn's shacking up with my little sister, Marissa, and even though I love giving them hell, I actually really like him and am thrilled that they're so happy together. "Oh, I'm sure he's got something to say."

"He spent a little time with the homeowner before he left. He's adding some outdoor lighting that wasn't on the original plans," he says, pulling my attention.

"They're adding more lighting? Where?" I ask, pulling out my drawings and laying them out on the tailgate.

"Here," he says, pointing to the area at the very back of the property. I made a quick note on the drawing since it'll be my job to fix the groundwork after they bury the wiring. "So have you met her yet?" I glance at my friend, not really sure who he's referring to. "The homeowner. She's hot," he adds with a smirk.

"No," I reply, rolling up my drawings and placing them back in the truck cab. "I dealt with her lawyer through the entire thing. I think I ran into her when I was leaving earlier, but we haven't officially met yet."

"Seriously, smokin' hot, bossman. She brought out lemonade to us all. I'm kinda hoping she's here every day. Damn sure makes the afternoons a little brighter, if you know what I mean," Jonas says, a wide smile on his face.

My gut clenches and for some unknown reason, I find myself unrolling the drawings. They were approved a week ago by K. Dunnington. I had assumed the homeowner was a man, but now that I look at the handwriting, it's delicate and curvy. I don't know why I can't seem to shake the feeling I'm missing something here. "Did you meet the husband?"

"Nope, never showed up. I assume he's at work. You can't afford a house like this and the massive work we're all doing and not have a husband working his ass off somewhere," Jonas adds, and while I understand his point, that's not always true. There are plenty of women who work their asses off, make good money, and could probably afford a place like this. Though, I do admit, it would be difficult for anyone on a single income.

"All right, I'll update tomorrow's work list for you, since you had the setback today. It'll be at the office in the morning," I tell my employee.

"Sounds good, bossman. No Max tonight?"

"Not tonight. He went back with his mom last night." I don't tell him I already miss the hell out of my son. If I could, I'd have him with me all day, every day.

"I thought about heading up to have a drink later. You wanna come?"

"No, I better not. I have to update the schedules for the rest of the week and make a few client calls," I tell him. The office side of work takes a lot of time, and being in the peak busy season, I'm busting my balls just to keep up with it all.

"'Kay. Don't work too hard," he teases, a smile on his face, knowing full well I'll be up late again tonight.

"See ya," I say, heading toward my truck cab. Before I get there, I decide to head back and check the spot where Rhenn will be installing lighting. If I know my future brother-in-law as well as I think I do, he probably already has it laid out with paint. I can check out the markings and make sure it aligns with what I already have in my head.

With my drawings in hand, I head toward the backyard, the sound of the ocean becoming more pronounced as I go. Everyone's already gone for the day, but they left their messes behind. There's material all over the back deck for the kitchen remodel and two new windows leaning against the siding. There's a large dumpster in the driveway for all of the old building material, but there's still a small pile of scrap by the back door.

I glance around quickly, confirming my guys cleaned up after themselves before heading to the very back of the property. Pink paint marks the route Rhenn will use to dig a trench and run the wiring for the new lights. When I get to the back, I can already see what they're envisioning. There's a small clearing with a breathtaking view of the ocean. I can practically picture the small benches or swing back here, with a few lights to illuminate the path. Solid idea in adding it, I agree, pleased to enhance this area of the yard. I make a few notes on my drawings, and roll them back up.

As I get ready to turn and head back to my truck, a familiar scent blows in with the breeze. It's gardenia and honeysuckle, and the sweet aroma reminds me of a happier time. The memories come flooding back and I hate the longing that starts deep in my chest. Closing my eyes, I let the salty breeze wash over me, fighting against the reminiscences. God, I hate I can still smell her, feel her as if she were standing right beside me.

Opening my eyes, I gaze out at the sea, wishing things could have been different. No, I'm not wishing away my son. He's the best part of my life and I wouldn't go back and do everything over again if it meant losing him, but wishing for…closure. Needing it, actually. I never got it. Never heard why she left in the middle of the night. Never was told what I did wrong. Never had the chance to make it right.

Maybe being back here, I'll finally have it.

Knowing I have a ton of work to do and only a little daylight left, I slowly turn my back to the ocean, desperately looking to put some distance between me and the honeysuckle. When I turn around, I see a woman. Her long blonde hair is piled high on her head and her gorgeous hazel eyes are wide in shock. Soft pink lips are gaped open as she stands not ten feet away from me, a look of surprise and horror written all over her beautiful face. She's as stunning as I remember in my dreams. She stands there, the house she grew up in as the backdrop, as tears fill her eyes. It's hard to breathe and even harder to keep myself from rushing to her, taking her in my arms.

But I don't.

I can't.

As much as I want to, I don't move a muscle.

The entire world has shifted.

Everything has changed.

My Kate has come home.

Chapter Four

Kathryn

First thing I noticed when I found the man standing in my backyard was his posture. He was tense, rigid even, as he gazed out at the vast ocean, but there was something so…familiar about him. He's tall—very tall, actually—with lean hips and long legs. My mind instantly flashes back to the man in the truck from earlier today. He felt familiar too.

It must be this place. I knew being home would conjure up ghosts I wasn't prepared to deal with, but needed to vanquish just the same. This is my chance, my do-over, and if that means I'm going to have to go to war with memories to finally live my life as my own, then so be it.

That's what Dad wanted.

Tears burn my eyes and I force them away. I will not cry. I've done enough of that, and I'm not about to start now. That's why I'm out here, actually. It was time to get out of the house for a while. The sandy beach and the rolling waves were calling my name, so I found a pair of flip-flops that would have made my mother have a coronary, and headed out the back door.

I noticed the man right away. I waited for the familiar fear to bubble in my chest, the anxiety to take over, but it never came. Instead, I felt…relief. It's weird the way your body can respond and the way your mind can ease just by being in the presence of a stranger. I watched him for a few moments as he wrote on a rolled up drawing he carried with him. I could sense he was part of a team, most likely the landscaping or electrical.

Then he gazed up at the sun and let the warm, salty breeze blow across his face. I knew what he was doing, because I had done the exact same thing the night before. It was the reason I talked to the electrician about adding a light back there. I could already envision a small private seating area, complete with shrubs and potted flowers. A private outside reading nook, as I deemed it.

Or maybe I'll use it for something else.

I don't let my mind go there. It's hard enough to get through the day without thinking about the *other* thing I had lost all those years ago.

My gift.

Something draws me to this man, this stranger. I find myself taking tentative steps in his direction until I'm standing about ten feet away. That's when he slowly turns around and my heart stops beating. The shock steals the very breath I breathe as blue eyes the same color as the ocean stare down at me.

My Jensen.

He looks the same, yet so very different. His eighteen-year-old baby face is replaced with stubble and tanned skin from spending time in the sun. Subtle lines crease the corner of his eyes and his full lips are dry and cracked. His shoulders have muscles he didn't have back when, and through his tight T-shirt, I can see hard planes and swells of years of manual labor. Oh, yes, the years have been good to Jensen Grayson.

Suddenly, I find it hard to inhale. My vision starts to blur and the familiar panic starts to sweep in. My chest burns as I close my eyes, willing the panic to subside. It doesn't, of course, and I place my hand out, needing to touch the ground. Strong arms wrap around my upper arms and help guide me down. The grass tickles my legs, but it's a welcome feeling as I concentrate on breathing in and out.

"Look at me, Kate," he says, his voice strong and firm, yet brimming with fear.

When I open my eyes, I'm comforted by those deep blue orbs that are both gentle and pained. "Can't. Breathe." I pant, my chest working hard.

"Keep your eyes on me," he whispers softly, holding my gaze with his intensity. "That's it, Butterfly, deep breaths. In through your nose and out through your mouth, nice and slow." I do as he instructs, keeping my eyes locked on his. "You got it," he adds when the pressure in my chest starts to subside.

It's then I realize his hands are rubbing gentle circles over my upper arms. His touch causes a reaction to my body, but it's not like the panicked one from a few moments ago. "Thank you," I whisper hoarsely as my breathing starts to even out. The spots in my vision are gone, leaving mortification in its wake.

"You okay?" he asks softly, the deep timbre of his voice jolting my frayed nerve endings like never before.

I nod my head and close my eyes. "I will be." The words are out of my mouth before I can stop them, and to be honest, I'm not sure if they're meant for him or me. I *will* be okay. After the divorce, the move, and still dealing with the aftermath of my father's death, I'll be okay. Now this? Running into the love of my life in my backyard after more than a decade? I'm not one-hundred-percent sure I'll be okay, but I'm hoping that I will. Someday.

"What happened there?" he asks, taking a seat across from me and crossing his legs.

Embarrassment tinges my cheeks. "I, uh, sometimes have panic attacks."

His mouth opens in shock and slowly nods his head. "Since when?"

Since when? How about since I left Rockland Falls in the middle of the night without warning or so much as a goodbye? How's that for an answer?

Instead, I go with, "A while."

Again, he slowly nods his head as if he's just taking it all in. Me, showing back up in town and on the job he's apparently working, no less. I'm sure he's reeling from this revelation as much as I am. Of course, he didn't dive full-on into a panic attack. No, those little treats are just for me.

Jensen stares at me, his blue eyes seeming to assess everything about me. I wonder what he sees, but am too afraid to ask. I'm sure he doesn't like the woman sitting before him any more than I do. Sure, she's still a pretty girl, but I'm willing to bet that's clouded with hurt and deceit. Yes, I deceived him the day I told him I loved him and wanted to spend the rest of my life with him. A lie? Hell no, but a deceit nonetheless since it didn't happen.

I open my mouth, but no words come out. I'm sorry seems too cliché, even if I truly am. His gaze drifts up and over me. I'm not sure if he's staring off into space or at the massive house in the background.

Finally, he seems to take pity on my inability to form words. "So, you're the new owner?" he asks, still looking over my shoulder.

"Yeah. My dad left it to me," I state, wondering if he even heard the words over the pounding of my heart.

This draws his eyes back to me in confusion. "Left it to you?"

I nod. "In his will."

A pained look crosses his face. "Jeezus, Kate, I'm sorry. I didn't know."

I give him a small smile. "It's okay." I glance over my shoulder at the structure behind me. "Six months ago. Massive heart attack."

"And your mom?"

I roll my eyes as I turn back to face him. "She's fine. Living in the new penthouse in New York City she bought from Justin Timberlake." She sold the home she had shared with my father almost as soon as he was buried. Mother claimed she couldn't live in the house anymore without him, but I think she just wanted to be closer to the action. Mother thrived on attention and the who's who of New York City, and the family home they owned in a gated community wasn't good enough for her.

His eyebrows shoot to his hairline. "Well, I'm still very sorry for your loss. I wish I had known," he says almost absently.

I don't reply, because, frankly, I don't know what to say. Should I have called him? It had been more than eleven years since we had talked, and I didn't want the first thing I said to him to be about my dad's passing. Besides, I doubt he would have come to the services. They were in New York, after all. A long way from Rockland Falls, North Carolina.

"I would have paid my respects. He was always good to me," Jensen says, the slight Southern drawl of his North Carolinian accent so pronounced. God, I've missed the sound of his voice.

"He liked you," I whisper, the memories of my past threatening to make a revisit.

"He was a good man. Tough, but fair."

Nodding, I sit there silently, trying to figure out what to say next. Again. There's so much I want to say, yet I have no clue how to actually say the words. My mind is still reeling and my body humming with something that feels a lot like desire, though it's been so damn long, I'm afraid I wouldn't know what that feels like anymore. Yet, here I am, so close to the first boy I ever loved, and my entire body is alive. We're sitting so close I can smell the mixture of sweat and soap off his skin. Instantly, I'm reminded of high school

Jensen—the boy who played in the dirt but kissed me like I was the only girl on the face of the Earth.

I'm pulled from those thoughts by the vibrating of a cell phone. It's not mine, since I left it sitting on the kitchen counter. Even though Charles agreed to the divorce, he's not-so-subtly trying to remind me of how amazing we were together via text message. The problem is we never really were amazing or even great. Sure, we had our moments, but I truly believe we had both settled. He wanted the Stepford Wife, and I wanted what I had lost.

It didn't work out for either of us.

Jensen pulls his phone from his pocket and glances at the screen. He goes rigid the moment he sees the message, his fingers hovering over the screen.

"Everything okay?" I ask.

My question seems to cause him more tension as his entire body tightens. He looks from the screen to me, as if he's not sure what he's supposed to do. "Yeah, uh, I just need to make a quick call." I watch as he jumps up and heads back to where I originally found him.

The moment he greets the person who answers, I stand up and go to move away. His voice carries over the sound of the distant waves, though I can tell he's trying to be quiet. "What do you mean you can't find the baseball? I packed it in his bag." He's silent for a few moments as he listens to whoever's on the other line. "Fine, I'll run home and check." Jensen ends the call and stares out at the water.

I should definitely move away as if I wasn't just eavesdropping on his call, but for some reason, my feet are rooted in place. In fact, instead of stepping back, I find myself walking forward—toward him. Once I'm only a few feet away, realization sets in.

He'll check when he gets home.

Meaning…someone needs something, something at his house.

Probably a house they share.

I don't recall a ring on his finger, but that doesn't mean anything. A lot of guys don't wear a wedding ring, especially those around machinery or who do manual labor. While I had always prayed for happiness and love for Jensen, now that I'm staring at him in the face, the pit of my stomach feels like it fell to my feet. It's an odd feeling knowing your life didn't turn out the way you had hoped, but the one person you always wished would find a happy life has found just that.

Without you.

I swallow over the lump in my throat as he turns around. Since I had walked toward him, I'm standing uncomfortably close, but he doesn't seem to notice. He slips his phone back in his pocket and grabs the discarded clipboard near his feet. "I need to go," he says, yet doesn't move a muscle.

Nodding quickly, I try to push back the tears that burn my eyes. *I will not cry, I will not cry.* "Of course. It sounds like your wife needs you at home." Saying the words aloud burns my throat and pulverizes my heart.

"Ex-wife," Jensen says, a bite in his tone.

My heart stops beating as I glance up at those impossibly blue eyes. "Oh."

"Ashley and I have been divorced just over a year," he says, pulling his phone from his pocket and swiping at the screen. I'm not sure what he's doing until he hands me the device. When I glance down, I see a smiling Jensen holding a smaller version of himself. I instantly smile at the obvious love this father and son have for each other.

"Max. He's four."

"He's you," I reply, still smiling down at the image on the screen. They look so much alike it's almost scary.

"He is," Jensen replies, his own smile evident in his words. When he takes the phone from my extended hand, our fingers graze, shooting electric currents through my bloodstream. His eyes widen, as if maybe he felt it too, but it's quickly dashed away as his face turns serious. "I need to head home. Max is missing his favorite baseball and I need to see if he left it at my place."

I nod, unable to find words. A deep sadness suddenly sweeps in at the thought of Jensen leaving. We've barely reconnected, but I'm not ready to let him go. There's still so much to say, so much to talk about.

"We'll be back at seven tomorrow morning. We made great progress on the removal today. Tomorrow we should have the rest of the old cleared out and ready to plant new," he says, standing tall and easily slipping into work mode.

Of course.

That's why he's here.

"Good," I reply, my voice hoarse, as I wrap my arms around my chest to ward off the sudden chill.

He glances my way once more, his own internal battle evident in those soulful blue eyes. I want to speak, but I just can't. For someone who's made a decent living off of bullshitting with words, I can't believe how much I've been struggling today. Yet, I know what the reason is, and he's standing just over six feet tall in front of me.

"I'm sure I'll see you tomorrow," he says, watching my every move.

Again, I nod. I seem to be doing that a lot lately.

He doesn't say goodbye, a realization that hurts more than I could have possibly imagined, but turns and heads toward the side of the house. I only watch him go for a few seconds before it becomes too painful. Instead, I turn to the ocean and watch the waves crash along the sandy shore.

It feels like hours as I stand there and watch the water, but in reality, it's mere seconds. Seconds I can sense eyes on me. Unable to fight it any longer, I slowly turn and find Jensen standing at the edge of the house, next to a large pile of fresh dirt. But he's not looking at the earth. No, he's watching me.

Our eyes connect for several heartbeats before he finally turns and walks away.

Breathing a deep sigh of relief, I gaze back to the ocean, the sound of his truck firing to life echoing off the waves. I stand there for a while, running through the day, the construction, and finally, seeing Jensen for the first time in more than a decade.

He was always the best looking boy in school, but now, Jensen Grayson is all man. A gorgeous man, at that. He obviously got married to a woman named Ashley and has a son, Max. The happiness that radiated through the wallpaper photo on his phone was evident, and reminds me of a time when I used to be standing beside him in photographs.

Pushing those thoughts aside, I head back to the house. I have a lot of cleaning I want to do yet this evening and more furniture to go through. Some of it'll be off to the resale shop soon, but there are a few pieces I'm keeping. Yet, as much as I try to forget finding him standing in my backyard, I just can't seem to move past it. Or the look on his face when he realized I was the new owner. Or the feeling that came over me when I thought he was married. Or the look of angst on his face when he pushed his emotions aside and walked away.

That's the image that keeps replaying over and over again in my mind.

I knew coming home might lead me to running in to him, eventually. I definitely didn't expect it to happen so soon—or conjure up those ghosts I thought had been long buried. But here we are, shovels in hand, and those ghosts standing right next to us.

Good thing I'm a strong, independent woman, right? I can handle this, working side by side for the unforeseeable future. Who knows, it might actually do me some good. Maybe I'll finally be able to let go of the past that's been holding me back.

Maybe now I'll finally be free.

Chapter Five

Jensen

My heart is pounding so hard in my chest I'm sure everyone within a two-mile radius can hear, and my mind? Holy shit. I can't believe the new owner of the Elliott mansion is none other than Kathryn Elliott. *My Kate.*

Seeing her today sent me back more than a decade when she was my everything. Her long blonde hair, her striking hazel eyes, and that familiar scent of honeysuckle. It all brought me right back to a time when an eighteen-year-old boy spent every chance he got wrapped up in the girl he loved.

But Kate isn't a girl anymore, and I'm no boy.

I have twelve years' worth of hurt, fear, and even love under my belt. No, I haven't felt all of those simultaneously, but in some ways, they all go hand in hand. You can't have love without hurt, and in most cases, you can't have hurt without love.

Knowing that Kate is back has me driving as fast as I can home, not even caring I'm speeding. I have no idea how to process this revelation. A big part of me wants to call Garrett for a beer. And by beer, I mean shots of Jack until everything is numb and dark. The other part wants to turn my truck around, walk back down to where I saw her, and throw my arms around her.

That's the reaction that scares me the most.

Instead, I focus on Max and finding that damn baseball. He keeps it in a round case, ensuring the ball remains in good condition. Not that we can't get another one signed by Sawyer Randall—he *is* married to my cousin, after all. It's the point that it's *this* baseball my son loves so damn much. I'd hate for him to lose it.

Lacey Black

Pulling into my driveway, I head inside to search for the ball. I come up empty, knowing it's got to be in his bag. I made sure I put it there myself. He may have pulled it out of the bag, but I doubt it. He was too worried about making sure he tied his new pair of tennis shoes. Even though he's four, Max insisted on a pair of laced shoes for the upcoming school year. When we were in the department store, I told him I would only buy them if he would learn to tie his shoes, which he readily agreed. It took him a few tries, and even then, he still fumbles a little, but by the end of our weekend, he had the gist of it and was trying his own shoes.

When I realize it's not here, I decide to head over to Ashley's. It's gotta be in the bag. I park on the street, knowing I won't be staying long. As I knock on the door, my ex-wife comes around the corner, a wide smile beaming across her face.

"Jensen, what a pleasant surprise," she coos, obviously happy to see me, as she opens the door and allows me to enter.

"I came to help find the baseball," I state, shoving my hands in my pockets.

"Oh!" she says, her eyes wide with excitement, "Good news! We found the baseball!"

Of course she did.

"Well, that's good. Was it in his bag?" I find myself asking, hoping that I was successful in masking my annoyance.

She reaches out and sets her hand on my forearm. "Silly little ball was mixed in with his blanket," she says with a giggle. "Since you're here, why don't you stay for dinner? I'm sure Max would be so excited to have you stay. Plus, I made pot roast, your favorite."

Does anyone else sense that I've been played here, or is it just me?

"Umm," I start, but am cut off when I hear small feel running down the hall.

"Max, your dad is here and he's staying for dinner," Ashley hollers to our son.

"I can't stay," I state, but it's too late. Max comes around the corner and flies into my arms.

"Daddy! You're staying for dinner?"

Exhaling deeply, I glance at my mini-me. "Yeah, Buddy, I'm staying for dinner."

"Yay!" he hollers, throwing his arms in the air in victory. And in his hand? The damn baseball.

"Why don't you go wash up for dinner," Ashley tells our son, still beaming up at me like she won the fucking lottery. Obviously, today is a good day on the Ashley rollercoaster.

Deciding to play nice for the sake of Max, I put him down and follow. "Come on, Buddy, let's go wash our hands."

After we both make sure we're clean to eat dinner, we head to the kitchen. Ashley is humming a song that sounds a lot like the one we danced to at our wedding reception, a happy little grin on her pretty face.

"Anything I can help with?" I offer.

"Will you grab the cottage cheese from the fridge?" she asks, taking the pan of pot roast, potatoes, and carrots over to the small dining room table.

While I grab the small carton of Max's favorite side dish, I pour him a small glass of milk and head to the table. First thing I notice is the table is set exactly as it used to be when I still lived here. Me at the head of the table and her directly across from me. Max's spot is nestled right between us. He's already seated in his booster when I set his cup of milk down in front of him, and I watch as he takes a few greedy gulps. The boy loves milk.

Dinner is nice, if not a little on the painful side. I can't help but wonder if this was a setup, considering she made one of my favorite meals. I have a hard time believing she made pot roast and all the trimmings for just Max and herself. Ashley drones on about her day, as if us all eating together is completely normal, but as much as I try to focus on what she's saying, my mind is back at the Elliott mansion.

I can't believe Kate is back and living in that house. How long would it have been before I found out that tidbit of information? Would she have sought me out or would we have just casually run into each other at the supermarket? What if I hadn't gotten that job and it was weeks—months—before I realized she was living just three short miles from me?

"Are you okay? You seem a little distracted," Ashley says, interrupting my thoughts.

"Oh, sorry. Just a busy day at work," I tell her, taking another bite of my food.

"I'm sure you're crazy busy. I barely ever saw you in July and August," she reminds, bringing up the past with a pained look. It was always one of her reasons to bitch. She hated I was always dirty, but even more so that I spent so much time working my business. I was always busy, but the summer months were the worst.

"Yeah," I reply, not really sure what else to say. It's not like we haven't had this fight before many times over, and frankly, we're divorced, so it doesn't really matter anymore.

"So where are you working?" she asks, surprising the hell out of me. Ashley never asked about my work, didn't really care that much.

"All over, really, but I just started to work on the mansion on Coast Drive," I answer, moving my food around on my plate.

I can feel her eyes assessing me from across the table, but I don't look up. Instead, I shovel a little more meat into my mouth, praying this dinner ends quicker rather than later. "Someone bought the Elliott mansion?" she asks, and yes, there's definitely something snippy in her tone.

My mind immediately goes the woman who now owns the house. I don't want to start a war with my ex, even though it's really none of her business who now owns that place. But the truth is, she's always felt threatened by Kate. Not physically, of course, but by her memory. Ashley went to school with Kate and me, so she knows all about our history. She knows about the plans we had made that never were carried out. She knows all about the pain I carried around after Kate's abrupt exit from town.

She knows everything, and that's why I keep the new owner's name to myself.

"It looks like it," I answer, not ready to get into the specifics of the Elliott mansion. Besides, I don't really have many of the details myself, other than Kate's dad passing away and leaving her the house.

"Wow, well, it will be good to see new life to that old dump." *It's anything but a dump*, I think to myself. Sure, it needs some work, but the house is still as beautiful as ever.

So is the owner.

Shaking that thought out of my head, I make it through the rest of dinner, thankful that the house isn't brought back up again. I help gather up the dirty dishes, taking them over to the sink, when Ashley suggests I help Max with his bath. Our son is instantly excited, running off to get his favorite squirt toy ready, so there's not much hope of me trying to sneak out of the house now.

Sighing in resignation, I head off to the bathroom. At least I can hide out there with Max instead of in the kitchen with Ashley. I let him play for a bit before grabbing the shampoo and scrubbing down his head. I can feel the gritty sand, which makes me smile. Max loves playing in the dirt as much as I always did, and I never fail to find some dirt or sand on his scalp. After a thorough scrubbing and rinse, he gets out and heads to his room where he finds his Captain American pajamas. Grabbing a book off the shelf, I read through it before his eyes start to droop.

"One more?" he asks, snuggled into my side.

"Not tonight, Buddy. I'm gonna head home so you can get some sleep," I tell him, placing a kiss on his forehead.

"Night, Daddy. Love you," he whispers.

"Night, Buddy. Love you too," I tell him, slowly crawling out of his bed and pulling the lightweight covers over his body. He snuggles in, and almost drifts off instantly, the Sawyer Randall baseball still in his hand.

Flipping off the light, I head back to the kitchen, ready to tell Ashley goodbye. When I get there, I find it mostly dark, the light above the sink providing just enough light that no one trips or runs into anything if they get up in the night. She's not in the living room, and it looks like the house is already locked up for the night. There's only one place she can be, and my stomach churns with dread as I head that way.

The door is cracked open and low light spills through the doorway. I already know what awaits me on the other side. She's tried this shit before. It didn't work then, and it sure as hell isn't going to work now. I push open the door with little fanfare and spot my ex-wife immediately. She's lying on the bed, wearing a white and pink nightgown that reveals a lot more of her skin than I should be seeing. In fact, I can see her nipples poking through the lace and her bare pussy is on full display.

"Ashley," I groan, and not in the excited way she's expecting. "Don't do this."

"Don't do what?" she asks, a coy smile playing on her plump lips. "Welcome home my husband after a long day's work?"

I close my eyes, hating what's happening. I've known this woman long enough that whatever is about to come out of my mouth is going to be wrong in her eyes. She's played this game our entire adult lives, and frankly, I'm tired. I just want to go home, get a little work done, have a beer, and fall sleep—alone. Now, I have to deal with my ex as I navigate today's landmine field, and that's sure as fuck what this is. No matter what I say, what I do, it's going to blow up in my face.

"Ashley, I'm going home." I exhale loudly, planting my hands firmly on my hips, and keep my eyes focused on hers.

"You are home, silly," she coos, running her hand down the white lace that covers her left breast.

"I'm not. We're divorced. This isn't happening," I tell her with conviction.

She smiles from her position on the bed. "That's not what you said last time," she whispers, an annoying giggle spilling from her lips.

My mind goes right back to that night, more than eleven months ago, when she tried this same shit. Only that time, it worked. I got caught up in the good, reminiscing about happier times. Next thing I knew, I was in her bed and hating myself the next morning. And speaking of the next morning, when I tried to politely remind her we were divorced and anything between us wasn't happening again, she threw a picture frame at my head and called me every name in the book. She also made my life hell for the next month when it came to Max, using him as much as she could as a pawn to get to me.

We finally got back to a cordial place, and now this. We're right back to where we started. Only this time, I'm not fucking her. No way, no how.

"Don't be silly, Jensen. We've always had chemistry in the bedroom."

I won't deny that because it wouldn't be true. She's right. We've always clicked between the sheets, but that doesn't mean I'm ready to jump back between them.

"Ashley, please. I'm going home, alone. Our marriage is over."

"Maybe so, but we can still have a little fun on the side, can't we?"

"No," I answer right away, needing to get the hell out of here, and fast. "Have a good night. I'll lock the front door when I leave," I tell her, turning away.

"So, that's just it? You're gonna tease me all night, act like we're one big happy family, and then just leave?"

Sighing, I keep my back to her as I say, "Yes, Ashley, I'm leaving. I want to get along with you for the sake of Max. You're his mother and I want to continue making sure he's number one to both of us, but this idea of us getting back together, even for just a night, isn't happening. Besides, we've moved on. You even went out on a date with Riley."

She doesn't say anything, but I know what's coming. I move my body out of the doorway before it gets smacked with whatever is readily available on her nightstand. I just barely get out of the way before the remote slams into the wall, popping the lid off and shooting batteries down the hall. "Bastard! I hate you! Riley meant nothing! I was using him to get a rise out of you!" she screams, no doubt going to wake up Max.

I keep moving though, needing to get out of the house as quickly as possible. Making sure the front door is secure behind me, I head to my truck. My long legs get me there quickly and my shaking fingers start it even quicker. I'm driving down the road before I can even process what the fuck just happened.

"Jeezus," I mumble, heading in the direction of my home. Only, when I get there, I don't pull in the driveway.

I keep going.

Visiting my mom is out of the question, even though I could really use her advice right now. She's probably already in bed, since she gets up at four and starts her day at the bed and breakfast. I could fire off a quick text message to Jonas and see if he's still out, but I really don't want to head to the bar. That's the last thing I need, actually. Samuel will bore me to death, explaining the ins and outs of prepaying your funeral before I even sit on the couch, and Marissa is probably with Rhenn, doing something I don't want to think about my little sister doing.

So that's why I find myself stopping in front of my older sister, Harper's, place. Harper's always had a pretty good head on her shoulders, and she's kickass with advice. My boots are heavy on her front steps as I raise my hand to knock on the door. Snuggles starts to bark, her stubby little tail wagging as soon as she sees me on the opposite side of the screen door.

"Hey, man," Latham says, unlocking the door and holding it open. "Come on in."

"Sorry to just drop by unannounced. I was in the area," I tell him vaguely.

Harper's boyfriend watches me, his eyes assessing and reading. There's no doubt he already know there's something more than just me being in the neighborhood. "Your sister's in the shower. Wanna come out back with me and have a beer?" he offers, nodding toward the door in the kitchen.

"Sure," I answer, shoving my hands into my pockets and following. Snuggles is already there, clearly having heard the words out back.

Lacey Black

Latham grabs two bottles of beer from the fridge and heads out to the deck. I take a seat on one of the chairs, anxiously opening the brew he hands me. It's a beautiful night, the stars high in the sky and a full moon just over the trees. I can't help but wonder when the last time I just sat around and looked at the stars was. A month ago? Hell, six months ago? It's hard to tell when you're up to your eyeballs in paperwork and spend every spare minute of time you have raising a son.

"So? You gonna tell me what has you all tied up?"

I glance over at the man shacking up with my older sister. Latham Douglas owns the hardware store beside my sister's lingerie shop, and honestly, he's a pretty good dude. I hope one day he'll become an official member of the family, though that's probably a long ways off. All I know is that my sister is over-the-top happy now that they're together, and for that, I'm grateful.

"Ashley."

He relaxes back in his chair and takes a pull from his beer. "Ahh, the ex. I should have known." Latham kicks his feet out straight, and as soon as Snuggles finishes sniffing all over the backyard, she lies beside his outstretched feet.

"She called me tonight because she couldn't find Max's baseball. I had personally packed it in his bag, but I ran home and tore up the house looking for it. When I didn't find it, I went over to her place because I knew it had to be there."

"Let me guess, it was?"

"Right where I had put it."

"And?"

"She told Max I was staying for dinner. He got all excited, so it wasn't like I could just leave and risk disappointing him," I shrug, now knowing that's exactly what I should have done.

"I'm guess you stayed and it was the wrong decision?"

60

"Definitely. To her, it meant we were one big happy family again. I found her lying on her bed in lingerie," I confide, taking a much bigger drink of my beer.

Latham whistles. "The fact that you're here and not there," he starts, leaving the rest of the sentence open.

"Means I didn't fuck her."

We're both quiet for a few moments, lost in our own thoughts. When I hear soft footfalls in the kitchen, I know my sister is about to join the party. Harper pushes open the door, her eyes glued to her boyfriend. I instantly notice what she's wearing and avert my eyes. Obviously she's not expecting a late night visit from her brother or I'm sure she wouldn't have just walked outside in a long satin negligée.

Latham, God love him, opens his mouth (probably to tell her that we have company), but then notices her outfit. His eyes are wide with excitement, and maybe a little amusement.

"Get ready, Mr. Douglas. I'm about to give your penis one hell of a hug with my vagina," my sister croons, walking over and straddling his lap.

"Jeezus," I groan, trying to burn that image out of my head.

Harper yelps and turns my way. "Jensen?" she gasps, pulling at the lace on her nightgown that covers her breasts. I, of course, avert my eyes because if this is my last sight on earth, no way in hell do I want it to be of my sister wearing something sexy and talking about vagina hugs.

Latham laughs, pulling her into his chest and kissing her forehead. "We have a visitor, honey."

"I see that," she grumbles, throwing her leg over his and standing up. "I'll be right back," she adds as she hurries back inside, hopefully to put on more clothes.

"Cockblocker," Latham teases, a wide smile on his face.

"I'm gonna go," I say, standing up.

"No!" Harper yells from inside the house. "You've already ruined the vagina hug, so you might as well stay and finish your beer. I'll be out in a second."

"Can you stop talking about your...vagina," I beg, shaking my head and chugging the rest of my bottle. Latham, the bastard, just laughs.

"So. What's up, little brother?" Harper asks a minute later, returning to the back deck wearing shorts and a T-shirt, as well as carrying three fresh bottles of beer. She hands me a new one and takes the other two to Latham. As she hands him a fresh beer, she sits down on his thigh, this time facing me.

"Can't a little brother stop by and say hello to his big sister?" I ask, taking a smaller drink from the new bottle.

"He could, sure, but something tells me that's not the case." She gives me a knowing grin and waits for my reply.

I go ahead and fill her in on what happened tonight at Ashley's place, hating she's getting all worked up over the drama with my ex. But Harper is loyal, and for a while, considered Ashley a friend until Ash started pulling this kinda shit when our marriage was ending.

"What a crazy bitch," she mumbles, taking a drink of her own beer. "I can't believe she's still pulling this crap. She's so hot and cold."

"That she is," I exhale, glancing off into the dark night. My mind is reeling with everything that happened today. First with work, then with discovering Kate is back in town, and then this bullshit with Ashley. My mind is toast.

"How's everything else going?" she asks, leaning back against Latham's chest and watching me.

This is the part where I could tell her it's fine. I've already shared all of the night's drama with Ashley, so I'm sure she'd think that's the reason I stopped over. And she'd be correct—it was the main reason. But there's more. God, there's more to this shitshow story, and I don't know how to process it.

So instead of finishing off my drink and leaving them to *do* whatever it was they were about to do, I find myself opening my mouth and spilling the rest of it. "Actually, I met the new owner of the Elliott mansion today." Without finishing the beer, I set the bottle on the table and rest my elbows on my knees.

"Okay," she says, drawing out the word. "Everything okay? You still have the job, right?"

I laugh humorlessly. "Oh, yeah, I still got it. There's no getting out of it now, even if I wanted to. I've already signed the contracts and the work has begun. It's just gonna be hell working there when Kathryn Elliott is on the opposite side of the walls."

Her eyes widen in shock. "Kathryn? As in *your* Kathryn?"

"Not my Kathryn, remember? But, yes, they are one and the same."

"I don't understand," Harper says, her blue eyes turning concerned.

"Apparently, her father passed away and left her the house. She's moving into it," I state, keeping it to the basics. Actually, I only know the basics, so that's all I can say.

"Holy shit, Jensen, and you saw her?"

I nod my confirmation. "We had a brief conversation. She had some sort of panic attack when she saw me."

"I don't believe it," she mumbles, my sentiments exactly. "What are you going to do?"

Standing up, I answer, "What can I do? She's the homeowner. I'm the landscaper. There's nothing there anymore."

Liar.

Lacey Black

"Liar," Harper states with a grin. "If there wasn't, you wouldn't be here."

Know-it-all.

Crossing my arms, I stare down at my smug sister. "Fine. It was hard seeing her. It's going to be hard tomorrow too. It's been twelve damn years, and now all of a sudden, she's back. I hate it. I hate that just the sight of her affects me the way it does, but at the same time, I'm… I'm happy," I say, that final word barely a whisper.

Harper stands up and come to me. "Of course, you'd feel both of those things."

"But I shouldn't," I insist, making Harper shrug.

"Maybe, maybe not. Did you get to talk to her?" she asks, giving me a pointed look that lets me know she's not meaning about landscaping or the weather.

I shake my head.

"Well, Jensen, I believe you're never going to truly move past this until you talk to her. Maybe that's exactly what you need for closure. Find out why she left and then move on. You've been in this crazy state of limbo since the summer after your high school graduation. Even when you moved on with Ashley, you were still closed off." My all-too-knowing sister glances at her boyfriend. "Take it from me, don't just assume shit. Talk it out and then move past it." Her blue eyes meet mine. "And you and Kathryn are a decade past time to talk."

I sigh knowing there's nothing she said I can dispute. "You're right," I confirm aloud.

"Of course I'm right. Your big sister always is!" she bellows, a beaming smile on her pretty face.

"Bullshit," Latham coughs, making her turn and glare at him.

"Excuse me?" she asks, a hint of humor in the way she glares at him.

"I didn't say anything, Sweetheart. I just had a little tickle in my throat," he replies, wide smile on his smug face.

"No vagina hugs for you," she tells him before turning back to face me.

"And that's my cue to leave," I tell them, throwing my half-full beer bottle in the outside trash bin.

"It was nice to see you, man," Latham says, standing up and throwing his empty in the trash too. "Stop by anytime."

As I head around the side of the house to the driveway, I hear my sister holler, "But maybe call first. Next time, we might be in the middle of the vagina hug."

I almost reach my truck before I turn back around to face them. They're standing on the edge of the porch, laughing grins on their faces and their arms around each other. "If Latham is able to stop and answer the door, I'm pretty sure he's not doing it right," I tease before realizing what we're really talking about.

"Oh, he does it right," Harper confirms, making me wince.

"I'm out, and I'd appreciate never talking about this again," I wave off as I slip into my truck and head for home.

A home that's quiet.

A home that's not really a home, not without Max there.

The fact I'll be trapped inside the walls with nothing but my overactive imagination doesn't settle well with me, but there's nowhere else for me to go. It's late and I'm tired. My bed is calling to me. I'm just pretty damn sure I won't be alone in that bed. No, there'll be a ghost beside me and all of the memories she's resurrected.

It's going to be a long night.

Chapter Six

Kathryn

How I've managed to survive this week with only seeing Jensen a handful of times is beyond me. Well, that's not true. It was actually pretty easy, considering I hid inside the house under the impression of working. Not that I wasn't up to my eyeballs in dust bunnies and dirt, but it was definitely a convenient excuse not to go outside during the daytime.

The house is slowly coming along. Very slowly, actually. I started cleaning my old bedroom, which is where I'm now sleeping. I was only able to stay at the bed and breakfast in town for a few days, just enough time to get one bedroom and bathroom ready for occupancy. The electrician was kind enough to make sure power was still on in that wing of the house and the contractor helped ensure the relocated fridge and washer and dryer were working too.

I've moved on to the other bedrooms, once used by guests. Actually, now that I think about it, we rarely had guests. But here I am, tearing apart the bed, taking down dusty curtains, and giving the rooms a deep clean. Each bedroom has an en suite bathroom, so I've taken the time to clean those as well before moving on to another room. After one week, I've completed my bedroom and two of the guest rooms.

Now that it's Friday evening, I'm exhausted. Like bone-deep exhausted. But without the kitchen ready to use, I have limited ways to cook food. That's why I've eaten out or brought home take-out way more than I'm used to. Sure, I have some fresh fruits and vegetables in the fridge, and even a few blueberry muffins in my room for breakfast, but without a stove or microwave, I'm limited on my dinner options.

That's why I'm heading out to grab a quick bite.

Pizza.

That's what I crave, which is weird because I haven't craved something like pizza in years, but just the thought of Pizza Castle has my mouth watering and my stomach growling.

As I head out the front door, I notice all of the fresh landscape work around the front entrance. I've avoided looking out the window to see what Jensen has been up to, but loved to take a stroll around the property to see his progress. Today's work included planting new flowering trees and ornate shrubbery around the front entrance. I also notice he has the fountain cleaned out and taken apart. Jensen told David, my attorney, that he would take a look at the pump and plumbing to see how extentive the damage was, but anticipated having to bring in someone else to fix it. That's exactly like the young man I knew so many years ago. He loved tinkering around with things, figuring out how they worked, and trying to fix them himself, if possible.

I'll have to ask if he was able to get the old fountain going.

The drive to town is quick, but finding a parking spot near the pizza joint isn't. In fact, I have to drive around the block twice before I get lucky and someone pulls out of a spot. With my purse in hand, I hop out and head down the sidewalk. There are people loitering around. A few families and couples strolling near the old band shell and town square, which brings a smile to my face. The only time I did that was with Jensen and his family. My parents barely had time for me, let alone to take me to the park or milling around town. They had companies to run and fundraisers to organize.

When I reach the gazebo, I find myself stepping inside, my fingers grazing against the old, well-maintained wood. A smile crosses my face as I recall my very first stolen kiss, right here in the middle of this gazebo. We were sixteen and had just left the homecoming dance. The night was still young, the air cool and crisp. Jensen threw his suit jacket over my shoulders as we strolled down these very paths that snaked through the town square. When we reached the gazebo, he pulled me into his arms. His fingers had a slight tremble to them as he softly lifted my chin and gazed into my eyes. I knew what was about to happen, the anticipation almost more than I could bare.

Then he kissed me.

Soft and sweet, the perfect first kiss for two young kids.

I push those memories aside and step out of the gazebo. Making quick work of retracing my steps, I head just down the block to the pizza joint, the smell of oregano and garlic becoming more pronounced with each step I take. I pull open the familiar red door and step inside. A smile instantly crosses my face as I glance around, realizing nothing has changed in the twelve years I've been gone.

"Can I help you?" a friendly young girl asks from the hostess stand.

Glancing around, I realize the place is packed with families waiting by the door to be seated. "Actually, I'd like to place an order to go, if that's okay?"

"Of course," she says politely, handing me a menu. "We could seat you, but it may be a twenty minute wait."

I wave her off. "No, that's okay. I'll take it to go."

It only takes a few seconds to find what I'm after on the menu. "I'll take a personal pan veggie pizza with extra mushrooms and a side salad with Italian."

The hostess jots down the order and gives me a smile. "I'll run this back. Should be about fifteen minutes or so. Have a seat," she says, then gives me a brighter grin. "Well, if you can find a seat, that is." Then she's off, taking care of my order.

I glance around the foyer, noting the décor on the walls and avoiding the faces, in case someone from my past is near. When I gaze into the full dining room, that's when I feel it. The hairs on the back of my neck stand on end, and even though I haven't spied him yet, I know he's here. I can sense it.

Unable to fight the urge to look, my eyes finally connect with those ocean blue ones I've been avoiding. He's sitting at a booth, staring directly at me—into my soul, is probably more accurate. My heart starts to gallop and my breathing comes in short little pants. No, I don't feel the onset of a panic attack, but I definitely feel something strong (primarily between my legs).

Jensen gives me a tentative wave and a small smile. It's awkward, at least it is for me. I mirror his actions, trying not to let my nervousness show. Unfortunately, my arms feel stiff and my wave is anything but fluid, and let's not get into my smile. I probably look all teeth, with my strained, fake smile in full force. I've seen that look before. It's been photographed and published in newspapers all over New York, mostly while I'm on Charles's arm.

Suddenly, he waves me over and before I can even try to figure out what I'm doing, my legs are carrying me there, through the dining area and toward his booth. It sits on the back wall with an old version of the Monopoly board game on the wall.

"Hey," he says softly, the deep timbre of his familiar voice wrapping around me like a warm blanket.

"Hi."

"I'm Max," a loud voice calls from across the booth. My eyes connect with the much younger, much shorter version of the man across from him.

"Hi, Max. I'm Kathryn." Now, my smile is genuine. The little boy is the cutest little guy I've ever seen, and it's not because he looks so much like his dad. His eyes are wide and expressive and his smile could melt the glaciers in Iceland.

"Do you like pizza?"

Again, I smile as I reply, "I do. I love it. Do you?"

He nods emphatically. "It's my favorite."

My grin is automatic. Heck, I'm not sure I've stopped smiling since I walked over here. "Let me guess: extra cheese?"

"And mushrooms! Lots of mushrooms!" he bellows with excitement.

"Shhh, inside voice," Jensen instructs with a small grin, making Max sit back down in his seat.

"Can I tell you a secret?" I ask, leaning over to where the boy is sitting. When he nods and his eyes light up like little sapphires, I confess, "Mushrooms are my favorite too."

"See Dad? Kate like mushrooms too!" Max tells the older version of himself across from him. My heart starts to jump in my chest when the young boy refers to me by the nickname no one uses.

No one but his dad.

I glance over to Jensen. He's smiling softly at his son as he replies, "I know she does." Then those blue eyes connect with mine and I feel it down to my toes. Jensen clears his throat and adds, "Do you want to join us?"

My mouth opens, but nothing comes out. Part of me is ready to decline. I don't want to interrupt his dinner with his son. And besides, how awkward would that be? My vote is for pretty damn uncomfortable. But then there's the other part of me—the one ready to say yes, to reconnect and enjoy a meal with an old friend and his son.

An old friend who's seen you naked more times than you can count.

I'm still not sure which answer I'm going to give when I see the hostess approach. She's carrying a small pizza box and a white paper bag, presumably with my salad inside. With a friendly smile, she hands me my order. "Here you go. You can pay at the front counter. Oh, are you joining them? Would you like for me to get you a plate?"

As I open my mouth to decline, I'm stunned by the response that comes from the table's occupant. "Yes, that would be great," Jensen says on my behalf.

When she rushes off to get me a plate, I turn stunned eyes toward the man at the table. "I don't want to interrupt your dinner," I tell him.

Instead of replying, he just scoots over in invitation. Something tells me this is a horrible idea, but that still doesn't stop me from slowly lowering myself into the booth beside him. Heat radiates off his large body as our shoulders brush, igniting a fire deep in my blood that has been long dormant. This is most definitely a horrible idea, yet here I am, sitting beside Jensen Grayson after a twelve-year absence, and do you know what?

I like it.

A lot.

Max starts chatting immediately as the hostess returns with a plate for me and a large pizza for the rest of the table. I smile when I see the pie, half covered in meat and the other half in just mushroom. Funny, that's exactly how we used to order it back when we were dating in school.

I try to focus on what the kid is saying, but it's hard. He's chatting a mile a minute, completely unaware of the tension that surrounds the table. I'm pretty sure a big part of it is sexual, but I'm

71

not about to vocalize it. Instead, I watch as Jensen effortlessly places a slice on Max's plate and cuts it into smaller pieces. Then, without breaking stride, he opens my box and pulls the small four-slice personal pizza out, placing it on my plate. Then, and only then, does he finally place two meaty pieces on his own plate.

"Do you like baseball, Kate?" Max asks, pulling my attention across the table.

"Oh, uh, I haven't really followed sports," I tell him with a sheepish grin.

"I love baseball. I got a ball from my cousin, Sawyer," he says, producing a baseball covered in a small round case from his lap. "I'm gonna be a ball player, just like him when I get bigger."

Taking the offered item, I spy a name scrolled between the stitching on the ball. "Who is Sawyer?" I find myself asking as I hand the prized item back to Max.

"He's married to my cousin, AJ. Sawyer Randall used to play for the Rangers," Jensen confirms as Max takes a big bite of his pizza.

"Wow, that's pretty neat," I reply, mostly to Max. Then I glance at Jensen and add, "I don't remember cousins."

Those piercing blue eyes find mine, stealing a bit of my breath and a lot of my sanity. "Actually, we discovered a whole new side of the family we didn't know about," Jensen says, and tells me all about how his mom had a much older brother who she rarely saw or spoke to. To find out Jensen has six female cousins, all with families of their own, is a little surprising, but he seems completely happy about the expansion of his family.

"That's pretty amazing. I'm glad you were able to connect with them," I tell him, finishing off my second piece of pizza while he talks, completely ignoring the salad that I definitely should have started with. I can still hear my mother's voice, whispering in my ear, that I should always eat salad. A lady never indulges in carbs, like pizza and pasta. She taught me at such a young age how to move food around on your plate to give the appearance of eaten food, and I hated it. I always craved a big bowl of macaroni and cheese or even a large slice of pizza, even if my hips didn't agree with it.

"Thank you for inviting me to join you," I say as I drop my napkin beside my plate and place the remaining two slices back in the pizza box. With those two pieces plus the salad, I can take it back to the house for a meal this weekend.

"You didn't each much," Jensen says, glancing down at his demolished half of their pizza.

I shrug. "My appetite isn't big," I tell him, which is partially the truth. I've never been a big eater, at least not recently. Years of beating 'small portions' into my head has trained me to only consume a little bit of food, especially in front of company. But that pizza? My mouth watered as I ate the first two slices, careful not to just shovel it in my face like I used to in high school.

The other part of it is the fact it was a bit nerve-racking eating in front of Jensen again. He's always had a hearty appetite (comes from manual labor) and never shied away from devouring his food. Even now, sitting next to him with so much left unsaid, leaves a slight flutter in my belly and makes it hard to eat. He's not intimidating, per se, but mostly just makes me a little uneasy. Like when you're eating in front of some dignitary. You're constantly afraid you'll dribble food down your chin or slurp your soup too loudly. You spend the meal trying to behave to the extreme, focusing completely on being polite and worrying about making sure you don't have spinach in your teeth.

That's how it feels to eat with Jensen again.

"Can you come to the park with us tomorrow? We're going to play baseball and run the bases!" Max grins from across the table, his wide eyes full of wonder and excitement.

"Oh, uh, I'm not sure what I have going on tomorrow," I answer, knowing that's a lie. I had planned to tackle the living room tomorrow, complete with airing out the house since the construction workers won't be there.

Max doesn't say anything, just nods his head. He looks so much like his dad with his assessing, serious eyes that sparkle like sapphires when he smiles. A pang of longing hits directly in my chest, causing a hitch in my breath.

"Well, I should head home. Thank you, again, for allowing me to join you," I say, sliding out of the booth and grabbing my purse. I reach for the bill for my to-go pizza and salad, but before I can grasp the slip of paper, Jensen snatches it up and grins victoriously.

"I've got it," he says, taking his own ticket off the table as well.

"No," I insist. "You don't have to do that."

He stands up beside me, my eyes darting upward to meet his. "I want to. What are friends for?" he asks, but his smile doesn't reach his eyes.

Friends? We haven't been friends in years, more than a decade, actually. The last time we spoke, it was about post-graduation plans and his summer job. *Friends* don't leave in the middle of the night and never return a call. *Friends* don't walk away from someone they love without so much as a goodbye.

No, I was the worst friend in the world.

He deserved better.

"Thank you," I rasp over my too-dry throat, blinking away the threat of tears.

Jensen helps Max out of the booth and heads toward the front counter. He pulls two twenties from his wallet and tells them to keep the change as the tip. Then, with his son's hand tucked in his, he exits the restaurant, holding the door open for me as we go.

Outside, the air is warm and slightly sticky. There was a touch of humidity coming from the ocean today, something I didn't miss while in New York. Actually, that may have been the only thing I didn't miss while I way away.

He stops on the sidewalk, a signal this is goodbye. Part of me doesn't want tonight to end. Part of me wants to hang on to this olive branch of friendship we've extended with both hands, but part of me knows there's no going back, not when hearts are involved. "Thanks for the pizza," I say lamely, holding my leftover food tightly in my hand.

"You're welcome." His eyes watch every move I make, and I can't help but wonder if he can still read my thoughts like he so easily did back when we were young.

I glance down at his mini-me and offer him a smile. "Max, it was lovely to meet you," I say, extending my hand and shaking his much smaller and slightly sticky one.

"Bye, Kate! Come play with us soon!"

I can't help but smile. It's a lovely thought, really, but saddening at the same time since I know I'll probably never play with this little boy. "Thank you for the invite. Enjoy your evening," I reply. My eyes connect with Jensen's before I slowly turn and walk away.

"Hey, Kate?" Just the sound of his voice saying my name again does things to my heart.

"Yes?" I ask, turning back around to face him.

He opens his mouth, but quickly closes it. He watches me for a few seconds before finally saying, "I'll see ya soon."

Nodding quickly, I turn back around and head to where I left my car, all the while wondering what it was he was going to say. That's the problem with us, really. So much to say, yet no words are spoken.

As I climb into my car, I can't help but wonder—when will I see him again? *Probably at the house when he comes to work, silly. You did hire him to do a job.* But that doesn't stop the kernel of hope popping to life, the deep-rooted longing starting to bud. At the end of the day, Jensen and I will never have what we had before, but what if we gave that whole friends thing a chance? I mean, I haven't had a real friend in I don't know how long. Sure, it may be uncomfortable, but what's a little awkwardness between former lovers? Maybe, just maybe, I'll see him and Max again when it's not work related.

A woman can hope.

Chapter Seven

Jensen

"Ready to go, Buddy?" I ask Max, as I gather up our bag of baseball supplies. Really, it just consists of a tiny glove, a much bigger one for my hand, a small bat, and a few balls. The tee is in the garage and I'll grab that before we head to the truck.

As I get everything loaded up, including a small cooler with a couple bottles of water and some fruit snacks, my phone rings. I almost ignore it. I hate losing even a few minutes of time with my son, but when I see the number, I know it can't wait.

"Hey, Pablo. What's up?"

"Sorry to bother you on a Sunday, Jensen, but I'm going through your order for tomorrow's delivery. Are you sure you only need fifty edging stones? From the picture you painted in my head, I would have thought the order would be much bigger than that."

I know right away that something is wrong. Pablo owns the concrete business the next town over that I use for all of my stone and gravel. "No, that can't be right. Those edgers are supposed to expand the entire front of the house. No way should it only be fifty," I reply, rubbing my forehead. I picture the design in my own head, seeing the subtle rise in the retaining wall so that it looks like waves along the shore.

"That's what I thought. I've got plenty in stock, but was hoping you could give me a better picture of how many you're looking for. I could send a few pallets with Tommy on the truck, but they'll just be in the way if you really don't need that many."

I pull out my clipboard and realize right away something is wrong. Half the sheets are missing, including the finalized design, which includes the list of required materials I sent over to Pablo. I close my eyes, trying to recall the last time I saw it when it hits me.

Kate's place.

Wes and I had used them Friday to outline the layout in preparation for this upcoming week's work. The ground is now bare, ready for my favorite part of the job—the build. At the end of the day, I was so busy trying to avoid Kate when she was outside talking to Rhenn about lighting around the landscaping I must have thrown it all in the small job trailer I keep on-site with my tools. The plans have to be there.

"I don't have them in front of me. Can you give me twenty minutes and I'll call you back?" I ask Pablo.

"Sure thing. I'll be here for another hour or two, getting everything lined up for you and everyone else." Pablo's business is the go-to place for concrete and landscaping needs. And not just big orders. A lot of locals prefer to patronize his place, rather than drive to the big box store a few towns away.

"I'll call you back," I tell him before hanging up and clipping my phone on my belt. "Come on, Max. We've gotta make a quick stop by Daddy's jobsite before we hit the baseball field."

Lifting him into the truck, I help him get fastened in his car seat, his signed baseball resting on his lap. I throw the truck in reverse, pull out of the driveway, and head toward the Elliott mansion. On a Sunday afternoon. When Kate is probably there. My heart does a happy little beat at the prospect of seeing her today. Ever since I invited her to join us for pizza Friday night, my body has not-so-subtly reminded me of how much she impacts me. Even now, I'm half hard in my shorts at the thought of seeing her.

Pushing all thoughts of Kate and my wayward cock out of my mind, I talk to my son about tonight's game. The Cubs are visiting the Rangers, and we have a TV date to watch the game. This will be an epic battle for him. Ever since he found out, earlier this summer, Sawyer used to play for the Rangers, the Rangers have been his second favorite team, right behind the Cubs. I try to make it a big deal for him, including making chili dogs and nachos for dinner. He gets a kick out of it, pretending we're actually sitting in the stadium instead of my ol' worn couch, but even as excited as he gets, he'll still be sound asleep by the end of the fourth inning.

I pull up to the house, keying in the temporary code we were all given at the start of this job. "This your work?" Max asks from the back seat of my truck, his eyes wide and eager as I drive up the lane.

"This is where I'm working, Buddy."

"Can I play in the dirt?" he asks, taking in all the bare soil. My kid is one-hundred-percent me and loves to dig and play as much as I did (and still do).

"We don't have time today if we want to get to the ball diamond and hit the ball," I tell him, pulling alongside my small trailer. My plan is to jump out, unlock the door, and find my paperwork. Unfortunately, Max takes it upon himself to unbuckle his belt and climb out of the truck. "We're not staying, Max. Get back in the truck," I tell him as I find the right key on my key ring for the lock.

"I wanna see," he says, coming around to where I stand. He doesn't say a word as I open the lock and pull open the door. It's dark inside the trailer, but fortunately, it's plenty light outside. "Shovels!" he bellows, reaching for the tool on top of the pile.

"Max, let it alone or you'll hurt yourself."

"I dig," he answers, trying to pull the shovel from the trailer.

"I thought we were going to play baseball."

"I work and play, Daddy," he says, a huge grin on his face as he drags the shovel outside.

I close my eyes and take a deep breath. One thing I've learned about kids is they're like yo-yos in regards to their attention span. One second he's ready to play baseball, and the next he wants to do something completely different.

When I open my eyes, I glance toward the house. I'm off to the side, my equipment and supplies kept as far away from the impressive front entrance, but still within view. All of the windows are open, the curtains fluttering in the breeze. The door is open too and soft music filters through the doorway. Clearly, the owner is home, and the last thing I want is for her to come out and find us in her yard on a Sunday afternoon.

Glancing back over at my son, I find him already digging the tip of the shovel into the raw dirt. There's a toothy grin on his face as he tries to lift, his small body not strong enough yet to elevate the dirt-filled shovel. He gets such a kick out of moving the earth, something I know all about. My own smile plays on my lips as I watch him drag the shovel, pretending to move big clumps of dirt and clay. In reality, he's barely digging a hole deep enough to plant a perennial.

"I'm a little surprised to see you here on a Sunday." The voice comes from behind me, soft and delicate. My body coils tight and my cock jumps to attention, clearly very happy to know she's near.

Turning around, I come face-to-face with Kate. "Yeah, sorry. I needed to grab some of my paperwork I left in the trailer." Glancing back over my shoulder to my son, I add, "Max decided to help with the landscaping."

Her smile is instantaneous and infectious. It lights up the world brighter than the sun and does dangerous things to my heart, like remind me of how much I used to love the feeling I got every time she flashed that grin my way. There was a time where I would do anything to see that smile, give anything she wanted. Now, as I gaze over at the very smile that's so very familiar, yet slightly different, I can't help but feel the same way.

And I definitely shouldn't feel that way.

"Hello, Max," she says.

"Hi, Kate! I'm digging!" he hollers over his shoulder, not breaking his stride as he moves the shovel.

"Yes, you are, Maximus," she says, a little giggle slipping from her lips as she watches.

My son stops and turns to face her. "My name's not Maximus. It's just Max."

"Are you sure it's not Maximilian, Just Max?" she asks, putting her hands on her hips and tapping her foot, her pink polish covered toes on full display.

Max busts into a fit of laughter, making both Kate and me laugh right along with him. "It's not Maximilian, silly. Just. Max."

"Well, Just Max, I'm so happy you stopped by to help with the landscaping. Don't tell your boss, but I was a little concerned about that dirt pile right there," she says, glancing my way with a coy grin. "So thank you for fixing it for me."

"You bet! I'm a good fixer!" he yells, turning his full attention back to the earth.

I take a step in her direction, instantly assaulted by her familiar scent. "I'm sorry about this. We'll be out of your way in a few minutes."

She waves me off. "It's no problem. The buzzer sounded when you used the code so I knew I had company."

"I was planning to just get the papers and sneak out without disrupting your Sunday afternoon," I tell her, keeping an eye on my son and his yard work.

"Really, I don't mind the interruption. I was neck deep in dust bunnies anyway, but the sitting room and the media room are both cleaned out," she tells me, a proud smile on her face. "Oh, is there still the resale shop on Main? I have tons of furniture I'd like to donate."

My eyes connect with hers once more. "Donate? I think that stuff in there is probably worth a little cash. You could probably sell it or something," I suggest.

"Could you imagine the look on my mother's face if she knew we had a garage sale here?" she asks, her eyes full of humor and light.

"Oh, she'd shit a brick, for sure," I reply, immediately regretting my crude use of language.

Kate must sense it, and quickly speaks. "You're fine. I never minded a little foul language back when we were together."

Now my heart is hammering in my chest as I recall the first time I said the word fuck in front of her. I instantly felt guilty for cursing in front of a lady, especially someone as wealthy and worldly as Kathryn Elliott, but she didn't seem to mind. Not in the least. In fact, she threw her arms around me and begged me to say it again, this time, while I was pounding into her sweet pussy.

My face flushes, and when I glance over, I realize hers is too. Clearly, I'm not the only one taking a dirty trip down memory lane.

Clearing my throat, I turn toward my trailer. "I'm going to grab my papers and make a quick call."

"Don't worry, I'll keep an eye on Just Max," she says, already heading over to where my son is digging in her yard.

I easily find what I'm looking for and dig out my phone. When I have the material list in front of me, I place the call, relaying the correct information to Pablo. He promises he has enough material on-hand, and I'll see the delivery truck by ten tomorrow. I'm not the first delivery, but I'm close. That means I'll be able to start really building her yard in less than twenty-four hours.

When I hang up, I head to where I left my son and my ex. They're not there, but it only takes me a few minutes to find them.

Out in the middle of the yard, where it's flat and bare, ready for new sod, are Max and Kate. Digging.

"Uhh, guys?" I ask as I approach from behind. Speaking of behind, Kate is bent over, her hands buried in the dark earth, and her beautifully round ass on full display. My cock jumps and starts shooting inappropriate messages to my brain about all the things it wants to do to that ass.

Kate is the first to glance my way, just over her shoulder in a manner that doesn't help talk down my wayward dick. A smile plays on her lips, her eyes full of laughter as she holds up a small clump of dirt. "Hey."

"Daddy, we're digging for treasure!" Max yells, furiously moving the soil from its smooth, flat stage to a clumped-up pile.

"Treasure? How do you know there's buried treasure here?" I ask, smiling at their filthy appearance, yet wondering how in the hell I'm going to get him home and into the tub without tracking mud all over the place.

"Kate said there was!" he yells, returning to his ferocious excavating.

I walk up to where Kate is wrist deep in the ground and whisper, "There is?"

She just grins over her shoulder and quietly replies, "Well, there might have been a few quarters recently dropped out here."

"Recently?"

"Like…within the last five minutes?" she laughs.

"I found something!" Max shrieks, pulling our attention to where he holds something high above his head and jumps up and down.

"What did you find?" Kate asks, watching intently as Max holds out his palm and displays the grimy, yet somewhat still shiny treasure. "Oh, it's a quarter!"

"Can I keep it? Like a pirate?" Max asks, turning wide eyes to the woman beside him.

I'm just about to open my mouth and tell him it's not appropriate, when Kate says, "Of course, you can, Just Max. All good pirates get to keep their booty."

I can't help it. I snicker.

She glances my way, her delicate eyebrows arching toward the heaven. "Really?"

Now, I'm laughing hard, but only because of the exasperated look on her face. "You said booty."

She rolls her eyes. "You haven't changed at all."

I take in her somewhat dusty and wrinkly clothing, the dirt now coating her manicured nails and smudged on her cheeks, and the wild strands of blonde hair spilling from the clip at the nape of her head, and I can't help notice beneath all of that, she's still the same Kate. "Neither have you."

We spend the next twenty minutes digging in the dirt together until Max finds four quarters. He's extremely pleased with his loot, but promises Kate he'll take them home and put them in his piggy bank. The entire time, she was right there, helping sift through the earth and find the treasures she haphazardly dropped in the dirt. With a smile from ear to ear from my four-year-old, Kate leads Max to the hose over by the garage where us workers have been cleaning up our hands at the end of the day. She helps him scrub up his hands before doing the same to hers. My hands are surprisingly clean, considering all I did was hold the discovered treasures as he was finding them, but I go ahead and wash the soil from them too.

"Well, that was fun. Thank you, Just Max, for helping me clear the buried treasure out of my yard."

"You're welcome, Kate. If you need more help, just call my daddy and I'll come help!"

She glances my way, a warm smile playing on her lips as she replies, "Deal. I'll be sure to call your daddy if I need more assistance."

Max seems very pleased by this, even though I'm not so sure about it. I mean, I know Kate is being wonderful with Max and he seems to be eating up the extra attention she's giving him, but I'm not so sure it's a good idea. At the end of the day, she's a client. A client whom I have a very deep-rooted past with, and I'm just not sure it's wise to let Max get too close.

Getting close to Kate again isn't in the cards, but there's also no denying this strong magnetic pull I feel every time she's near. Considering it's only been a handful of times, something tells me I'm in serious trouble where she's concerned. I'm not the person I was twelve years ago, but I'm not sure I'm strong enough to fight it either.

And if the look on my son's face is any indication, he's already in too deep.

Chapter Eight

Kathryn

The house is quiet as I make my way down the hallway toward the closed room at the back. My mind has been a jumbled mess of questions with no answers ever since Jensen and Max left. After we dug in the dirt and found the quarters I dropped, things between us got a little awkward. It's like the easygoing friendship we so effortlessly slipped into suddenly changed when we realized we weren't friends.

Not anymore.

That's when I felt the change, especially from Jensen, and when I felt his discomfort, that's when the shift happened within me. For the first time since I saw him standing in my backyard, anxiety nipped at my chest, threatening to overcome me. I was able to hold off the attack, mostly by focusing on Max (or Just Max as I will now call him). It wasn't necessarily because of his presence, but mostly because of the feelings he conjured up inside me, and if the way he reacted were any indication, I'd say the same happened to him.

Maybe without the accelerated heartbeat and the slightly labored breathing.

Max was ready to go play baseball by then, and even though he adamantly insisted I come along, he finally relented with a promise from me to join them soon. With Max secured in his child seat, Jensen threw me a wave, a quick "see you tomorrow," and took off to the park to play with his son.

And I was left alone in my giant house with walls that haunt me.

But I'm determined to make this house my own. Much of the furniture is being donated, and next weekend I'll be traveling around to buy a few new pieces of my own. Thanks to the sizable inheritance from my dad, as well as my half of everything in the pending divorce, I have plenty of money to put into this house and whatever else I want. Even though this place holds a few of my worst memories, it also holds many of my best, and those far outweigh the negative.

Home.

That's what this place is.

My home.

And I'm determined to make it just that.

That means biting the bullet and opening the final door. The one I haven't had the guts to access yet. I know what stands on the other side of this solid oak door, and I'm not sure I'm ready to face it. But it has been two weeks since I've been back home and if I don't do it now, then when?

No, it needs to happen now.

With a shaky hand on the doorknob, I give it a slight twist, only to find it locked. I pull out the master set of keys and try several before the lock releases. The door creaks loudly as it swings, a mocking groan of admittance. It's dark inside the room as a dank, dusty scent assaults me. I stand in the open doorway, not really seeing anything, yet seeing everything. My past is here. My passion. My love.

I reach for the switch and give it a flip. The room is bathed in light and a cry slips from my lips. The room is a mess; nothing like I remember in my dreams. The books are still on the walls, shelves and shelves of hardbacks and paperbacks. Classics, mysteries, and some romance. Books I used to read cover to cover late at night or under the shelter of shade beside the pool. Books I used to get lost in when my parents went to their many charity functions or some tropical getaway.

Appearances.

It was all about appearance to them, but to me, it was torture. I'd much rather have stayed home, devouring my books and spending time at the easel, and when I was finally old enough to do so, they stopped using me like a flashy new toy to show off to their rich friends.

I also spent time with Jensen. Throughout high school, he became my solace, my one true friend. He knew me better than my parents, better than anyone in the world, and my parents hated that. Especially my mother. He was too…blue collar. A working boy from a working family. While my father busted his ass in the business world, providing for his wife and young daughter, that was different because their circles were different. Not bad (at least to me). Just different.

That's one of the things I loved most about him.

He didn't care about the money that backed my family name. He didn't care how many square feet the house was or how much money was donated to local charities each year. He didn't use me to swim in the pool on a hot summer's day or pretend to be my best friend just to get invited over for a sleepover. He wasn't like the girls I went to school with. No, they weren't all like that, but when so many of them proved to have ulterior motives, I stopped looking for the real ones.

Until Jensen.

My legs are shaky as I step inside the room. The old desk is there, littered with papers of no importance left behind. An old photograph of me in a tutu adorns the left corner beside an old phone. It's covered in grimy dirt and cobwebs, but I can still see the faded pink of the outfit I wore when I was five. My father's desk sits regal and proud, just like the man I remember. Flashbacks of phone calls and contract reviews fire through my brain and it's almost as if he's sitting there now, surrounded by his work.

And in the corner, a young girl paints.

I don't know when the tears start to fall, but they do nevertheless. Big, fat crocodile tears slide down my cheeks, unchecked. My legs carry me toward the place I found so much comfort and joy. The canvas still sits there, covered in more than a decade's worth of abandonment, the colorful work half-finished.

I cover my mouth as a sob escapes my lips. I had forgotten about this painting, but now that I see it, the memories return. My father was on the phone, arguing with whoever he was talking to, while I sat on my stool, tuning him out completely. My eyes bounce between the canvas and the ocean outside. This room, though technically his, had the best lighting. Floor-to-ceiling windows with so much natural light that it was an artist's wet dream.

When I was nine and discovered my love for painting, I took over this space. Of course, Daddy gave it up easily when he saw the beauty my young, untrained hands could bring to life. My mother, on the other hand, hated my painting. She never understood how I could spend so much time "doodling" instead of using our name for philanthropy all over the state of North Carolina. Not to mention the fact I usually found myself covered in flecks of blues and greens, reds and yellows.

It was my source of escape, of pure joy, until it was ripped away from me.

Like Jensen.

Now, I stare at the piece I started more than twelve years ago, a half-finished piece of the backyard. It is the exact view from this very window, if the backyard would have been maintained over the years. The pool house is there, along with the massive pool. The ocean

Lacey Black

is in the background, peaceful and calm, as the sun slowly begins to drop and night starts to settle in. And on the beach, a young couple, their hands entwined as they made promises of forever to each other.

Unkept promises.

It was to be his birthday gift. The moment we stood on the beach and vowed to spend the rest of our lives together. I captured it so vividly in my mind, I came home later that evening and began to put it on canvas. I spent two days working on that painting, and had several more to go, but knew I'd have it complete in time for his birthday the coming weekend.

I never got to finish it because the next night, we were gone.

And I never picked up a paintbrush again.

I have to turn away from the painting as the powerful memories it evokes are too painful to bear. My breathing is choppy, partly because of the dust stirred up by my admittance into the room and partly because of the panic attack. I feel it coming, hard and rough. Reaching for the chair, I slowly lower myself to the floor. I try to slow my breathing, but it's not working. Nothing from the training the physicians gave me is working.

White dots pepper my vision as I reach for my phone. I don't know why, but my hands are moving before I even have time to realize what I'm doing. I pull up my contacts and find the newest entry that was added when I began the remodel phase of the house. New View Landscaping. Of course, at the time, I didn't know who'd be on the other end of that call, but now that I know?

I hit connect.

It rings twice before his deep voice filters through my cell phone. "Hello?"

I don't reply. I try, but the words just won't roll off my thick, heavy tongue. I suck in a breath, but it's strangled and refuses to inflate my lungs.

"Kate?"

The way he says my name causes tears to prick the corners of my eyes.

"I'm here, Butterfly," he says, the distant sound of something falling to the floor echoing through the phone. "Take a deep breath for me, okay?"

"Tr...tr...trying," I gasp, finally able to get that singular word out. The memories of the childhood nickname come back, both painful and catalytic. He said it represented me, a butterfly ready to spread her wings and fly. Be free. Unfortunately, freedom wasn't exactly what my life had entailed.

"Good. Are you sitting on the floor?" he asks, making me nod my head. "I can't hear you, Butterfly, so just listen to my voice, okay? If you're not sitting on the floor, make sure you're seated. I want you to close your eyes and concentrate on my voice. Deep breaths in through the nose and out through the mouth."

I focus on his words and do as he instructs, just the way he did last week in the backyard. The first deep breath into my lungs is like a cool dip in the pool on a hot summer day. He must hear my gasp and lungs fill with sweet oxygen, because I can practically feel him relax on the other line.

"Good job, Kate. Keep taking those deep breaths, okay? You should have seen Max today after we left your place. He smacked that ball off the tee every time he got up there, but his favorite part is running the bases. He likes to pretend the catcher is hot on his heels as he's running to first, a huge smile on his face. When he gets there, he just rounds the base and keeps going. He makes it all the way home, where I'm waiting to try to tag him out. I never get him though," he says, a small chuckle spilling from his lips.

He paints a beautiful picture of a boy and his father playing baseball on a Sunday afternoon. I can visualize the scene as it plays out, Max giggling as he tries to beat his dad to home plate to score the winning run. Before I realize it, my breathing is back to normal and the panic has subsided.

There's even a smile playing on my lips.

"Are you there, Kate?"

"I'm here," I whisper, exhaustion starting to rake through my body as I lean back against the wall.

"You okay?"

Exhaling deeply, I answer honestly. "Yeah."

I will be.

"What happened?" he asks, the sound of a chair scraping on hardwood filters through the line.

I open my eyes and glance around. The hauntings of my past are there still, watching and waiting for me to fall. My eyelids are heavy, but I keep them open—force them to stare down my past, instead of fleeing the room like I'd prefer. I sit, and stare, and eventually, I talk.

"I came into the library." I knew just saying those words aloud would probably be a good indication of why I ended up calling him in the middle of a full-blown panic attack.

"Had you been in there before tonight?" he asks.

I shake my head, but then catch myself again. "No. The door was locked and I stayed away."

"So, you opened the door and what did you see?"

I close my eyes again and picture the room as I entered. "Everything. The books, his desk, my...my painting. It was all there, exactly as it was when we left." He's quiet for a few moments, and I start to wonder if he's still there. Instead of asking, I keep talking. "When I saw it, it was like a splash of cold water on my face. Everything came back so vividly, so painfully. The shock, the sadness, the anger. The entire room was as if we'd only left for a few days. Well, except for the substantial amount of dust and grime all over everything."

"There's a lot there, Kate, that I won't pretend to understand. Maybe, someday, you can explain it to me, but I don't think that's a conversation for tonight," he says, and I have to admit, I'm appreciative I don't have to rip off that particular Band-Aid tonight as well. "Is there something you can do to relax? Maybe you can finish that painting," he offers easily, making my heart clench in pain.

Before I even realize it, a tear slips down my cheek. "I can't." The voice sounds so raw, it barely sounds like my own.

"Why not?" His own words are guarded, as if he wants to know, yet is preparing himself to receive the blow.

I glance over at the dirty canvas, sitting on the easel, the hurt so close to bubbling to the surface once more. "I haven't painted since the night we left."

Jensen's startled inhale comes through loud and clear. "Seriously? Kate…how…why?"

I shrug, even though he can't see me. Getting into this deep conversation isn't something I'm interested in doing right now. All I can think about is climbing into a hot bath and soaking in as much lavender bath salts as I can safely use. "I guess, I guess I just never had anything worth painting."

That was the truth. When we left, I left my muse behind. The one who brought me joy and laughter. The one who held me close and kissed me as if I were the only woman in the world. The one who loved me with his entire heart, and then some.

"I'm sorry to hear that. You were a brilliant artist, even at such a young age. I guess after you left I pictured some big-time gallery person stumbling upon you and insisting you sell your work in sold-out shows across the state of New York."

I can't help it, I snort a laugh. My mother would have been so mortified. "There was no gallery or shows. Everything was just…different after I left."

Again, I'm met with silence. "Maybe someday you can tell me about it."

A small smile pulls at the corner of my mouth. "Yeah, someday."

"Are you feeling better?" he asks after a few more moments of quiet.

"I think so. I can't believe I had that attack. I'm sorry to call you on a Sunday evening. You were probably getting Max ready for bed or something."

I can hear him get up from the table and turn on the faucet. "You're fine. He fell asleep during the third inning of the Rangers game. I had just got him settled into bed when you called."

"Well, I'm thankful I didn't wake him."

"Kate?"

"Yeah."

"You can call me any time you need help, okay? When you have an attack or just need someone to talk to, I'll answer."

My heart pounds in my chest. "Are you sure that's wise, you know, considering everything?"

Jensen sighs. "Probably not, but I don't give a shit. We weren't exactly a conventional couple back in the day, so there's no reason to start that shit now. I'll always be your friend, Kate. If you need something, I'm here."

"Thank you," I whisper hoarsely, his words pulling so much emotion from my body. "I appreciate that. I haven't exactly had a lot of friends."

"Well, you've got me, okay?"

"Okay," I reply, not really knowing if that's a good idea or not, but I won't turn away the chance at rebuilding the broken friendship we used to share. Even if all we'll ever be is a fraction of that bond.

"All right, Butterfly, up off the floor and close the door behind you. You can try to go in that room another day. What's on the agenda for the rest of the evening?" he asks casually. You know, like friends do.

"Actually, I'm going to have a bath. I brought some of my favorite products with me from New York. Ever since I knew I was moving back home, I could picture that big claw-foot tub I used to love to soak in. I think tonight, of all nights, it's calling my name." Jensen makes a strangled sound on the other end of the line and the hairs on the back of my neck stand up. "What? What's wrong?"

"Nothing," he insists, clearing his throat.

"Obviously, it's something. You just sounded like you were choking. Are you okay?"

"I'm fine, Kate. Just fine," he repeats, the words tight and full of tension.

"I don't believe you. Just say it," I insist.

"I shouldn't."

"You should."

"Drop it, Kate," he groans, as if in pain.

"No, I won't. If something's wrong, just tell me."

"You don't want to know," he argues.

"I do! Say it."

He huffs out a choppy breath. "Fine, do you want to know what's wrong? I was picturing you in the bathtub, naked and wet and all sudsy and now my pants are so tight they hurt."

The words he said register, but not completely. It takes a full ten seconds or so to really catch my brain up on the fact Jensen is…hard. And thinking about me, in the bathtub. My mouth goes completely dry and my heart rate spikes, and it has nothing to do with the residual effects of my earlier panic attack.

"You're… um… wow…"

That's all I got.

"Yeah," he says. "Now do you see why I didn't want to say anything?" he huffs.

A blush burns up my neck and settles on my cheeks. "Well, I do apologize for causing you some… discomfort. That was not my intention when I mentioned a bath."

Jensen is quiet for a few moments before whispering, "Do you remember the night your parents went out to that Save the Whales fundraiser at the museum? You gave me a key the day before at school. I told my mom I was headed to Garrett's house to watch the football game, which is actually quite humorous because the Broncos don't play on Saturday nights.

"Anyway, I went to your house and climbed up the stairs to the second floor. Where did I find you, Butterfly?"

I know exactly what memory he was talking about the moment he started his story, so it's easy for me to answer his question. "You found me in the bathtub."

"I did. You were naked and touching yourself."

"Only because I knew you were about to step into the bathroom. I had been waiting for you."

Jensen growls, a low noise that goes straight to my lady parts. "We…" he starts before clearing his throat. "We shouldn't talk about this."

I shake my head, agreeing. This is definitely not a trip down memory lane either one of us needs to be taking right now. "No, definitely not." Saying it aloud doesn't ebb the ache I suddenly feel between my thighs.

Jensen clears his throat again. "Good night, Kate." The words come out all gravelly and hoarse.

"Good night, Jensen," I whisper in a voice that doesn't even sound like mine.

Then, I hang up, even though I don't really want to, already knowing there's only one man I'll be thinking about when I touch myself in bed later tonight.

Chapter Nine

Jensen

Ashley was waiting at the door when I dropped off Max, and I could feel the frigid cold front even before I stepped inside the house. Apparently, she's still pissed as hell. While I'd much rather forget all about her attempt to seduce me back into our former marital bed, she's chosen a different path. This one will involve her throwing anger and guilt trips my way for the unforeseeable future.

Good times.

"Good morning," I say politely, but she completely ignores me.

"Hi, Maxie. How's my boy? Did you have a good weekend?"

"Duh best! We played baseball! And I found treasure," he adds with excitement, digging in his pocket for the four quarters he put there after he got dressed this morning.

"Treasure?" she asks, a giggle spilling from her lips that grates on my nerves. "Let me see." Max places his four prized quarters in her hand. After a few seconds of examining them, she wrinkles her nose and says, "These are just regular quarters."

I want to thump her upside the head.

"Nope, they're treasure from Kate's yard! I dugged them up with Daddy's shovel."

Fuck.

Ashley tenses before handing the quarters back to our son. "Kate?" she asks, her wide eyes never leaving our son's, even though I can feel the wrath building behind those big eyes.

"She lives in the big house. We dugged in her yard and found them," Max says casually, putting his treasure back in his pocket.

"Dug them," I correct my son before adding, "Why don't you run to your room and put your clothes and stuff away. Take the money out of your pocket and put it on your nightstand so it doesn't end up in the wash."

"Okay! Bye, Daddy! See you tomorrow," he says, throwing his arms around my legs and hugging me tight.

"Bye, Buddy. I'll see you at the school." Tomorrow is Max's first day of four and five-year-old preschool. Even though it's Ashley's day with him, I'll be meeting them at the school and walking him in.

When his hurried feet disappear into his room, I turn my attention to my ex-wife. Her eyes are full of fire and I can already tell she's gunning for a fight. Instantly, I can tell this isn't going to end well. While Ashley no longer has a voice in what happens in my personal life, we've always tried to understand anything involving our son would require transparency on our parts. When she dates, she tells me. That could be to try to make me jealous or simply because we both want to know who's going to be hanging around Max, but either way, we try to be as transparent as possible.

Of course, I have yet to date since the divorce, but whatever. The one time I tried didn't go so well. The woman my sister, Harper, set me up with was nice and all, but I could tell the moment she walked in it wasn't going to be a comfortable evening.

"Kate?" Ashley asks, her voice dangerously close to a high-pitched shriek.

"The new client. Max and I stopped by the house yesterday to pick up some paperwork. While I was on the phone, the homeowner took him over and helped him dig in the yard. No big deal," I reason, knowing full well she's not going to let my explanation slide.

"Where does this client live?" she asks, crossing her arms over her chest and throwing some serious eye-daggers my way, killing me multiple times in just a fraction of second.

And here we go…

"I'm not fighting with you, Ashley. I have to get to work," I reply, avoiding her question entirely. I know the moment I confirm what she suspects, our cordial relationship is out the fucking window. "You look nice, by the way. Have a good day at work."

Then, I hightail it out of there so fast, you'd think my ass was on fire.

I know this isn't the end of it. The compliment may have been a last-ditch effort at peace before the war breaks out. She won't let this drop for a second. I just pray she doesn't give Max a hard time when she discovers the woman we spent part of the afternoon with—the same woman who shared dinner with us Friday night—is the very one who stole my heart when I was sixteen and never really gave it back.

Fun times for all.

* * *

It's not a fun afternoon, that's for sure. Our large mower took a crap and the new parts weren't in stock at the tractor supply store. It'll take forty-eight to seventy-two hours just to get them in and then another day for the shop to put them on. The delay put Jonas a few hours behind and it was only worse once I ran one of the smaller back-up mowers to his location to finish the job.

The plants started to arrive today, which would normally put a smile on my face. However, when the North Pole Arborvitae arrived instead of the Stewartsonian Azaleas, I knew my afternoon was truly fucked.

After a quick call to the nursery where I purchase all of my product, I try to wrap my mind around the layout and design, wondering if I can incorporate the shrubbery that arrived into the scheme. The North Pole Arborvitae is a hearty, fast-growing plant that will work well in most conditions. They require some regular pruning to keep their shape, and they're perfect for privacy.

"You look to be in deep thought." Her voice filters over the distant sound of the ocean, and the sawing on the back patio, soft and tranquil.

My eyes connect with hers and my heart rate kicks up a few hundred beats. Will I ever *not* feel something when I look at her? This gut-clenching desire that swirls in my belly and thunders through my veins like an approaching tornado?

Probably not.

"Sorry, I was," I respond, glancing back out at the backyard.

"Problems?" she asks, coming to stand beside me.

Normally, I wouldn't bother to discuss the issue with the homeowner. I'd tell the nursery to send the right shit, and that's that. But something pulls deep inside me, begging to tell her all about my day. My soul calls to her, just as much as it did every day all those years ago, and I don't know what to do with that.

I know I should excuse myself to deal with the shrubbery mess. I know I need a little distance between the sweet honeysuckle permeating from her skin and the salt in the air. I know I shouldn't open my mouth and tell her all about my shit day, but even knowing all of that, it doesn't stop my lips from moving before my brain has a chance to catch up.

"The wrong shrubs arrived today. I can't use them for what I had planned around the patio."

"Can you send them back?" she asks.

Lacey Black

Nodding, I confirm. "Yeah, I can. They're really nice bushes, but not what I envisioned in the space. Since they're already dug up, they'll have to try to sell them right away, but that's not really my problem." I shove my hands into the pockets of my blue jeans and gaze back out at the vast yard.

"Can you incorporate them somewhere else?" she asks, bringing a voice to what I've already wondered.

"I don't know."

I hear her walk off, but keep my gaze on the new seating area we're building at the back of the property. The last thing I need is to have a problem with my dick perking up at the sight of her ass. It was hard enough (pun intended) after our phone call last night. So hard, in fact, it took two showers to relieve the ache I had in my balls. Just the thought of her in that damn bathtub was enough to send every ounce of blood I possess to one concentrated area.

Stepping toward the sitting area, my mind starts to picture the new space we're creating. I want to give her privacy from those in the water, yet award her a great view of the ocean at the same time. Not as easily done as it is said, considering you can't see through shrubbery.

Unless…

"What are you thinking?" she whispers, coming to stand beside me, the softness of her arm brushing against mine.

"What if we plant the bushes here," I say, drawing an imaginary line with my hand that runs the complete northeast side of the new space. "It will create a wall, of sorts, between your property and the neighbors." There's already plenty of space between the Elliott mansion and the much smaller house to the north, but it would create a little more privacy when said neighbors come down to the beach.

"Keep talking," she encourages.

"I'm thinking if we plant them along this property line, you'll have a little privacy in your new seating area, while still giving you the unobstructed view of the ocean. We'll keep those shorter shrubs over here," I add, motioning to the place where the yard meets the beach. "This way, you can still watch the waves. Plus, I'm creating a walkway that'll worm through this part here. I think it'll be the perfect private oasis for you."

Excitement courses through my blood as I take in the slightly altered picture I've created in my mind. Yes, I think this will work. Kate still gets the private area she was looking for, and I can use the plants the nursery accidentally delivered. It's a win-win. Especially if I get the product at a considerable discount, which I'm sure I can arrange, considering they won't have to try to sell them quickly on clearance.

"I love it." Her words are a balm to the very pain I carry deep down in my soul.

Turning back to face her, a smile plays on her lips, matching the one on my own. "Okay, I'll make the adjustments and call the nursery," I tell her, reaching for my cell phone to let them know of the change in plans. I'll still use the gorgeous flowering shrub they'll deliver tomorrow, but I'll be able to use the wrong ones too.

I glance around, the itch to dig tingling up my spine. Everyone is gone for the day, including the other contractors. "Would it be all right if I stayed a bit and got these in the ground?"

"Sure," she replies with a shrug.

As soon as she gives me the okay to hang around and keep working, I head to my truck for a few tools. Tossing them in the bucket of my small tractor, I steer the machine to the backyard. I'm surprised when I come around the corner and find Kate there, carrying a folding chair. I stop the tractor and jump off, anxious to get these bushes in the ground.

When I glance her way, she gives me an unsure look. "Is it okay if I watch?"

My heart does a little gallop in my chest. She used to show up when I was working in high school and watch me mow. She always said it was relaxing, watching me do what I loved. My tongue is thick and I'm not sure if words will actually spill from my lips, so I just nod instead. Kate settles into the chair, looking around to make sure she's not in the way. She is, but I'm not going to tell her that. I can maneuver around her and work from the opposite side. The good thing about this phase of the project is the canvas is clear and unobstructed for the most part.

I get to work, clearing a spot for my tools and readying the shrubs for planting. It doesn't take me long to fall into my zone, all while keeping Kate in my peripheral vision. She doesn't move much, just watches me work.

Since the ground is already prepped for planting, I have the eight new plants in the ground fairly quickly, even while working solo. As I start to fill in the holes around the roots, I catch movement out of the corner of my eye. Kate gets up and heads to the house, probably desperate for something to do other than watching me work. I'm sure she's bored out of her mind.

As I head up to the house to grab the hose, I'm surprised when she returns to her chair, carrying two glasses of what looks like lemonade. When I place the water source at the line of new shrubs, she gets up and brings me a glass.

"I thought you could use this."

"Thanks," I tell her, drinking the cold, sweet liquid down all at once.

A giggle spills from her lips. "I guess I was right."

"Yeah, I may have been a little thirsty," I tell her, wiping my sweaty brow with the hem of my T-shirt. The movement draws her eyes, and there's no mistaking the way she gapes at my bare stomach.

Her eyes meet mine and the cutest blush burns her cheeks. She doesn't avert her eyes, though. No, my Kate holds my gaze, not backing down for a second, even after being caught ogling my abs.

When she finally speaks again, she asks, "So no Max tonight?"

I walk over and adjust the hose, moving it down the line. "He's with his mom," I answer. She watches me closely, probably waiting to see if I'll elaborate more, before going back to her chair off to the side. "Go ahead and ask."

Our eyes meet and there's no hint of surprise in hers. "Who is his mom?"

I grab the shovel off the ground and pretend to adjust some of the wet dirt. It's not really necessary, yet I feel like I need to do something with my hands. After a few minutes of awkward silence, I give her my full attention, putting my weight on the handle of the shovel. "Ashley Tatum."

This time, her shock is very evident. "Ashley Tatum? You married Ashley Tatum?"

I slowly nod a reply. "Sure did."

Her mouth gapes open, clearly not expecting me to confirm I was married to one of the school's biggest bitches. Kate and Ashley always had snide words for each other, mostly on Ashley's part. Though, if I was around, Ash tended to be nice as pie. The moment I stepped away, however, she'd turn up the bitch factor to one hundred, always giving Kate a hard time about her perfect grades, her abundance of money, and her perfect life. Only those close to her (namely, me) knew the real story behind all of that. Behind it all was a miserable girl who just wanted to forge her own path and do what she loved instead of what was expected of her.

"Wow," she replies, clearing her throat, "I have to admit, I'm a little shocked by that."

I hold my position and look to the side. The water is gorgeous this evening as the sun starts to drop behind the house. "She seemed different," I confess. "When I returned from college, I spent a couple of years working for old man Parkinson. He was set to retire soon and took me on as his apprentice. I learned a lot of shit from him in a short time, and I knew owning my own business was where I was headed. Ashley was a year behind us in school and returned after things started to take off for me." I shrug. "Everything wasn't always great, but it was good for a while. The best part about it is Max."

She smiles up from her chair. "He's pretty awesome. He's definitely the spitting image of you, but now that I know who his mom is, I can see her in him as well."

Talking about my son makes my own smile come fast and easy. "He *is* pretty fucking awesome."

"So you've been divorced for..." she asks, leaving the end open for me to fill in the blank.

"Almost a year. We were separated for about six months before that."

"I'm sorry to hear that, but as someone who very recently went through her own divorce, it can be quite freeing to finally let go of something negative or a bitterness that has a hold of you in life."

I knew she was married. The different last name was a pretty damn good indication of that, but to hear her confirm it? It kinda makes me a little rage-y, which is completely not like me. Yet, it feels a little bit like jealousy bubbling up in my chest and I don't know how to explain it. She's not mine and hasn't been for a long damn time. "I kinda figured, since Dunnington is listed on the contract."

She nods, but doesn't immediately elaborate. Just when I think she's not about to continue, she speaks. "Charles Dunnington III worked for my father. After college, it was expected of me to join the family business. I hated it, and Daddy knew it. But I tried to make the best of it, you know? Charles was Daddy's right hand and I was told our partnership would do wonders for the business." She says it so matter-of-factly that it comes more of a shock than the actual words she speaks.

"Partnership for the business?"

Kate shrugs her bare shoulders. "Mother made it very clear our relationship would be important to my father and his company."

"So she pushed you into marrying someone you didn't love?" Again, anger sweeps through my chest at the idea.

"Yes and no. I met Charles when I was young and vulnerable. I thought I was in love with him, but I wasn't, not really. Not the kind of love a woman should have for the man she marries. He was comfortable."

"But was he really?"

She looks at me with those piercing hazel eyes that look a shade lighter than the bark of a sycamore tree in this light. "No, not really."

I watch her for several long seconds, both of us coming to terms with the mistakes we've made in the past and the repercussions we live with now. Our lives, while ripped away from each other, took similar paths. No, my life was still as blue collar as it could get, but the deep-rooted pain and longing was there for both. Together, we found solace in someone else, someone who wasn't right for us.

The end results were the same.

"Do you want to stay for dinner?" she whispers, pulling me out of my thoughts.

I shouldn't.

I should go home and grab some sleep. I have to meet Ashley and Max at the preschool tomorrow for his first day. There's a small stack of bills on my desk that require my attention. Yet, for some reason, I find myself disregarding all of that, instead replying, "Sure."

Gathering up my tools, I ignore the feel of her eyes on me and the happy little gallop in my chest. That warning sign that tells me not to get too close? I brush it aside too. Instead, I clean up my mess and head to the back door, where I find Kate gathering up food for dinner.

I'm staying.

I shouldn't, but right now, there's nowhere else I'd rather be.

Chapter Ten

Kathryn

I'm nervous. I'm not sure why, exactly, but I am.

Wait.

Yes, I do.

It's the fact Jensen Grayson, the man who stole my heart in high school and never gave it back, is now sitting at my new island, watching me cook chicken breasts in my new chef's kitchen. It was one of the features I insisted on when I decided to update the space. The old kitchen was formal and stiff. Plus, it reminded me of our housekeeper, Ingrid, and the fact I saw her ass bent over the countertop, the man standing behind her making her moan in pleasure definitely not her husband. He was the old landscaper, in one of those totally cliché ways.

Now, this almost complete kitchen is mine. I'm not the best cook, but I'm learning. Okay, so I can barely cook at all, but no one needs to know that. How hard can it be to throw a few chicken breasts on the stove?

"Umm, Kate?" Jensen asks softly, getting up from the stool and meeting me on the opposite side of the island. I can feel the heat from his body as he stands behind me, a mixture of dirt and sweat filling my nostrils.

"Yes?" I ask, my voice all crackly and high-pitched.

"Do you know what you're doing?" he asks, a hint of humor in his voice.

I glance over my shoulder and then back at him. "Of course I do," I defend, ready to argue until I see the smoke starting to billow from the fancy six burner stove in front of me. "Shit!" I holler, turning off the heat and reaching for a towel. I wave it back and forth to try to move the smoke before it hits the detector on the ceiling.

Jensen starts to laugh as he reaches around me and pulls the chicken from the heat source. Clearly, I'm unable to do something as simple as grill a few chicken breasts. Hearing him laugh should upset me, but it doesn't. Instead, I find myself laughing right along with him, something only he could make me do when faced with one of my failures.

"So, clearly cooking classes weren't in order while in New York," he jokes, grabbing the towel and waving it around more.

I run over and open the back door, thankful when the smoke starts to dissipate quickly. "Umm, no. No cooking classes, though clearly, I could have used a few."

Jensen stands at the counter, his hip leaned casually against the marble top. A smile plays on his lips as he crosses his arms and watches me. He looks so much the same, yet completely different. He's older for sure, but his mannerisms and his smile is everything I remember from my time in Rockland Falls.

"Come on, Gordon Ramsay. We'll call this your first lesson," he says, heading over to the fridge as if he's done it a thousand times before.

He makes himself at home as he takes a pork loin and some vegetables out, setting them down on the counter. Fortunately, I picked up a few things at the store to keep in the fridge, even if I didn't know how to fix them. My plan was to pull up YouTube cooking videos, but this is probably better right? I watch as he quickly washes his hands and grabs the cutting board and knife. He works silently as he seasons the loin with salt and pepper, adding crushed red pepper to the top before placing it on a pan. Once the oven is preheated, he places it inside and sets the timer.

With the meat in the oven, now he turns his attention to me. "That'll take about forty minutes or so. Let's get these cleaned and cut up. I love this big double oven. It'll come in handy when cooking the vegetables," he says, washing his hands a second time before turning to me.

Jensen reaches for me, gently taking my upper arm in his warm, callused hand and moving me until I'm standing directly in front of him. His body produces heat like a furnace and I can feel it all the way down to my bones. My blood starts to zing through my veins as he places the cutting board and knife in front of me.

"Can I trust you not to accidentally chop off one of these pretty little fingers?" he asks, taking my hand in his own and almost rendering me completely speechless. I nod frantically, the words just not able to slide through my parched mouth. "Let's cut up these Brussels sprouts. Slice off the end, like this," he instructs, showing me how, "and then cut them in half, like so."

Looks easy enough. He leaves me to it, while preheating the bottom oven. Jensen takes a minute to wash four potatoes, trimming off the ugly parts, before setting them next to my board. When I have the sprouts cut, he places them in a bowl and adds coconut oil, salt, and pepper, before stirring it all together and spreading them out on a cookie sheet. Watching Jensen breeze around the kitchen is actually quite the turn-on. I never thought having a man who could cook would get me all hot and bothered, but here I am, practically panting like a dog in heat, and getting lost in his effortless movements in tight jeans as he cooks us dinner.

My word, that ass...

"Cube those, but leave the skins on," he interrupts the naughty train that was silently barreling down on me.

I do as he instructs, careful to keep my breathing under control, all while watching him out of the corner of my eye. Somehow

I manage to not slice off a finger, considering my attention is definitely diverted. He barely says a word as he rinses off the potatoes and gives them the same treatment as the Brussels sprouts. Once they're seasoned and spread out on a pan, he places it all in the oven below the loin.

Then he turns, his eyes lasered in on my position. My hands are suddenly fidgety, like I don't know what to do with them, so I hold them tightly at my waist. Jensen doesn't move, doesn't give anything away on his handsome face. I have no clue what he's thinking, something I used to pride myself in being able to figure out, but now, I don't know if I'm just out of practice or if I just don't know the man as well as I knew the boy.

The air shifts, warmth spreading through the room and my blood like someone turned up the heat. My breath catches in my throat and before I know it, he's moving, approaching with the confidence I've always admired in him. His eyes bore into mine as he pulls me into his arms and presses his lips to mine, hungry and fierce.

At first, I'm almost in shock. As far as fantasies go, this one's been at the top of my list for a really, *really* long time. But as Jensen sweeps his tongue across the seam of my lips, I realize it's not a fantasy. Not at all. This is real. Jensen has his arms around me, pulling me tightly against his hard body, and he's kissing me with a decade's worth of pent-up frustration.

This kiss is everything. It's alive, breathing and feeding, consuming me in a way only his kisses could ever do. My mouth opens easily as his tongue slides inside, tasting and devouring. Blood swooshes in my ears as he lifts, setting me atop the counter. My legs instantly open and wrap around his trim waist, while his hands are pinned between the globes of my ass and the hard surface I'm sitting on. I can feel his erection pressed firmly in the apex of my legs and it only grows (pun intended) when he pulls me tightly against him.

Lacking any control over my own body, I tilt my hips and grind against him. A low groan crawls from his throat, but he doesn't break the kiss. His lips are firm and rough as they devour my own, ensuring this kiss is one I won't be forgetting anytime soon. My pulse is pounding, blood is pumping, and my body is begging for more. More friction. More touching. More Jensen.

But before I can beg him to remove every scrap of clothing between us, he rips his lips from mine with a groan that borders desire and pain. "Shit," he pants, closing his eyes and resting his forehead against mine.

His heavy breathing mixes with mine as I struggle between reeling back in the desire coursing through my body and continuing to grind against him. I know exactly which way my needy body is leaning, that's for sure. This ache between my legs is only growing more intense by the second.

"We shouldn't be doing this," he whispers as he opens his eyes. They're still dilated from desire, but it's the look of pain that grabs my attention and won't let go.

He's right.

We shouldn't be doing this.

His words ring in my ears like a siren, and suddenly, I feel embarrassed. I'm practically climbing my ex-boyfriend as if he were a tree in the backyard, while imagining the dirty things he could do to me on this very counter. The burn moves up my neck and lands in my cheeks as I drop my hands from gripping the back of his T-shirt.

Jensen pulls away and walks to the opposite side of the kitchen. It's as if he can't get far enough away from me, not that I blame him. Confliction is etched all over his handsome face, and that pains me even more. I did that to him.

Then my eyes drop to his pants and the tightness they possess, and I realize, I did that too.

"I'm sorry," I whisper, wrapping my arms around my stomach, wishing his arms were still around me.

"For what? I'm the one who kissed you."

My eyes connect with his from across the room. "I'm not talking about the kiss." My heart tries to pound out of my chest as my words seem to register. We haven't talked about what happened twelve years ago. I've been avoiding it like the plague, but I don't think I can live without saying it any longer.

He averts his eyes for a second, his mouth moving as if he's trying to figure out what to say. Needing to get this out, I let the words spill from my lips. "I'm sorry I left in the middle of the night and you never heard from me again. If I could take it back, I would. Something...something happened and I still don't completely understand it. My dad stopped me when I came home that night from our date and told me we were leaving." I feel the burn of tears, but forge on.

"Mother was already packing what few belongings she was taking. I was informed I needed to gather my things because we were moving to New York. I tried to call you, but it just went to voicemail. When Mother came in my room and saw me waiting to leave you a message, she took my phone and smashed it.

"I was barely able to gather up a few things before I was ushered to a waiting car. The next thing I knew, we were boarding Daddy's jet for New York. It all happened so fast, it was like a dream. A nightmare, actually. I couldn't remember your number since my phone was broken and there was something clearly going on between my parents. The tension was so thick between them you could practically see it."

I take a deep breath, steeling my back as I forge on. "I decided to give it a day or two to calm down before I asked to go back. Even though they had their heart set on me attending Princeton that fall, I was ready to tell them I had enrolled at North Carolina State with you."

That day comes back to me as if it had happened yesterday. My parents had no clue I wanted to stay local and study art instead of being carted off to Princeton and major in business management and real estate like my dad. Painting was my passion, my dream. It's all I wanted to do. Well, that and stay with Jensen.

But that was taken from me in the middle of the night.

"What happened?"

"Mother bought me a new phone and refused to allow me to pull my old contacts. I couldn't remember your number for the life of me, even though I had called or texted it a dozen times a day for a few years. After a few days, I got online and found the number for your mom's bed and breakfast. Before I could call, she told me you didn't want to speak to me anymore." The words are barely audible as I relive the worst time of my life.

"What? Why would she say that?"

I shrug my shoulders, keeping my eyes on the fancy new tile I just had installed in the kitchen. "She said..." I take a deep breath and force myself to say the words. "She said you were using me, to get our money."

"The fuck?" he bellows, pulling my gaze back to his. His face is a mixture of horror and disbelief.

"I didn't believe her at first," I insist, the tears spilling from my eyes like someone turned on the faucet.

He gazes at me from across the room before asking, "At first?"

"Yeah, at first," I whisper.

"What changed?" he asks, his voice shallow and unsure.

"The letters."

"Letters?" he asks, clearly very confused about what letters I'm referring to.

"The ones between you and your father."

Perplexity is written all over his gorgeous face as he tries to follow, but I don't understand why. How could he have forgotten about the letters he wrote back and forth with his dad, talking about how he didn't love me and was in it for sex?

"Butterfly, I'm trying to understand what you're saying, but I have to be honest. I don't know anything about any letters. The only letters I wrote were to you and they were all sent back to me in a bundle with a note you didn't want to hear from me again."

Now it's my turn to look confused. "I never got any letters, and I definitely didn't tell you to leave me alone."

"I got them all back about two months after you left. When your cell phone was disconnected, I resorted to writing you letters. Your dad gave me your address," he says, shocking me all over again.

"What? I never received anything!" I insist, trying to figure out how he would have gotten them back if I didn't even see them.

And then, like a snake slithering up my spine, cold dread settles in.

"What did the note say that I supposedly wrote?" I ask, my eyes glued to his blue ones.

"That you were happy in New York and had already moved on." His words cut like a knife, the wound left behind fresh and gaping.

I start to cry harder now, my shoulders shaking with realization. "I never wrote that."

The warm touch of his hand against my cheek startles me. Jensen wipes away my tears with the pads of his thumbs and tilts my head up to look into my eyes. "And there were never any letters between my dad and me, Kate. I was barely speaking to him at that point in my life, let alone talking to him via mail about something as personal as my feelings for you."

His words make me cry all over again. Years—more than a decade—I spent wondering what I had ever done wrong, why I never saw Jensen for who he was. He had told me he loved me every day, so why would he tell me that and then tell his dad he didn't? I had been so confused and hurt.

Warmth and familiarity wrap around me as he pulls me into his chest. The worn cotton of his shirt becomes soaked as it mops up the tears I shed. "I can't believe this," I whisper, inhaling the scent that is uniquely Jensen.

He exhales, the steady beat of his heart grounding me. "Clearly, there's a bit of a miscommunication. I didn't write letters to my dad and you didn't tell me to leave you alone. Honestly, that makes me feel a little better. Not that I'm glad you disappeared on me, but at least I know it wasn't because you didn't love me anymore."

"And I'm glad to know you weren't using me until something better came long," I confess, speaking my biggest fear aloud for the first time.

His whole body tenses. "I loved you more than life itself."

Loved.

Past tense.

Even though our relationship has been over for many years, it still hurts a little to hear him confirm what we had ended.

We're both quiet for several minutes, but he doesn't let me go. He lets me cry until the tears subside, pulling as much comfort from his embrace as I want. When I pull away, I quickly wipe under my eyes, no doubt swiping away a day's worth of mascara and snot from my skin. Jensen grabs me a paper towel, and hovers in front of me as I clean myself up from my cryfest.

"You really got our address from my dad?"

The right side corner of his lips turn upward. He shoves his hands in his pockets, but stays close as he replies, "I did. It was after you'd been gone a few days. I was going crazy trying to track you down. I knew your dad had the big office in New York City, so I found the phone number and called him. Took him two days to call me back, but when he did, he explained the move was best for you. I didn't understand, and he didn't seem too keen on explaining it to me. He wouldn't give me your new number, just told me it was safer to give me your address."

"Clearly, it wasn't," I retort, tossing the used paper towel into the exposed garbage.

"Clearly," he agrees with a smile.

I'm lost in his sapphire eyes for several long seconds and I start to wonder what this all means for us. Can we go back to what we had before? Probably not. Can we move forward? God, I hope so. But I don't know where he stands on an *us*, and the prospect of asking him is enough to cause a small panic attack.

"Don't," he says with force, taking my face in his hands and turning me until we're looking at each other. "Don't go there. We can't go back, only forward," he adds, putting into words the questions running through my head.

"Forward."

He nods. "Forward. We'll start with dinner Saturday night."

"Dinner? With you?"

He grins that lopsided boyish grin I fell in love with all those years ago. "Yeah, with me. I mean, we've already had pizza together last week, and we are having dinner together tonight, so this won't be anything we haven't already done twice in the last seven days." Before I can open my mouth, he keeps going. "The Falls Festival is this weekend, and I'd like to take you."

The Falls Festival? As in the biggest town gathering in the county? Where everyone, and I do mean *everyone*, will see us?

"The festival is this weekend?" I ask, recalling how much I used to love going to the festival. The games, the rides, the food. My dad used to take me when I was a child, but when I was in high school, it was always Jensen who was by my side. The thought of going again—and with him, no less—has me all sorts of excited.

"It is, and we're going. I'll buy you a corndog and lemon shake-up," he tells me, grinning like a loon.

"And an elephant ear. I need an elephant ear too, or no deal," I tease.

"You drive a hard bargain, Butterfly, but I think I can swing an elephant ear for the lady too." His hands run up my legs and rest on the outsides of my thighs. My skin tingles where his thumb draws little circles on my bare skin.

I'm about to accept his offer, when something else jumps to mind. "What about Max?"

"It's his weekend with his mom. I have him most weekends, except for the last weekend of the month. We flip our schedule for that week."

"So, it'll just be the two of us?"

"Well, yeah, and about four thousand other Rockland Falls residents," he quips with a chuckle.

"Yeah, and them too." I reply, realizing I'm actually a little disappointed his son won't be joining us. "I just meant if it means you had to find a sitter for Max, he can just go with us. I wouldn't mind."

The breathtaking smile he gives me causes little butterflies to take flight in my stomach. "I love you want to include him. If it were my weekend, we would definitely be taking him with us. He loves the festival. I'm actually a little sad he won't be with us."

Lacey Black

"Maybe next year," I say without giving it a thought. Then, I realize what I said and hope he doesn't take it as an insinuation we'll still be hanging out this time next year.

The timer on the oven sounds, alerting us that our dinner is ready. "Come on," he says, helping me down from the counter. "Let's eat."

Chapter Eleven

Jensen

The Saturday morning sun is fierce, but the shade of the old oak trees along my mom's driveway provides just enough cover to make the heat bearable. I'm on the small walk-behind mower, since Wes has the bigger one across town. We got it back earlier in the week from the repair shop, running better than it has since it was new.

When I'm finished mowing, I pull the hedge trimmers from the small trailer behind my truck and get to work making sure everything leading up to the business front looks immaculate. I fell in love with landscape maintenance and design by working this very property, and that love has definitely continued into my adulthood. This place is one of my favorites in the entire county, only second to the sprawling landscape and glorious blooms at the Elliott mansion.

As I'm raking up the trimmings from the yard, Mom comes out, carrying a glass of lemonade. "Hey, you," she says, setting the glass down on the small table beside the swing.

"Hi, Mom. How's your Saturday going?" I ask, piling up the scraps and leaning the rake against the porch.

"Good. Rhenn and Marissa took off in the boat for the weekend, so I'm manning the B&B," she says, nodding toward the glass.

I take the steps up and have a seat beside her on the swing. The lemonade is refreshing and much appreciated on this warm August day. "Thanks for this," I tell her before finishing the glass.

"Warm out here," Mom acknowledges, gently rocking the swing back and forth. "Big plans for the rest of your Saturday?"

I use my longer legs to rock us, trying to decide how much to tell her. She's always been a human lie detector, especially when we were younger. But there's also the fact Mom quickly became the one I could talk to about anything. When my dad left to screw half the younger population of Rockland Falls, including my good buddy's very married mom, any relationship we had was severed like the sharp cut of a knife. The easygoing, natural bond I had with Dad was replaced by one with Mom, the parent who was there in person day in and day out. Maybe that's why I find myself finally spilling all of the details about the Elliott mansion and discovering Kate as the new owner.

She doesn't say anything as I recall the panic attack or the late night phone call. She just listens, letting me spill my guts, and waiting. "We're heading to the Falls Festival tonight. We're going to be seen together."

"Does that bother you?" she asks, finally speaking for the first time since I started my story.

"No." I'm surprised by how true that is. I know everyone in town is going to be there, and there's no doubt they'll recognize Kathryn Elliott right away.

"Then what's the problem?" she asks softly, sipping her own lemonade.

"It's still comfortable with her. I'm surprised at how easy it is, like no time has passed."

She nods slowly. "Well, she was always very special to you." Now, it's my turn to nod. Mom doesn't need me to confirm her statement. She already knows it's the truth. "Well, I'm not going to tell you what to do or how to live your life, but I am going to tell you to be careful. You two have a lot of history, and there's some pain behind it. Just take it slow."

"I will, Mom. Besides, there were some things that happened back then that may have played a part in the hurt." Then, I tell her about my returned letters and that she says she'd never seen them, let alone returned them. I explain how she was told I didn't want her anymore and to stay away.

"I never trusted that her parents weren't involved in more than they should have been. Her father always seemed to be a decent man, but her mother? Well, she was a bit more conniving and underhanded. It doesn't surprise me if they somehow played a part in what happened back then."

We spend the next ten minutes swinging, talking business, and even about my siblings. When it's finally time for me to gather up my tools and pack up for the day, she pulls me into a hug. "Follow your heart, Jensen."

The air thickens in my throat. "I will, Mom."

She nods and turns to head back inside. "Oh, and bring my grandson over for dinner when you get him back. I've missed him."

I offer her a smile. "You just saw him last week," I remind.

She huffs out a breath. "That was last week. Now I want to see him this week. Bring him over," she instructs, leaving no room for argument.

"I will," I assure.

Before she slips through the door, she adds, "And go ahead and bring that pretty Kathryn too. I've missed that girl."

She doesn't wait for a reply, just disappears through the screen door. Kate and I spent so much of our time together I forgot how much it hurt my mom too when she disappeared. If I bring Kate around, I'm not only subjecting myself to more potential heartache, but my family too.

Especially Max, who already seems completely enthralled with her.

I guess I'm just going to have to take it slow and keep myself guarded. I'm pretty damn sure my heart wouldn't survive being ripped out a second time.

* * *

"What first?"

"Do you have to ask?" Her eyes light up with excitement as she gazes across the town square and the midway games positioned in the streets. I know what she's looking for, and there's no missing the happiness that crosses her face the moment she spots it. "Oh my God, they still have it!"

I chuckle as we make our way through the masses of Rockland Falls residents. Many offer me greetings along the way, but I don't stop. With a friendly grin and a hello, I follow behind Kate as she makes a beeline to the Ferris wheel. "I take it we're riding that first," I holler over the Skee-Ball noise and the carnival music.

Kate slows just long enough for me to buy two wristbands for unlimited rides. I've never been much of a ride person, but with Kate, I always found myself stepping out of my box. Frankly, I could never tell her no.

Apparently, that's still true, if the way my stomach turns a little queasy is any indication.

We make it to the end of the line, which, fortunately, is only a few people long. I try to ignore the odd looks from those who pass us, no doubt, everyone recognizing the woman at my side. Even if she's been gone more than a decade, Kathryn Elliott looks very much the same as she did all those years ago. If anything, she's even more beautiful with her faint laugh lines outlining her eyes and her blonde hair turning a slightly darker shade.

"Everyone is staring at me," she whispers, twisting her hands together at her waist.

"They're staring at me," I tell her, knowing we're both right.

She glances around again before turning those hazel eyes on me. "I didn't think about what everyone would be saying when they saw us out in public together."

"Fuck 'em," I insist, hating she's suddenly very conscious of the many eyes turned her way. The more she notices, the more agitated she becomes, and all I can think about is her having a panic attack in the middle of the festival. "Hey," I say, taking her hand in mine to offer a little comfort. "They're gonna talk just like always, okay? We're just two people enjoying the evening together, going on rides and stuffing our faces with greasy food."

That makes her smile a little. "But we're two people who have a… past."

I shrug. "True, but none of them matter, right? Whatever happens, wherever this *thing* between us goes, it's not about them. It's about us. Two friends, reconnecting after a long absence."

Kate snorts in a very unladylike manner. I fucking love it. "*Friends*. I don't think I've ever pictured my friends doing dirty things to me on the Ferris wheel," she says before suddenly realizing it. Her face turns a very dark shade of red and her sexy little mouth falls open in shock. "Holy shit… I didn't mean… What I meant to say was…"

I step forward, nice and close so I can smell her perfume, and reply, "That's okay, Butterfly. The things I'd love to do to you on this Ferris wheel have been playing through my mind for the last several minutes. All of them dirty," I confirm, remembering how I let my hand slip up her skirt and beneath her panties our final year of high school. She was so fucking wet already, I thought I was going to come in my shorts on contact.

Her blush only intensifies, making my cock hard. Before she can reply, the carnie clears his throat behind us. When I gaze his way,

I realize we're next in line and the car is waiting. "We're up," she whispers hoarsely, slowly turning and walking up the stairs.

"Oh, we're definitely *up*," I reply quietly enough so no one hears me. With a quick, as discretely as possible adjustment of my pants, I follow her into the waiting car and pull the safety bar down.

As soon as the car starts to move, my stomach drops to my shoes. Did I mention I'm not a fan of heights? Kate would remember this, of course, yet shows not a single ounce of remorse as she grins ear to ear and gazes out over the festival square in downtown Rockland Falls.

"I forgot how beautiful this place is," she whispers, almost absently to herself.

"It is," I confirm. It's part of the reason I never envisioned myself leaving. Well, besides the fact my family is here. But even before Max came along, I never pictured heading off to make a home somewhere else. It was always Rockland Falls, with its quaint small shops and overly nosey neighbors. And when my son came along, I knew I'd be here for the rest of my life. "Did you ever miss it?" I ask as we start to round the top of the wheel.

"Every day," she confirms, turning her eyes from everything below us to me. The moment they meet, the anxiety I feel about being fifty feet above the earth starts to slip away. "Not just because you were here, but because this place was my home. It was a hard transition from here to New York City. I didn't handle it well."

"The panic attacks?"

She nods. "Yeah."

"I'm sorry to hear that." Before I realize what I'm doing, my hand is holding hers, offering comfort and peace. We're both silent as the wheel reaches the bottom and then continues back to the top. Her hand is still nestled in mine, between us on the seat, as we fall into a familiar and easy rhythm of companionship and friendship. It was always so damn easy between us.

As we reach the top for the third and final time, she speaks again. "There's been a lot of changes since I left. All of those buildings have had a facelift."

"That one there," I say, pointing to the newest updates in downtown, "is my sister Harper's shop."

Kate's eyes light up. "Oh? What kind of shop?"

"Lingerie," I confirm.

I expect her to be embarrassed by this revelation (I was, admittedly, at first), but the look that crosses her face isn't one of discomfort. No, this look is more of curiosity. "Really? I can't wait to check it out," she replies, and I can already tell she means it.

"The shop next door is her boyfriend's."

Kate glances that direction, but the angle is off since we're already descending. "The hardware store?"

"Douglas Hardware. Bud retired last month and his son, Latham, took over. They actually purchased the space between them and are sharing it."

"A hardware store and a lingerie shop? Together? There's some *Fifty Shades of Grey* joke in there, right?"

I chuckle, because, yes, I've heard the jokes about rope and lubricants down the aisle from the crotchless panties. "There have definitely been a few dirty jokes made in recent weeks," I verify as the carnie starts to let riders off. We're stopped about halfway down when the atmosphere starts to thicken, and I'm pretty sure it has nothing to do with the late August night air and everything to do with the fact I want to kiss this woman again more than I want my next breath.

"I'll have to check it out."

Lacey Black

"Do that, and let me know if you need any assistance." The implication of my words hangs heavy between us as the car makes a jolting stop at the base of the Ferris wheel.

The man at the helm of the ride doesn't seem to notice the heavy sexual tension surrounding us, or he chooses to ignore it. The moment we step off the ride, he's scanning the wristbands of the next group of ride-goers.

"So, what's next? Corndogs? Lemon shake-ups? The Tilt-A-Whirl?"

Groaning, I respond, "I forgot how much you like to eat and then get the shit shaken out of you."

She laughs, a breezy, earthy sound that fills my soul with wonder and excitement. "That actually sounds very gross. Let's hope you didn't mean that in the literal sense."

"Uh, no, definitely not literally. I just forgot you enjoy spinning and flying through the air," I reply.

"And you don't like that," she replies, matter-of-factly.

I'm stuck in her intoxicating gaze. "Hate it."

"But you always did it."

"For you." My cock twitches in my shorts.

"For me," she ratifies. Kate glances around, realizing we've stopped in the middle of the street. "Oh, look! The House of Horrors," she bellows, pulling me from my Kate-infused sexual funk and practically dragging me toward the mini haunted house, where the line is a bit longer than the Ferris wheel.

It takes us about ten minutes before it's our turn to ride through the small, dark haunted house. A couple of teenage boys are in the car in front of us, loudly joking around about how scary the ride is. It reminds me of the way my friends and I used to behave on this ride. Well, at least until I was seated beside Kate. Then, all I wanted to do was be all cool and try to steal a few kisses in the dark.

128

Speaking of kisses...

We jolt as the ride moves, my arm instantly going to rest of the back of the seat as I used to do when we were kids. We creep through a rickety old door, ignoring the neon sign about danger ahead. Instead, I focus on the way Kate nestles into the seat, her upper back hitting my arm the same way it used to. My fingers twitch to move just a few inches, to caress the soft skin on her arm, but I refrain. The truth is we aren't kids, and we aren't together. There's no reason to start groping her in the middle of the haunted house.

Until she looks at me.

There are shadows since the place is bathed in darkness, with the exception of the flashes of light accompanying skeletons, zombies, and mummies, but even then, there's no missing the look on her face. It's a look of longing and mischief; the same look she used to give me all those years ago. It's familiar and yet so foreign, but piques my interest in that challenging manner. Like she's daring me to kiss her.

A challenge I fully accept.

With teenage boys pretending to be scared at our ambiance, my arm moves, pulling her against my overheating body. She gazes up at me with wide, needy eyes, already licking her lips in anticipation. Something deep inside me pulls, a subtle reminder I shouldn't be doing this, that there's no going back. Now that I feel her in my arms again—for the second time this week—I know I'm truly and royally fucked.

Not that I'd want to backtrack at this point anyway...

"Do you remember when we used to make out in this ride?" I whisper, ignoring the loud spooky music blasting through the speakers around us.

"I remember you getting to second base for the first time on this ride," she replies, eyes sparkling like diamonds under the strobe lights.

Oh, I most definitely remember that too. A boy never forgets the first time he felt a boob. Chuckling, I add, "I recall that too. My palms were sweaty with nerves." I move ever so slightly, lining up our lips.

Her breath fans across my face. "Are your palms sweaty this time?" she dares, my cock jumping with excitement in my shorts.

"I don't think so, but there's only one way to find out."

"I agree. We should definitely find out," she pants.

Kate's eyes flutter shut and my mouth moves, claiming hers in a hard, fierce kiss. The softness of her lips is so fucking enticing, so fucking sweet, so fucking right it steals any logic that may try to slip into my brain, reminding me we're still in a fairly public place. All that goes right out the window when she opens her mouth and her tongue slides against mine.

My hand moves, gently slipping beneath her top and gliding its way up the smooth skin of her side. When it reaches her bra, I find her nipples already hard, pressing firmly against the coarse lace material. As I graze my fingers over the hardened peaks, the sweetest fucking gasp slips from her lips.

My mouth devours hers as my hand cups her breast. They're definitely fuller than they were when we were younger and a lot more sensitive, if her mewls of pleasure are any indication. I move the material aside and slip my palm against the warm skin. Her body practically ignites as she seeks out the sweet friction of my hand. When I pinch her nipple, she detonates, her needy cries sending tingles down my spine that land heavily in my balls. I'm pretty sure I could take this woman right here, right now, in the middle of the world's cheesiest ride, and not give a single fuck about witnesses or repercussions.

Unfortunately, it's as she's seeking out more contact with my hand when I realize our dark ride is coming to an end. I pry my lips from hers and rip away my hand, helping right her bra and top just as we're bathed in light once more. The ride jerks to a stop, the young kid manning the exit giving me a knowing smirk.

I stand up, my own legs a little shaky, and offer assistance to Kate. Her lower limbs are in even worse shape than my own, which makes for a fun exit from the ride. Not to mention her lightly mussed hair, the fact her shirt is slightly askew, and her lips are swollen and red. I try to save face a little, glancing over to the young guy and saying, "She's not much of a ride-taker."

He laughs right in my face though, and whispers, "Looks like she enjoyed the hell out of the ride."

Of course, Kate hears his comment and gasps beside me. I can tell she's ready to fire off a quick-witted retort, and decide to save a little face, pulling her along beside me. "That was rude," she replies when we're walking away from the House of Horrors.

I snort. "Rude, but true. You look a little…excited," I reply, my voice dropping dangerously low.

Her eyes dilate even more and her pinked cheeks turn a shade darker. Instead of trying to deny the state of her appearance and her body, she leans in and whispers, "Well, I have always loved that ride."

My balls tighten painfully as I gaze down at her. Every time we've fooled around on that ride flashes before my eyes. I'm a millisecond away from dragging her back in line for a second trip when I hear a familiar voice break through the lust-filled fog choking me.

"Daddy!"

I glance to the side just as Max launches himself at my legs. Snatching him as he flies through the air, I feel the weight of my ex-wife's judgmental eyes almost immediately. Choosing to ignore her at the moment, I focus on my son. "Hey, Buddy, are you enjoying the festival?"

"Yeah! I ate a big corndog and cheese fries," he tells me, a toothy grin on his happy face.

"I can tell," I laugh, noting the dried cheese left behind from his dinner.

"Kate! Can I come over and find more treasure?" he asks, giving all of his attention to the woman at my side.

"Hey, Maxwell! You can come over any time and look for more treasure," Kate replies, returning my son's warm smile and giggle.

"My name's not Maxwell," he laughs. "It's just Max!"

"Well, Just Max, the invitation stands," she agrees before turning her eyes to my ex-wife. "Hello, Ashley."

It's the first time I glance at the woman I share a son with, and the look on her face is exactly as I anticipated. It's a mixture of anger and shock, most likely because I never confirmed the Kate Max talked about was the Kate from my past. Now, there's no denying it, since they're face-to-face.

"Kathryn," Ashley bites out as if just saying the name has left a horrible taste in her mouth. "When did you get to town?"

"A few weeks ago," Kate replies politely.

"Well, it's good to have you back. I'm sure Jensen was *very* pleased," she says, glancing my way. Then she turns back to Kate with a spiteful grin and says, "And obviously, you've been very *pleased* recently too."

I can't help the gasp that slips from my mouth at her insinuation. No, she's not far off course, but who actually says something like that, and with our son in earshot? Kate doesn't stoop to her level, though. She just civilly smiles and adds, "It has been a very pleasant visit with Jensen and Just Max. I've enjoyed spending what little time I have with them."

Ashley turns her glare my way. Max, fortunately, seems completely oblivious that his mom is a mere one step away from punching me in the face. Ashley was never a violent woman—I wouldn't have married her if she was—but there has always been this underlying issue when it came to Kate. There was always a jealousy there, smoldering beneath the surface. Even though she had nothing to worry about, since Kate was long gone from the picture when we got together, she just always hated what I had before her.

Now, it's liable to only get worse.

"Well, I'm sure you two have more important things to do, so Max and I will leave you to it," Ashley says, taking Max by the hand and guiding him away from where I stand.

"I'll see you Monday morning, Buddy," I tell my son, eager to have him back at my place. The reversed week is always a little harder, since we each have him for a longer period of time right before or after, but we make it work. Normally, I would pick him up after school on Monday, but since it's the Labor Day holiday, I get him in the morning before his mom goes to work at the hospital.

Max runs back to me, throws his arms around my waist, and squeezes. "Love you, Daddy. Bye Kate," he hollers with a wave before running back to his mom. Ashley manages one final icy glare before turning and disappearing into the mass of people.

"Well, that was fun," Kate says beside me.

"She hasn't always been so...unfriendly. You're taking that well," I tell her, turning my attention away from the crowd and back to the woman at my side.

She shrugs. "What am I going to do? Be all hard and snappy? Max doesn't need to see that, and frankly, what happened between the two of you has nothing to do with me."

I'm afraid she's a little off base. When I look back on my marriage to Ashley, I know I never really gave her my entire heart. She received only part of it, by no fault of her own. No, the fault behind my failed marriage rests solely on my shoulders, even if she did make it quite difficult from time to time. I'm the asshole in this picture, and that's okay. I deserve it. I'll never regret marrying Ashley, though I do wish I had gone about everything a little differently.

Sensing the heaviness of the moment and the weight of my thoughts, Kate offers me a smile and reaches for my hand. "Come on, you owe me a corndog."

Chapter Twelve

Kathryn

My stomach is positively stuffed to the gills, carbs be damned. Between the foot-long corndogs, lemon shake-ups, and the elephant ear, I couldn't eat another bite. Just the thought of ingesting more food is enough to make me want to puke.

"Look, fried Oreos," Jensen says, pulling me along toward the food truck, my hand still comfortably nestled within his much bigger one.

"Uhhh," I groan miserably. "Jensen, I seriously don't want to even think about more food right now."

"But this isn't food, Butterfly. This is deep fried Oreos," he says, and for some reason, it sounds totally naughty when he says it. Like he's seducing me…with food.

"No," I reply, shaking my head adamantly. "I couldn't possibly eat another bite."

Suddenly, I'm moving, being pulled gently forward until I'm practically pasted against his rock-hard chest. My breathing hitches as I press firmly against the rigid planes of his midsection, his free hand wrapping around mine. "What if I did all the eating?" he whispers and my thighs clench. I can feel the wetness flooding my core, no doubt rendering my panties completely useless.

"Oh my God, did you just say something dirty?" I hear what sounds like a choking sound next to us and quickly turn my attention to our side. I recognize the woman right away.

"Harper. Don't you have anything better to do?" Jensen asks his older sister without taking his eyes from mine.

"Actually, yes, yes I do. If you're talking dirty I have *sooo* many other things I'd rather be doing. Like getting a root canal or maybe a bikini wax. Painful things that would hopefully dull the ache of hearing my little brother talking dirty to his ex-girlfriend," Harper says without breaking stride and moving to stand behind us in line. Finally, she turns her blue eyes to me. "Hi, Kathryn." It's polite, sure, but not dripping with friendliness.

"Hello, Harper. How have you been?"

"Couldn't be better. You remember Latham Douglas, don't you?" she asks, her eyes lighting up when she turns to the handsome man behind her. I definitely remember Latham. He was a couple of years older than me and played sports. Every female in the school knew who he was, but I specifically remember how he used to torment Harper. Well, maybe not torment, but there were definite buttons pushed—on both sides.

"Oh, yeah. Hi, Latham. Good to see you," I say, reaching for his hand. It's large and welcoming, but doesn't give me that warm, fuzzy feeling like when Jensen touches me.

"Good to see you too," he says, turning a pretty sexy smile toward the woman at his side.

"Jensen mentioned you two were together now. That's great," I find myself saying. Even if Jensen hadn't mentioned it, it's obvious, considering his hands are dangerously low on her hip, as he tucks her into his side, and looks like he wants to devour her.

"He wore me down," Harper shrugs, practically glowing with happiness as she gazes up at the big guy beside her.

"Wow," I reply with a big smile, but gently lean toward Jensen and whisper, "Didn't she once tell the school he was pleasuring himself on the football field with a traffic cone?"

"I knew that was you!" Latham bellows, pulling our attention (and everyone within a two-block radius) to his shocked face.

"Of course, it was her, love. You didn't think the rumor of you screwing a traffic cone came from anyone other than our sweet little Harper here, did you?" a woman says as she comes up to stand beside Harper, licking a chocolate ice cream cone. I know her instantly. Freedom Rayne was Harper's best friend in school. She was completely eccentric, and if her long, flowy shirt, braided hair with a ring of flowers around her head, and dozens of bangle bracelets are any indication, I'd say she hasn't changed a bit.

Latham wraps his arms around Jensen's sister and plasters his lips on hers. When he comes up for air, he says, "You're going to pay for that later, Sweetheart."

"I look forward to it."

"Okay, you're in public. Let's not get carried away and spoil my appetite." Jensen gives me a smile when he turns away from his sister and her boyfriend. "You remember Free, right?" he asks, nodding to the familiar woman who walked up.

"Of course," I reply extending my hand. "Good to see you, Free."

"You too, love. I didn't know you were back in town," Free says, taking another long lick of her cone.

"You're getting that all over the place." The man who walks up is as familiar as the man standing beside me. His older brother, Samuel, has always been as professional as they come, in his polo and Dockers. He was off to college most of the time I dated Jensen, but when he'd return home, his appearance was much the same. Now, it's clearly no different as he's wearing a charcoal gray suit and black tie.

"What the hell, Sammy? You're at the Falls Festival. Dig out the mothy T-shirt and shorts and live a little," Free chastises the oldest Grayson sibling as she continues to lap up the ice cream. She's definitely a messy eater, but a part of me is thinking she's doing it for fun.

Samuel's eyes flash as he watches her eat the cone, a look most probably would have missed. Heck, I would have missed it if I weren't looking directly at him. It was a look of desire, but was gone almost as quickly as it appeared. "I just got off work, Freedom. I just stopped in to see how the festival was going before heading home for the evening," he replies, shoving his hands in his pockets.

"Aww, you missed me? It's okay to admit you knew I was here," Free says with a shrug.

"Hardly," he replies before turning his attention to Jensen and me. "Is my nephew here?"

"Yeah, but he's with Ashley," his younger brother replies, grabbing my hand. "You remember Kathryn, right?"

Samuel's eyes are intense as he turns his gaze fully in my direction. It's like being instantly thrust under a microscope. He watches me, taking everything in from my casual appearance to the fact Jensen's hand is wrapped around mine. Finally, he replies, "I remember. Good to see you again, Kathryn. How long are you in town?"

"Uhh, actually, I live here now. I'm back in my old home," I tell him and watch as surprise filters across his face. Apparently, I've been able to hide my homecoming well, even though I have dozens of workers in and out of the property all day.

"Oh, well, welcome home. I'm sure everyone is happy to have you back," he replies, glancing at his younger brother with a look that conveys concern.

I tense, knowing everyone in this group thinks poorly of me. In their eyes, I left Jensen, never to be heard from again. They don't know I tried to reach out to him, that I cried myself to sleep for weeks. That when I finally did hear from him, it was in the form of letters that were found between him and his father. Hurtful letters that only ensured my tears continued for a lot longer.

Of course, I know now it was all an illusion, a mirage painted by someone evil to keep me away from the boy I loved.

"Well, it was good seeing you guys. We're grabbing some food and then I promised Kate one last ride on the Ferris wheel," Jensen says, pulling me to the window at the food cart in front of us.

"Let's go, Sammy. You're taking me on the Tilt-A-Whirl," Free says, tossing what's left of her sticky cone into the trash can, licking her hand, and grabbing a hold of Samuel.

The look on his face is quite comical as she puts her sticky fingers all over his suit. "I am *not* riding the Tilt-A-Whirl, Freedom," he demands, digging his heels in the ground.

"Oh, yes you are." Then, the craziest thing happens. She pulls him toward the big spinning contraption on the other side of the park, and Samuel...follows.

When I glance in the direction of where we left Jensen's sister and her boyfriend standing, I find them still there, watching. Well, specifically, Harper's laser eyes are pinned directly on me, a concerned look on her face. I can tell she's trying to figure us out, and frankly, *I* haven't even figured us out yet. There are still so many unanswered questions, so much time elapsed, and so much history stands between us. I don't have the energy to try to figure out what *us* means. All I know is I've had a great time together, catching up with an old friend, enjoying the festival I grew up attending.

An old friend who still makes my body sing with just the slightest glance...

Harper and Latham finally walk away, holding hands and chatting quietly to themselves. I know she doesn't trust me, and that's fine. If I were in her shoes, I probably wouldn't like the girl who broke my brother's heart either, but there's so much more to the story than what she knows. I just hope she gives me a chance to explain it someday.

The deep timbre of Jensen's voice pulls me from my thoughts, and I turn to find him paying the young woman at the food truck for the small tray in front of him. They're small discs covered in batter and deep-fried, with powdered sugar sprinkled on the top.

"Let's go over to the seating area. These need to cool for a second," he says, taking the tray in one hand and my hand in the other.

We worm our way through the crowd, Jensen offering greetings to those he knows—which just so happens to be about everyone there. We find one end of a picnic table open and have a seat. A family of five sits on the other side, three kids with sugar-covered lips smiling at us and bobbing their head to the music in the band shell. A small four-piece band plays a popular upbeat country number, one I recognize from the radio, though it's been so long since I've listened to this kind of music, I don't recognize the artist. My mother insisted on classical music or even original compositions from Broadway plays and musicals.

Jensen always loved country music, and that suited him. With the slightest hint of a Carolinian accent, the Southern twang and mix of guitar and banjo always reminded me of him, even when we were many miles apart. Early on, after we left town, I would listen to any country station I could find on my radio. If I closed my eyes, I could picture him sitting in the driver's seat of his old truck, me riding in the middle, and hear him singing along to whatever song was playing. After a few weeks, Mother became tired of my morose, forlorn mood and insisted I listen to something else. My radio was taken from my room and replaced with an MP3 player already prefilled with the music she preferred I listen to. *More worldly music fit for a young lady*, as she called it.

I hated that fucking classical music.

"Here," Jensen says, shoving an Oreo in my face.

I should probably take it from his fingers, but for some reason, I don't. Instead, I find myself leaning forward just a bit and taking a bite. The moment the warm, gooey Oreo hits my tongue, an explosion of chocolaty flavor fills my senses. "Oh my God," I groan in total sugar-coma pleasure.

"Good, right?" he says, his eyes bright and glued to my lips, which I'm sure are covered in the powdered sugar. The tips of his fingers are covered in it, and I have the strongest urge to grab his hand and lick it off.

Before I can do something as embarrassing as that, he moves his hand to his mouth and finishes off the Oreo, never taking his eyes from mine. The only time I avert my gaze is when it drops to his tongue as he licks the white powder from the corner of his mouth. The moment my eyes return to his, I see a fire burning just below the surface. The air is thick with sexual tension, and suddenly, it feels almost scandalous to be sitting in the middle of a family-friendly festival when all I can think about is licking powdered sugar off of Jensen's abs.

Okay, maybe not only his abs…

We finish the Oreos in silence, our gazes flitting between the small stage up front and each other. The moment he pops the last one in his mouth, I'm moving. I don't know what possesses me to, but I'm standing, gathering up what little trash we've accumulated, and turning toward the way we came. Jensen is behind me. Even though I don't feel him, I can sense his presence.

When we reach the edge of the grassy area, I drop our trash into the receptacle. Jensen's long legs easily bring him to my side, his warm hand slipping around mine as we walk. We don't engage in any conversation as he leads me to the side street where he parked his truck.

The ride back to my home is quiet. Neither of us speaks. I wouldn't know what to say anyway. *Please come inside and do me against the wall* seems a little inappropriate, but in the grand scheme of things, I'd be up for it, if the offer were on the table.

Jensen pulls into my driveway, enters in the temporary code for the front gate, and heads to the house. I almost roll down my window, desperate for a little fresh air. The combination of Jensen's aftershave and the thick sexual tension is stifling, making it hard to breathe. He parks in front of the doorway and hops out before I can so much as thank him for the evening. The passenger opens, flooding the cab with warm night air, as he extends his hand and helps me down.

"I had a great evening," I tell him, finally finding my words.

"Me too. It was good to hang out with you again like that."

I stop when I reach the front door and turn to meet his gaze. My heart is pounding in my chest like a snare drum, so loudly, I'm sure he can hear it from where he stands. My mouth is moving before I can stop myself, speaking words that are as true as the sun rising in the morning. "I missed you."

The corner of his lip tips upward ever so slightly as he steps forward, invading my personal space. I look up as his right hand skims around my side and gently grips my hip. He pulls me forward at the same time he takes a step so we're chest to chest. His left hand moves to my neck, his long fingers sliding easily along the smooth skin until he's cupping my jaw in his big hand. "I missed you too, Butterfly. So fucking much."

Then his lips are on mine. The kiss isn't soft or gentle. It isn't tender or sweet. This is raw, unabolished lust and desire. This is more than a decade of hurt and longing entwined together. This is a kiss that preludes into something dirty, something powerful. This kiss is everything.

Jensen nips at my bottom lip causing me to gasp in pleasure. The moment I do, his tongue sweeps in, tasting and licking. His hold on my hip tightens, branding me with his heat through my clothes. My body sways in his direction, immediately coming in contact with the hard length of his erection entombed in his shorts. I'm ready to throw caution to the wind and drop my clothes—hell, drop to my knees—right here in the middle of my front porch.

Before I can loosen his belt, his lips are ripped away from mine. Gasps for air fill the night sky as I open my eyes and try to focus on his gorgeous face. He looks conflicted as hell, a heady mixture of desire and confusion. It's like he wants me, but maybe doesn't want to want me. That's a sobering thought.

I take a step back, hating the distance instantly. Jensen runs his hands through his hair, his wide eyes never leaving mine. "Shit, that got out of hand quickly. I wasn't going to kiss you."

Well, then…

Clearing my throat, I tug down the hem of my shirt, wishing it helped cover how exposed I feel—and I'm not talking about my skin. I'm referring to my heart. "Oh, well, no harm, no foul," I say in a shaky voice as I take another step back to the front door. Yeah, not at all confident and blasé as I was hoping for.

"Wait, shit, no. That didn't come out the way I wanted it to," he concedes, closing his eyes and glancing upward. "What I meant was I wasn't planning to maul you like an animal tonight. I was planning to do the respectable thing, give you a kiss on the cheek, and then leave."

I'm sure the look on my face conveys my confusion. "But…you had your hand on my boobs earlier."

He snorts a laugh. "Yeah, I know, and I was about two seconds away from having my hands on your boobs again."

A new confidence sweeps through me. He wasn't pulling away because he wanted to. He was pulling away because he felt like it was the right thing to do. Well, maybe, for once in my life, I don't want to do the right thing. Maybe, for once, I want to throw caution right out the window and live. Maybe, for once, I want to take something for me—because I want it.

Because I want *him*.

Taking a bold step forward, I gently take his hand in mine. His eyes dilate and his nostrils flare. I swear the man is a mind reader. I move my other hand to his chest, grazing my palm over the hard planes of his abs and up to rest on his pecs. "So, let me get this straight," I start, taking another step closer until we're standing chest to chest once more. "You wanted to be the polite, respectable man who would make any father proud, right?"

He swallows hard and nods his head.

"Well, maybe that's not what I want."

"What do you want?" he whispers, his hands moving to my hips, his fingers digging into the flesh of my lower back.

"I want you, Jensen. I've always just wanted you."

He places his forehead against mine and inhales deeply. "What am I supposed to do, Kate?" he whispers, his voice strained and tight.

"You're supposed to come inside with me, Jensen. But only if you want to."

"Fuck, I want to come inside with you more than anything," he confesses, his fingers flexing and biting my skin.

Going up on my tiptoes, I whisper, "Take me inside."

That's the only invitation he needs. Jensen practically sweeps me up in his arms and takes two steps until we reach my front door. I dig for the keys in my bag and turn the lock at the same time his hand grabs for the knob and turns.

Inside, I can still smell the fresh carpet, paint, and cleaning supplies, but I'm not paying any attention to the recent updates to the house when Jensen's lips lock on mine once more. This kiss is passionate, fierce, and dominating. He was always a take-what-he-wants kinda guy, and that hasn't changed in the slightest in adulthood.

The moment the door closes behind us, he maneuvers me until my legs are wrapped around his waist. He grinds his erection into the apex of my legs, and I swear, there are fireworks. My body is on fire and my blood pooling centrally between my legs.

"Jesus, Butterfly," he groans, gripping my ass and grinding into my core. "I can't…I can't even think."

"Don't think," I beg, gliding my lips along the smooth column of his neck. Jensen had shaved right before our evening out, and while I love the velvetiness of his tanned skin, part of me longs for the bite of a five o'clock shadow.

Especially on my thighs…

The engagement of the lock echoes through the foyer before he turns and heads toward the massive staircase. His long gait eats up the ornate stone flooring and he takes the stairs two at a time. I glance over my shoulder as he stops at the top of the stairs. Our eyes both dart to the hallway to the right—the one that leads to my former bedroom. There are more rooms down that way, but most of them were guest bedrooms.

"Left," I tell him, knowing he'll know where we're headed.

When I moved back into the home, I decided to take the master bedroom. There's no reason to keep it for my mom, since she says she'll never return to Rockland Falls, and it's not like my dad needs it anymore, right? The bedroom is massive, complete with seating area, his and hers walk-in closets, impressive en-suite bathroom, and private balcony. Honestly, it's way more space than I need, but it's gorgeous, nonetheless. Especially since I had the builder start here and do a little work to update the bathroom and tear down the old planked hardwood walls. They made it too dark for my liking, even with the floor-to-ceiling windows along the ocean. Fortunately, it only took them a few days to drywall and get them ready for paint. Throw in the decorator I hired to help give the room a facelift and you can barely tell it's the same room my parents shared when I was young. It's amazing what can be done in a week's time.

"Wow," Jensen says when he steps inside.

I look over my shoulder again and take in the room as if for the first time. There's a large bookshelf over by the seating area, where I've added plush gray chairs with turquoise pillows. I changed the hardwood flooring to a thick, rich carpet, and purchased a new California king poster bed with a light barn wood style headboard and footboard. The old dark walls are replaced with drywall, painted a rich shade of gray, and the bedding is a black and white chevron pattern.

"It's nothing like it used to be," I tell him, knowing he'll remember how formal the room was before, even though he only saw it in passing.

"It's so much better than it used to be," he says, walking us into the middle of the room. "This is comfy and perfect for you."

I smile. "Thank you."

"Do you know what would make this room even better?" he asks, those incredible blue eyes focused solely on me once more.

Glancing around the room, I try to find what could possibly make this room more amazing than it already is. "What?"

He slowly walks toward the massive bed. "You. Naked. In the middle of this bed."

The blush creeps up my cheeks and there's no stopping the spread of my grin. "Then you should definitely put me on the bed," I state boldly.

When his knees reach the bed, he gently sets me down, coming to rest on top of me. My legs are still wrapped around his waist, loving the way his erection presses in all the right places. "Stay right there," he whispers as he moves to sit on his haunches. With firm fingers, he runs his rough hands up my legs and unbuttons my shorts. They're gone, sliding down my legs, before I can even process what's about to go down. Then, he moves to my shirt, helping me sit up just long enough to pull it up and over my head before tossing it somewhere into the room behind him.

As I lie back down, I realize he's sitting there, staring at me. I'm in a light pink bra and panty set, one that probably cost more than your average computer. Money has never been an object to my family, and my mother made sure I always had the best of the best. Even undergarments. But it's the way he's looking at me now, with passion-filled eyes, like I'm a cool drink of water and he's been without for days, that has me thankful for the fancy lace and satin I'm wearing.

Though, if I'm being honest, Jensen has never cared about money. Not about the cost of the clothes I wear or the house I live in. It's one of the biggest draws I felt to him all those years ago. He couldn't care less about the designer name on the tag or the amount that was spent on the tiny scrap of material he now stares at. In fact, I'm almost certain he'd have the exact same look on his face if my bra came from Target.

"My God, you're beautiful," he whispers, his hand slowly caressing up my outer thigh and stopping at my hip.

Then his lips are on me once more in a kiss that's both fierce and tender. He claims my mouth with his own, taking his time to worship my plump lips. His hand is gentle as he slides it up to my breast, cupping the material in his large palm. My nipples pebble against the lace as his thumb slowly draws circles over the tight bud.

I'm a panting mess of hormones as his lips leisurely make their way down my jaw to my neck. They continue their southward trek down my body, stopping just long enough on my breasts to rain tender, open-mouthed kisses over the material. Then, he continues to move down, running his lips along my stomach, inhaling my skin and leaving a trail of goose bumps in his wake.

Finally, he reaches his destination. I know what's next because, even at a young age, Jensen never shied away from his desire to taste me. He always claimed it was his favorite part, to see me completely let go under his mouth. He was no expert back then, but we learned together what we liked and what we really, really liked.

Jensen slides my panties to the side and gazes between my legs for several long heartbeats before his eyes return to mine. The rapture and intensity between his blue eyes steals my breath and sends my heart pounding right out of my chest.

Then, he moves. With our eyes connected, he swipes his tongue along the seam of my legs for the first time in more than twelve years. I cry out, the contact almost too much and not enough at the same time. I've never felt so exposed, so vulnerable, so…worshipped.

And this is only the beginning.

Jensen doesn't give me a moment to breathe. He goes right after what he wants, which ultimately, is my pleasure. I know this, and yet it's still a huge shock for someone to put me first this way. I've only been with a few men since our time together, one being my ex-husband, and none of them compared to this man.

To Jensen.

His tongue slides between my folds, my body starting to quiver and shake. I can already feel an orgasm barreling down on me and he's barely touched me. I close my eyes, lost in the feel of his mouth as he licks and sucks on my most sensitive area. I'm startled as his finger is introduced into the mix. Not just one, but two. He presses them inside, slowly stretching me in the most delicious way. I rock my hips, the combination of his mouth and his fingers doing exactly what he was hoping they'd do. My body is pulled taut, my breathing almost nonexistent, and my heart racing.

"Look at me, Butterfly. I want your eyes on me when you come. I want you watching the moment you come on my face and fingers," he growls against my pussy. The hum of his words add fuel to the already raging inferno within me.

Again, I rock my hips as his fingers curl upward, hitting that magical spot inside of me that makes me see stars. "You like that?" he asks softly, pulling his fingers almost all the way out and making me whimper.

Just when I'm about to protest, he thrusts them inside once more, hitting that spot again and again. His mouth latches onto my clit, and that's all she wrote. I'm flying high above the clouds, floating in a sea of euphoria and pleasure, his name spilling from my lips.

I have no clue how long I soar, but it feels like forever. "You closed your eyes," he whispers, pulling my heavy lids open to rest on his fiery blue ones.

"I couldn't help it," I protest, not sorry in the least. A smile creeps across his lips and I realize it probably matches my own.

"I noticed," he says, kissing my inner thigh as he removes his fingers from my body.

I'm sated, spent, yet more than ready to see what he has in store for the next phase of our evening. I glance down at his shorts, or specifically, at the tent formed with the khaki material, and my mouth waters. He's thick and hard and so very ready, and I'd give just about anything to get my hands—and mouth—on him right now.

"Stop looking at me like that or I won't last five seconds."

I run my hands up his sides, pushing his shirt as I go. "Like what?" I whisper, scoring my nails into the sensitive flesh under his armpits, making him jump.

"You're playing with fire, Butterfly," he growls before nipping at my earlobe with his teeth and soothing the bite with his tongue.

"Maybe I want you to let go completely?" I taunt as I move my hands around to his back and dig into his skin.

The result is a shiver, followed by fire flaring within his eyes. He's dangerously close to losing control, and frankly, I'm not interested in his control. I'd much rather him lose it, just the way he used to back when we were younger. He'd never hurt me. Never. Jensen would rather hurt himself than me, but there was this wildness that lurked within he tried to cage.

Tonight, I want to unleash the beast.

All it will take is for me to drop the match.

I push up on my elbows and run my nose along his neck. His scent is simply magnificent. When I reach his ear, I whisper, "Take me, Jensen. Make me yours."

He inhales sharply and pulls my elbows, making me fall back onto the bed. I watch in awe as he reaches behind his neck and pulls his shirt up and over his head, disregarding it much like he did mine. He lies back on top of me, caging me against the mattress. Anticipation races through my blood and his mouth claims mine once more. His tongue sweeps in and out, mimicking what I want him to do with his erection. My nails grip his shoulders and my legs fall completely open.

Jensen's hand moves to my leg, tossing it over one shoulder. Even though he's still wearing shorts and I've got my panties on, I can feel just how hard and ready he is for me. He grinds himself against the wet lace until I'm practically shaking in his arms. Then, he rips his lips from mine, his heavy breathing mixing with my own. The intensity in his eyes burn into me as he says, "I'm not even close to being done with you."

Chapter Thirteen

Jensen

I'm practically shaking as I grasp on to any sliver of control I can find. I'm hanging by a thread and with her grinding her sweet pussy against my cock, I'm mere seconds away from losing it completely.

I let go of her leg and set it back on the bed. She looks positively edible in her fucking lace bra and panties. I'm sure they cost a pretty penny, yet the caveman inside of me would love nothing more than to rip them from her body. I won't, however, as hard as it may be not to.

Deciding to enjoy the view of her body just a little longer, I jump up and practically rip my button off my shorts trying to get them off. My slip-on shoes are gone, so there's nothing in my way as I push my shorts and boxers down at the same time. My cock juts from my body, painfully hard and weeping with precum.

Kate's eyes are glued to my body as I strip naked and reach for my wallet to retrieve a condom. I only have two in there, not that I expected sex tonight, but because I've always been one to be prepared. Back when Kate and I dated the first time, sex was always a spontaneous thing. We never knew when we'd find ourselves stripping naked (or sometimes not even stripping at all) and going at it like rabbits.

I've changed a bit since she last saw me naked, much like she has. I've always been on the leaner side, but now my skin is rougher, tanner, and my muscles much more defined. Kate is still the perfect combination of softness and curve, though she's definitely filled out a lot more in the last twelve years.

My eyes are glued to her as I sheath myself in protection. If I could hold out a little longer, I'd just sit here and stare at the beauty she is. The soft pink of her bra and panties is amazing against the delicate color of her skin, but I burn to see what she's like completely nude. Her pale skin against the black and white bedding is like a siren's call.

I slowly make my way onto the bed, feasting on the beauty before me. "Sit up," I instruct, loving how her eyes dilate with anticipation. As soon as she does, I unclasp her bra, letting the pale pink fall away. She's just as I envisioned her to be. Full breasts with hard, rosy nipples begging to be sucked.

As if knowing what I'm going to say next, she lies back down on the comforter, putting her legs together. My fingers glide along smooth skin as they trail up her legs. I've always been fascinated with her legs and that hasn't changed. She's fucking sexy as hell and I long to have them wrapped around my waist.

I toy with the satin along her hipbones, drawing out the anticipation a little longer. I can hear her breathing, it's choppy and heavy, and I'm pretty sure it matches my own. With my eyes locked on hers, I slowly pull the panties down her hips. I keep going past her thighs and calves until I'm maneuvering them around her feet. They're wet from earlier and I can smell just how turned on she is. My mouth waters for another taste, but I refrain. The only thing I want right now is to feel that sweet pussy gripping my cock.

When the panties are completely gone, I finally look down. She's bare before me, glistening and wet, only the tiniest strip of hair on display. I'll definitely have my mouth on her again, but not yet. Not now. I *need* her. Need to feel her wrapped around me.

"Hold on, Kate," I say, taking my position between her legs and throwing one over my shoulder once more.

Lacey Black

She seems to hold her breath as I line myself up. My eyes lock on hers once more as if seeking confirmation one last time. Kate nods at me, her hazel eyes a touch on the brown side, as she waits for what's to come (no pun intended). I have to fight my body's reaction not to just thrust forward, burying myself balls deep. Instead, I ever so slowly rock my hips until just the tip is surrounded with warmth and wetness.

The sweetest gasp spills from her lips as I push forward, inch by inch. She's tight—so fucking tight—and the moment I'm buried completely inside of her, I have to stop, take a deep breath, and try not to blow right then and there. I can feel her spasm around me, her own body tight with desire and need. I'm grinding down on my molars as I fight every urge I have not to just pound until I come.

Kate's face is a mixture of tension and pleasure. I move her leg and lie on top of her, taking her lips with my own. The moment I do, I can feel her body loosen around me. "That's it, Butterfly. Take a deep breath and relax," I whisper, trailing my lips down the delicious column of her neck.

She digs her nails into my back once more, the slight bite of pain an accelerant to my libido. "Move," she gasps, rocking her hips to try to create friction.

"Not until you're ready," I tell her, placing open-mouthed kisses along her collarbone.

"I'm ready. Please." It's a plea for more, one I'm more than ready to fulfill.

"You sure?" I ask, turning and locking my eyes on hers.

"Yes. Just…move."

A cocky smile creeps across my face as I prepare to give her—us—what we both need. Returning to my position on my haunches, I toss her leg back over my shoulder and grip her hips. Slowly, I pull out until I can see the glistening tip of my cock. When she goes to

154

protest, I thrust forward, rocking my hips and hitting that spot inside her that makes her scream.

"Fuck, Kate," I groan, holding her leg up and grinding my hips between her thighs. She places her hands above her head, gripping the pillow, and hangs on, and that's when my body starts to take over. My thrusts are out of control as I drive us both toward release.

The familiar tingle starts at the base of my spine and I know I'm out of time. Reaching down, I start to rub her clit, her pussy instantly clenching around me. Kate cries out, rocking her hips in rhythm. It only takes two more thrusts before she's coming again, squeezing the life out of my cock and screaming my name into the night. I follow quickly, my release hard and fast as I continue to pump into her tight body.

The moment the spasms subside, my entire body is riddled with fatigue, my own legs barely able to hold me up. Setting her leg to the side, I come down on top of her, my lips immediately finding hers. Our bodies are slick with sweat and our pants of exertion mix together, but I never remove my lips from hers. In fact, I'm pretty sure I could kiss this woman for the rest of my life and die the world's happiest man.

"You okay?" I whisper, grazing my lips along her full bottom one.

She moans a reply, a happy, sated little noise that makes my cock jump. Her eyes connect with mine, and there's no missing the shock and excitement there on her face. "Again?"

"Well, maybe not *right* this second, but yes, again. Very soon," I say, rolling to the side and taking her with me. My cock falls from its happy place as she curls against my chest. "I'm not the spring chicken I used to be. My recovery time is more like thirty minutes now," I confess, remembering back when I was eighteen and full of hormones, my dick could recover in about two minutes flat, eager for another round of loving Kate.

"So we have time to grab a snack?" she asks, her soft fingers sliding through the hair on my chest.

"You're still hungry? I thought you couldn't eat another bite."

She giggles into my neck and places a tender kiss on my skin. "That was before I burned off all the fair food calories."

Rolling her to the side so we're facing each other, I give her a slow smile. "I do enjoy burning calories with you."

Her eyes look greener now as she gazes up at me, her own grin playing on her lips. "Me too. I've missed you," she whispers, her voice dripping with emotion.

Pulling her back into my arms, I hold her close, reveling in the way her body fits against mine like a puzzle piece. "Me too, Butterfly, me too." Placing a kiss on her forehead, I add, "Let me run and get rid of the condom and then we'll go down and see if we can find something to eat."

As much as I hate to do it, I release my hold on her and get off the bed, not even caring I'm naked as I make my way to her bathroom. Inside, I toss the rubber in the trash and grab a washcloth from the closet. As soon as I'm clean, I take a second cloth, wet it with warm water, and return to where I left her in bed.

Her eyes are closed as I approach, a satisfied little smirk on her lips. She hasn't moved, her naked body lying angelically on top of the bedding. I can see the small of her back, one of my favorite parts of her body, and my cock starts to respond. Instead of going to her front side, I opt to walk around to the opposite side of the bed, where her back and pert ass are on display. I can see the slightest ridge of her spine right where it meets her ass and my mouth waters.

Crawling onto the bed, I set the washcloth aside and run my hands along those delectable ridges of her spine, cupping her ass in my big hands. She glances over her shoulder, a look of desire written across her face. That's all it takes for my semi-hard dick to become fully ready for round two.

I reach over and grab my wallet, pulling out the second condom. Definitely going to have to pick up more of those on my next trip to the store. I've got myself covered in a matter of seconds and return to my position behind her. Kate doesn't say a word, just hitches her leg up over mine and grinds her ass against me. I line up and slowly push inside of her body, her gasp mixing with my groan.

Just before I start to pump, she glances over her shoulder with lust-filled eyes and a coy smile on her sweet lips. "Thirty minutes my ass."

* * *

I pull into my former driveway and park. I've been looking forward to grabbing Max all morning, but not the part where I'll have to deal with Ashley. I'm not sure what version of her I'm getting today, but after Saturday night's display at the festival, I'm sure it won't be a pleasant one. Not now.

Not after the confirmation Kate's back in town.

At the festival, I was able to push all thoughts of Ashley and the pending confrontation I'm sure is coming. In fact, it wasn't until last night, when I returned to my own place, anyone besides Kate entered my mind. No, that's not true. A few times when we were lounging around the house, I thought about Max and wished he was hanging out with us, but then I'd start to question what was going on exactly between Kate and myself.

I still don't have the answer to that one.

We've both declared we missed each other, but that's the deepest we've gone. I'm not sure exactly how to dissect the feelings that come with her being back in town and back in my life. I'm not

Lacey Black

sure if sleeping with her was a good thing or not (okay, yeah, it was a very, *very* good thing) because I have no idea what comes next for us.

Okay, that's a lie too.

I do know what comes next.

A cookout today at my mom's house.

Yesterday, I hung out at her place for much of the day. Sure I might have screwed her six ways to next Sunday, but there was a lot more of the other stuff too. It was almost like getting to know someone, even though I already know her pretty damn well. But there's a void from the last twelve years, one I was anxious to fill, so we talked about New York, her parents, and her job, which she hated. We ate food at the kitchen counter, watered her new plants around the property, and snuggled on the couch while pretending to watch some girly movie. When the clock finally struck six, I knew it was time for me to head out. I was too comfortable there, which is why I forced myself to get up, kiss her long enough that she wouldn't forget it anytime soon, and then headed back to my own place for the night.

I only texted her once.

Fine, more than once. It started with a single text message, just to let her know I was home and thinking of her. That transpired into three hours of messaging before I finally fell asleep with a hard dick and a smile on my face. It was during that texting exchange I invited her to my mom's cookout for Labor Day. She refused at first, like I knew she would, but when I reminded her it was a holiday and no one was working at her place, I knew by her hesitated responses she was wavering. Then, I went in for the kill and told her my mom was making her famous four cheese macaroni with bacon.

That did it.

Now, after spending the day with my son, I'll be picking up Kate around three to head to my family's gathering. Mom won't care about the extra plate, but I admit, it may be a little awkward at first.

158

Kinda like it was at the festival when we ran into my siblings. They all loved Kate way back when, but that love dried up when she left town. Of course, they only know one side of the story, and I'll be sure to share the rest of it with them all so they don't treat her like an outsider or someone not welcome.

"Daddy!" Max yells as he barrels out the front door.

I take the steps two at a time, scooping him up in my arms as I go. "Hey, Buddy, did you have a good weekend with Mommy?"

"Yep! I won a monkey at the fessibal."

"Festival, and I'm glad. Are you bringing it to my house for the week?" I ask, setting him down when I step over the threshold.

"Yep! His name is George." Max giggles at the name, throwing his head back and giving a full belly laugh.

"Good morning, Jensen," Ashley sings, practically floating into the dining room.

"Morning," I reply, keeping one eye on my ex-wife as she sets her bag on the worn table. She's wearing nursing scrubs in a light green and comfortable walking shoes with her hair piled high on her head. Her makeup is subtle, yet knowing her as well as I do, I can tell she's put a lot of work into her appearance.

"So, he's already eaten breakfast and his bag is ready to go," she says, nodding toward the duffel bag at the door. When I turn back and face her, she's grinning widely. "I'll give him a call later tonight before bed, if that's okay."

"Of course it's all right."

"I assume you'll be either at home or your mother's?" she asks, fiddling with something in her purse.

I clear my throat. "Either. We're having dinner at mom's tonight and then we'll be heading home," I tell her. Max comes back to the doorway, monkey and prized baseball in his hands.

"Alone?"

When I glance her way, I can see the smile on her face, but it's deceiving. There's a glint of something dark, something hostile just beneath the surface. "You know, Jensen, we haven't really talked about the whole dating thing," she says, pulling a tube of nude-colored lipstick from the bag and applying a thin coat. The hairs on the back of my neck stand up.

I open the door for Max. "I'll be right out, Buddy. Why don't you hop in the truck and we'll get going?" I ask, watching as he runs to his mom and gives her a goodbye hug and kiss. Then, he runs out to my truck and climbs in the driver's seat like he's done a hundred times. After I make sure he's out of earshot, I glance back at my ex. "Dating thing?"

"Oh, you don't have to play dumb with me. We've been divorced for a while now and it's natural we'd both start dating again. I've had a few dates, but nothing too serious, but that doesn't mean that's not about to change," she replies with a shrug.

Before I can open my mouth, she continues. "The point is, I don't think we should bring our dates around Max."

"Okay," I reply, the word sounding more like a question than a statement.

"You know, we don't want to confuse him."

It's like the light bulb switches on. This is about Kate.

"Confuse him," I parrot.

"Are you being difficult on purpose?"

"I'm not trying to be difficult; I'm trying to figure out what you're talking about," I tell her, crossing my arms over my chest.

Ashley exhales loudly. "Dating. I don't want you to bring your *dates* around our son. He has a mother and I won't let you try to replace me," she spits out, the friendly smile from earlier very much gone.

"Replace you? I'm not trying to replace you. I'm not bringing any date around him."

"Kathryn Elliott? Or whatever in the hell her last name is now."

Called it.

"Kate and I are friends, Ashley. Not that I owe you any explanation, but we've only hung out in public once and that was the festival." I decide to gloss over the time we invited her to join us for pizza.

"She won't replace me," she bites, her eyes burning with anger.

"Of course she won't. You're Max's mom, Ash. I'd never try to replace you in his eyes," I reassure, trying to calm the storm brewing across from me, though it is true.

"Just in your eyes, huh?" she sasses, the hurt and anger still very much alive and well.

Exhaling, I close my eyes for a moment. What the hell am I supposed to say that won't piss her off further? Our relationship has been more of a ticking time bomb than anything else, especially in the last year. I don't want to hurt her. I don't want to fight or argue or anything anymore. I'm just...tired.

"Ash, what's done is done. We weren't right for each other. We tried. Maybe it was doomed from the beginning or maybe it happened somewhere along the way. I don't know. What I do know is we're tied together for the rest of our lives. We have an amazing little boy who needs both of his parents. We need to let go of the past so we can move forward and be the best we can for our son."

She snickers at me and throws her purse over her shoulder. "Sure, move forward. Easy for you to say when the one you've always wanted returns to town, huh? Should be no problem for you to *move forward.* Anyway, I'm not kidding about the dating thing. I don't want you to bring dates around our son."

I rub my temples as a full-blown monster headache starts to spread. "Ash, I won't bring random women around Max, but I won't keep Kate from him. She's my friend and the few times they've interacted, she's been great with him. He likes her."

My ex-wife snorts and rolls her eyes. "She bought him with money. Of course he likes her."

I know this conversation needs to be done, and the only way to accomplish that is for me to quit engaging. Kate didn't buy him, at least not the way Ashley is referring to. A few quarters in the dirt isn't like she bought him a new gaming system or a bike just so he'd like her. She was entertaining him while I was on the phone. Four quarters does not equal buying someone, but there's no reasoning with Ashley when she gets like this.

Stepping back to the door, I grab Max's bag and walk onto the porch. "Call my phone later when you're ready to speak with him. I'll make sure he's nearby."

"You do that," she replies as she follows me onto the porch, closing and locking the door behind her as she goes.

Heading to my truck, I find Max kneeling on the driver's seat, wheel in hand and pretending to drive. "Did you obey all the stop signs?" I ask my happy four-year-old.

"I wasn't really driving, Daddy," Max laughs, the sound a balm that soothes my soul.

"Well, that's good. I don't recall you getting a license," I say opening up the door to the back seat. "Climb over so I can get you strapped in."

"Bye bye, Maxi. Mommy loves you," Ashley sings over my shoulder as I get our son buckled into his booster seat.

"Bye, Mommy! Love you!"

Ashley doesn't acknowledge me, and that's okay. I'm more than ready to get out of here. Max and I have the day together, and I know just what we should do. We're going to grab the tee ball stuff and head to the park. I can pack a small cooler with a few peanut butter and jelly sandwiches and bottles of water. We'll make a morning out of it, swinging, sliding, and running the bases. Then, after lunch, we can head back to my place so we can get cleaned up and maybe relax a bit before I have to pick up Kate.

This day is definitely looking up.

Chapter Fourteen

Kathryn

I've almost worked myself into a frenzy. I talked myself out of going with Jensen and Max at least a dozen times. There's no reason for me to be in the mix of his family time on a holiday, right? Exactly! I'll just be in the way. Plus, his mom probably doesn't even want me around; you know, considering I broke her son's heart and all.

My heart is pounding in my chest when I hear his truck pull through the gate. I'm just going to politely tell him I'm not going. Maybe that I have a headache or something. Or a stomach bug! Those are contagious.

Before I can finalize my way out of this afternoon's festivities, the doorbell rings, startling me. Since I'm standing in the foyer, I take the couple of steps to the door and pull it open.

And my heart melts.

There at the doorway is Max Grayson, smiling up at me with a wide, toothy grin on his face, and holding a bouquet of handpicked wildflowers. "Hi, Kate! These are for you," he says as he thrusts the treasures in his hand at me.

"Oh, thank you so much, Maximo," I coo, reaching for the buds.

Max giggles before me. "It's not Maximo, silly! I'm just Max!" he hollers through his laughter.

"Well, Just Max, these may be the most beautiful flowers I've ever received," I assure him, taking a step back and allowing them to enter the house.

"Daddy helped me cutted them," he says as he quickly kicks off his shoes at the doorway.

"Cut them, and we're not staying, Max. We're just here to pick Kate up and take her with us to Grandma's," Jensen says, standing in the doorway with a grin on his face.

"Oh, about that," I start, glancing his way. I'm prepared to give him my *I don't think I'm going* speech, when Max comes up and takes my free hand.

"Come on, Kate. We'll put the flowers in water and then go see my grandma. She maked me some cookies!" Between the twinkle in his baby blues and the warmth spreading up my arm from where our hands are joined, I know there's no way I could ever tell him I'm not going now. I quickly realize I'd probably go anywhere with this little boy.

I smile down at him as I lead him toward the kitchen. "She made you some cookies," I correct, like I heard Jensen do, and ask, "What kind of cookies?"

"Chocolate chip!"

I gasp with a dramatic hand on my chest. "My favorite are chocolate chip," I tell him as I pull out one of the stools under the island.

Max climbs up on the stool and crawls on the counter. I don't say a word, just head over to where I *think* I put the vases. Fortunately, I find one in the second box I check and return to where I left my handsome little helper. I fill the vase about three-quarters of the way with water and step back while Max arranges the blooms in the vase.

"Perfect," I tell him when he places the last flower and turns my way.

"Looks good, huh? Do they smell good, Kate?" he asks and watches, waiting expectantly for me to take a big ol' whiff.

I make a dramatic show of inhaling. "They smell amazing," I insist, grabbing the vase. "I have an idea. Why don't we put them in the center of the dining room table?"

"Okay," he says, shrugging his shoulders and crawling off the counter.

It's the first time I notice Jensen leaning against the doorway, a small smile playing on his lips. The look he gives is part amusement and part longing. It makes my heart rate kick up a few thousand beats. "How about over here?" I ask when we reach the formal dining room. No, I'm not exactly a formal dining person even though I grew up eating most of my meals there. I'd much rather sit in the kitchen, around a small table where you can reach over and touch the people around you. Not some big, formal monstrosity of a table where you can't even pass a bowl of potatoes to the person next to you.

"Daddy, do you like it?" Max asks his father as I place the vase in the center of the table and turn it until the best side is facing the entrance.

"I love it. You picked great flowers, Max."

His son gives him a cheeky grin. I bend down and place a kiss on Max's forehead. "Thank you for the flowers, Just Max. I love them."

"I picked them, but Daddy had to cut them with his knife."

"Smart to let Daddy do all the cutting," I tell the four-year-old. "Now that we have the flowers taken care of, are you ready to go?"

Max nods feverishly and turns to head back to the foyer. His little hand slips into mine as we make our way to the front door. I can feel Jensen behind me, but he doesn't say a word. Instead, he just locks the door and follows us out. When we reach his truck, he helps his son climb up into the back seat and get buckled in. I watch, transfixed by the simple task of father and son securing a seat belt, until they're done and the door is closed.

Jensen reaches around me and opens my door. "Thank you," I tell him.

"For what?" he asks. It's the first time I realize we're standing close. Very close, actually. I could set my hand on his chest or maybe even step forward and feel his arms wrap around me. Our lips would be dangerously close too.

"For the flowers."

"They were Max's idea," he says, glancing to the side to where his son sits in the back seat. "They were growing wild in the ditch down the road and he thought we needed to stop and pick some."

"That's a sweet thing to do. Did you teach him that?"

Jensen shrugs. "Yeah. Last year, we stopped once on our ride home and picked some flowers for his mom."

"That's nice."

He nods.

There's a several second pregnant pause and my anxiety starts to kick up a notch. "I was going to try to get out of it," I blurt out.

He takes that half step in my direction, and suddenly, I can feel his body heat radiating against me. "Out of what?" he asks, though I think he already knows the answer.

"Today. I wasn't sure it was wise I come," I confess.

He toys with a strand of hair before moving it behind my ear. "I know we have some things to talk about, but I'm really glad you're coming with us. Max enjoys spending time with you, and frankly, I'd love to hang out with you too."

"He's an amazing little boy," I tell him, though I'm sure it's nothing he doesn't already know.

Jensen smiles softly before releasing my hair. His hand is suddenly cupping my cheek and running his thumb along my jaw. "Thank you for being so awesome with him," he whispers.

I start to lean forward before I even realize what I'm doing. "It's easy to do when he's such a great kid." My words are whispered, my breath bouncing off his lips.

And then those lips I've been longing to kiss since he left yesterday slide softly across mine. It's a tender kiss, yet one that packs quite the punch to my ovaries. I don't know if it's the kiss or the man with the magical lips and the fact he's an astounding dad, but something deep inside me pulls hard and it's like my biological clock actually starts to tick.

"Let's go! Grammy has chocolate chip cookies!" Max hollers from the back seat, making us both laugh.

"We better get going," I mutter. Though, I wouldn't mind exploring more of that kiss.

"We better or he's liable to climb behind the wheel and drive himself to Grandma's," Jensen quips. He takes a step back, putting a little distance between us, and helps me climb inside the truck. Before he pulls away, he leans forward and places a gentle kiss on my forehead. Without a word, he moves back and shuts the door.

Max chats the entire ride to Grayson Bed and Breakfast, so I don't even have another opportunity to get nervous. It's surprisingly comforting to sit there and listen to father and son chat about playing at the park earlier today. Apparently, Max wanted to go down the big slide, but the only way he would do it was if Jensen went with him. I only wish I would have been there to capture the moment with a photo.

When we pull off the road and onto the shaded lane that leads to his family's bed and breakfast, I start to break out in a sweat. All those nerves I wasn't feeling on the ride are now alive and well, furiously causing some major sweaty pits under my shirt.

Glancing around the property, I see it's in much of the same shape as I remember. The yard is lush and green and the shrubbery hedged perfectly, no doubt at the hand of the man beside me. The blooms are vibrant and colorful, even as we approach the end of summer, and the old garage looks freshly painted. The Grayson homestead sits proudly in the center of it all, a spacious house turned bed and breakfast.

There are a handful of vehicles here, but I don't see any sign of Jensen's family or of the guests who are staying. I'm glancing around the homestead, taking in the few changes they've made and pretty much lost in my thoughts, and don't even realize we've parked and the truck is shut off until Jensen appears at the passenger door.

"You okay?" he asks as he opens my door.

"Yeah."

Warm hands slide against my cheeks as he turns me to face him. "Breathe, Butterfly. No one's going to bite you. Don't look so scared," he says with a lopsided grin.

"I know that," I reply as I unbuckle my seat belt, but I'm not really sure that's the truth. I'm terrified one of them might actually bite me (figuratively, that is) for all of the heartache and damage I caused Jensen.

"Stop thinking about that," he insists, his thumb now caressing my bottom lip.

"I can't," I whisper, my tongue slipping out and tasting the tip of his thumb. His eyes flare before narrowing in on my mouth.

"You're making it real hard not to just throw you back in this truck and take you to the nearest bed," he whispers, careful the young ears behind him don't overhear.

"That wouldn't be so bad," I confess, not really minding at all if Jensen were to strip me naked and have his wicked way with me again.

"Naughty girl," he replies, leaning in and placing a tender kiss on my lips. "Don't worry about anyone else. No one is going to be upset you're here."

"I guess I'll believe that when I see it."

Jensen exhales. "It'll be fine. Besides, I've already talked to my mom about you."

Okay, I wasn't expecting that. "You have?"

He nods. "Saturday morning, before our date to the festival."

After a few long seconds, he doesn't elaborate. "And?"

"And she's happy you're back in town and can't wait to see you again."

"Even after...everything?"

"Yes, Kate, even after everything. There was a force keeping us apart, but it wasn't one of us, and frankly, we're the only ones who matter anyway. Just you and me," he replies with a shrug.

"And me! Don't forget me!" Max hollers behind his dad.

I can't help but giggle. "Yes, and Just Max. We can't forget him."

"Of course," Jensen says, smiling over his shoulder at his son. "You ready to go back and see Grandma?" he asks, resulting in Max jumping up and down and practically running toward the backside of the house. "As you can tell, he loves coming here."

With my hand tucked in his, Jensen helps me down from his truck and shuts the door. "I can see that."

He stops us before we get too far away from the truck and pulls me into his arms. I glance around, afraid someone might be watching. "It'll be okay, Kate. I promise."

Deciding to put all of my faith in this man, I give him a quick nod in agreement and go up on my tiptoes, placing a kiss on his lips. "Thank you."

"For what?" he asks, wrapping his arms around my waist.

"For just being you."

"That's easy," he says, bringing my hand up to his mouth and kissing my knuckles. "You bring out the good in me. I'm my best me when I'm around you."

I feel the slightest blush and can't fight the grin. As far as compliments go, that's a pretty damn good one. Hand in hand, we head in the same direction Max went, eventually emerging in the backyard of the Grayson Bed and Breakfast. The backyard is almost the exact same as I remember it, except for the updated flower gardens. The small cottage out back has been repainted too, and now boasts a welcome sign with sunflowers.

"That's where I live now." Even though it's been twelve years and she's a woman now, I recognize the youngest Grayson immediately. I always loved spending time with Marissa. We had a lot of things in common, from our love of books to our art. She was an artist with a whisk in the kitchen, while I was one with a paintbrush.

"Marissa," I reply, taking in the lovely young woman before me. My arms move, but I hesitate for a second. If she notices, she doesn't say. Instead, she pulls me into the biggest hug I've had in forever. "It's so good to see you," I tell her honestly.

"I've missed you," she whispers, pulling back and giving me a warm, friendly smile. "We all have." She glances to where her brother stands beside me, talking to the tall, built man with sandy blond hair. "This is Rhenn, my boyfriend, but I believe you've already met. He lives with me in the cottage," she adds.

Rhenn sticks out his hand. It's huge, wrapping around my hand and almost swallowing it whole. "We've met, Angel. I'm almost finished with her electrical job," the big guy says with a smile.

"Good to see you again, Rhenn. You've done an outstanding job at the house," I assure him.

"I'm glad you like it," he says, taking a pull from his beer bottle.

"The new outdoor lighting is wonderful. I can't wait for it to all be finished so I can go out back and use it all."

"I'm sure with the pool, spa, and outdoor barbeque area, it'll be amazing," he adds.

"The pool guy will be here tomorrow. He's going to inspect the waterlines, foundation, and the pump of the pool, as well as repair the fountain out front. As long as there's nothing seriously damaged, both will be operational and filled by end of week," Jensen states.

"I heard you put a lot of work into the kitchen. I'd love to see it sometime," Marissa says, her eyes lighting up at the prospect of visiting the big, gourmet kitchen that's almost complete at my house.

"Anytime. In fact, when the pool is done, we can have a pool party and you can check it out," I tell her.

"Pool party? I'm in," Harper says as she comes around the corner and joins our group.

"Harper in a bikini? I'm in too." Latham has an ornery smirk on his face as his eyes travel down his girlfriend's body. She's wearing a cute pink smock top and white Bermuda shorts.

"Give the girl some room," Mary Ann says, pushing through the small group until she's standing directly in front of me. "Come here, you." Then her arms are around me and I'm engulfed in a fierce hug. Jensen's mom smells like vanilla and cinnamon, a familiar scent that takes me back to a time when I spent a lot of my childhood with this family.

I open my mouth to say something, but my throat is closed. I'm choking on emotions and I'm not sure where they came from. Out of the blue, I feel overjoyed and elated to be here, wrapped in Mary Ann's arms. I blink rapidly, trying to will away the tears, but one slips out. She pulls back and smiles at me, her hands still holding me firmly by the arms. "Oh, don't you do that, sweet girl. No tears or you'll make me cry too."

"I'm sorry," I whisper, not really sure what I'm apologizing for. The tears or the past. Probably both.

Mary Ann scoffs. "Don't you worry about any of that. What's in the past is past. You're here now, and that's all that matters," she says with a wink. "Besides, I made the cheesy mac and cheese with extra bacon just for you."

"I can't wait," I reply, a smile playing on my lips.

"Now, I better get back inside before my grandson eats more than the one cookie I set out for him," she says, patting my hand and then turning and heading back to the house.

"You left him alone with the cookies?" Jensen hollers at his mom.

She turns and shrugs. "I'm Grandma. He can have whatever he wants."

Jensen groans and Harper laughs. "Just you wait. You'll have kids soon and you'll know what it's like to be completely undermined by the grandma factor."

A look passes between Harper and Latham and I can't help but wonder what it means. As far as I know, they've only dated for a handful of weeks and recently moved in together. But their attraction has been brewing for a long time. Even when we were in school, there was just something about their love/hate relationship that screamed sexual chemistry. It may have taken them a while to get here, but I have a feeling, just by watching them interact the two times I've seen them, they're forever.

"Oh, Riss, don't forget the Ladies' Night Out is set for Thursday night. Can you still whip up a few batches of cookies?" Harper asks her sister.

"Absolutely. I'll make you those new s'mores muffins too."

"That sounds amazing. Whatever you want, just let me know how much. I'm serving lemonade and bought a few bottles of wine from a North Carolina vineyard," Harper adds, her eyes connecting with mine. "Kathryn, if you're not doing anything Thursday night, you should come by the shop. Some of the small businesses have organized a Ladies' Night Out. I'll have some goodies to eat and some wine. Plus, I'm running a special on bra and panty sets."

I can feel the blush creeping in. There's just something about discussing bras and panties in front of Jensen and his family that makes me a little nervous. Obviously, Harper isn't fazed in the least. She tells her sister about some of the new items she got in as if she were talking about the weather.

"Seriously, come by the shop," she adds.

"I will, thank you."

Latham pulls her toward the coolers that are set outside, but before she's completely out of earshot, she hollers, "Anytime after seven."

I feel Jensen's hand on my lower back. "Looks like you have plans on Thursday night," he says.

My reply is a small smile and a nod. It makes me feel good to be invited to their gathering, even if it's only in the hopes I'll spend a little money. I realize I'm looking forward to Thursday night. I'm excited to shop at Harper's boutique and maybe even spend a little girl time with Jensen's sisters.

The rest of the afternoon progresses wonderfully. The weather is warm, yet the yard is shaded enough to provide comfort against the heat. A handful of guests staying at the bed and breakfast mill around and visit, enjoying appetizers and drinks Marissa prepared.

Samuel arrived a bit ago in a full suit. He said he just finished a funeral for someone I vaguely remember, but apparently had no desire to stop by his place and change his clothes into something more comfortable. When Freedom arrives a bit later, it's like the air changes. Samuel becomes tense (even more tense than normal), and even though he gives off the appearance of ignoring her, I catch the way his eyes casually follow her movements around the yard.

Latham and Rhenn fire up the grill and the guys seem to all congregate in that area. Marissa hovers nearby, but doesn't actually step in. I can tell she's not used to giving up control over a meal, but she does so when Rhenn takes the grill spatula, kisses her on the tip of the nose, and sends her off to sit with us under the oak tree. I split my time between visiting with those sitting around me and watching Jensen and Max play catch. They're off to the side so they don't hit anyone, and I can't get over how effortless their play is. I excuse myself from the group and make my way to where father and son are playing.

"Hey," I say as Jensen catches the ball in his mitt and throws it back to Max.

"Having fun?" he asks, glancing my way, but quickly returning his eyes back to the kid across from him.

"Yes. Today has been very relaxing and enjoyable," I tell him as the ball comes sailing back our way. Jensen easily catches it before tossing it back. "Wow, he's really good at that," I observe as Max snatches the baseball from the air and lobs it back to his dad.

"He is. He's been playing all summer. Here." Jensen holds out his hand, the ball between his fingers.

"Oh, no, I can't."

"You can't?" he asks, eyebrows arched toward his hairline.

"I've never really played," I reply, glancing to where Max stands, eagerly waiting for the ball.

"Really?" he bemuses, tossing it back to his son.

"Really. I hated sports growing up. The only ball I've thrown was in PE, and even then, everyone knew I couldn't play, so they never gave me the ball."

When the ball returns to Jensen, he pops off his glove and hands it to me. "Here, put this on."

I'm hesitant at first, not really wanting to embarrass myself by trying to play catch, but eventually slide the glove on my hand. He holds out the ball, which I take in my right hand, and then stands there watching.

"Well, go ahead and throw it."

"But...what if I hurt him?"

"Max? Are you going to intentionally throw the baseball to hurt him?" he asks, his voice gentle and calm.

"What? No!" I gasp, my eyes wide as I gaze at him.

"Of course you're not. Accidents sometimes happen, Kate, I'll be honest, but Max is a pretty good player. You throw it, he'll catch it."

"But..."

"No buts, Butterfly. Don't think. Just lock your eyes on Max and throw him the ball."

I exhale deeply, the weight of the ball in my hand feeling like a piece of lead. When I open my eyes, they lock on the little boy standing about twenty feet across from me. He gives me a wide toothy grin, his glove ready to catch whatever I throw his way. I take a step forward, raise my hand, and release the ball without giving it another thought. The ball goes sailing through the air, wide and to the right, but the little boy eagerly runs a few steps and catches it. The sound of the ball hitting the glove practically echoes through the yard like a cannon.

"I did it," I whisper, the smile on my face instantaneous.

"You did," he says, an encouraging, proud smile on his face. "Good job."

"What now?"

"Now you stand there and wait for him to throw it back."

"Throw it back? As in...catch it?" I ask, the panic starting to bubble to the surface.

"Yep, just catch it, Kate. You got this," he says, turning his attention to his son. There's a slight shadow across his jaw from today's hair growth and I can't help but think about how that very jaw felt Saturday night rubbing against my sensitive thigh. "Kate?" he asks, my eyes moving upward until they clash with his.

"Yeah?"

The slightest smirk spreads on his lips. "You better keep your eye on the ball, Butterfly."

"Oh!" I yell, turning away from the handsome man beside me and facing the four-year-old ready to hurl a hard baseball at my head.

Max is all business as he waits for me to get ready. I'm not sure how you get ready to catch a baseball, but I think I'm prepared as best as I can. I mean, I've got the glove up by my face to protect against any vital face injury. That's important, right? No one wants to take a ball to the nose like Marcia Brady.

Max starts to giggle as Jensen reaches over and gently pulls the glove from obstructing my view. "Just hold it right here. He won't throw it very hard, so your reflexes will have time to catch it."

"Are you sure? I don't want to get hit in the face," I say, doubting I should even be standing on this side of the game of catch. I mean, throwing the ball is one thing, but catching it in the glove (not with my face) is another.

"You'll be fine, sweetheart. Trust me. Trust Max."

Exhaling deeply once more, I hold the glove where he instructs and wait for the ball to come flying at my face. I watch as Max brings up his arm and asks, "Ready?"

I nod frantically and wait. The ball is tossed in my direction, not nearly as fast as I was expecting. I easily move the glove to the side to catch it. Unfortunately, the ball hits the tip of the glove and bounces off. "Damn it," I mumble, bending down and picking up the ball.

"It's okay. You did good," Jensen says in a total dad tone, like he's speaking to a child.

"No, I didn't. I missed it." I tell him, taking my stance again and getting ready to throw the ball back to Max. "Again," I tell him, anxious to catch it this time around.

I toss the ball and he doesn't have to move to catch it this time. It sails directly into his glove and before I know it, he's tossing it back. I have no time to think or prepare, just adjust my glove. But this time, the ball hits me square in the glove with a satisfying thump. "I did it!" I yell, dropping the ball from the glove as I do a little shimmy and shake in victory.

"Good job, Kate! Now you can play catch with me all the time!" Max yells, jumping up and down along with me.

I glance at Jensen. His eyes are hungry with desire as he watches my little victory dance. He takes a step toward me, invading my personal space, reaching down to pick up the baseball and whispers, "I knew you could do it."

"It must have been the teacher," I tell him, smiling like a loon.

"Ehh, it's the player," he says, handing me back the ball. "Better throw it back. Max is waiting."

And that's how I spend the next fifteen minutes.

"Dinner's ready," Mary Ann hollers from the porch, pulling everyone's attention. Jensen takes the ball glove from my hand and heads over to collect Max's. The little guy is already sprinting toward the food line, his grandma there, waiting with an empty plate.

Slowly, everyone makes their way to the porch and loads up their plates with delicious homemade food. I grab a hotdog and plenty of the cheesy mac and cheese with bacon, some fresh fruit, and baked beans before heading over to find a seat at one of the tables under the shade tree. Jensen follows behind, sliding onto the bench between

Max and me. Soon, everyone takes a seat and practically inhales all the amazing food Mary Ann and Marissa prepared.

"Emma and Orval want to come down next weekend," Mary Ann says, making Samuel groan. "We don't have any vacancy, though, and you know there won't be any in town either." She's referring to the other bed and breakfasts in Rockland Falls, and I can tell by the way she says it that there's more to this story.

"Orval is my mom's brother that I told you about," Jensen whispers beside me, referring to the long-lost brother his mother has.

"Our guest room is torn up, remember? There's no way we'll get the closet finished, walls painted, and new flooring in before Friday," Harper says with a shrug, but it's the glint in her sparkling blue eyes that I notice right away.

"And I'll have Max, so I don't have any extra room," Jensen adds, the corners of his mouth fighting to not turn upward.

"I'm busy," Samuel says, straightening his already straight necktie.

"Your work schedule doesn't have anything to do with family using your guest room," Mary Ann says gently.

Samuel scoffs. "The last time they used my spare bedroom, I found the plastic packaging for a vibrator on the floor and a note that said I was out of KY." Everyone at the table, with the exception of Max who's obliviously eating macaroni and cheese with bacon, bursts out laughing. "It's not funny. I don't even own KY."

"Oh, Sammy, liven up a little, will ya? Share your house. Buy them KY. They're family," Freedom adds, her bangle bracelets jangling as she reaches for the bowl of watermelon.

Jensen's oldest brother gives her a look of horror. "I am *not* buying KY."

"For them or for you?" she asks sweetly.

"Neither," he growls, adjusting the necktie once more. It's almost like a nervous thing he does when he gets riled up, and if there's one thing I've noticed in the last two hours, it's Freedom definitely gets him all sorts of worked up.

"They could stay with me." I don't know why I said it, but the words were out before I could stop them. Actually, no, that's not true. The fact is I have a huge house with umpteen bedrooms and no one else to share them with. A little company might be just what the doctor ordered.

Everyone stops and looks at me. I can tell I've overstepped. Their faces are a mixture of relief and horror, most likely because I'm not even a part of this family and I'm offering up bedroom space for some out-of-town family.

"You don't have to do that," Jensen insists.

"Yes. She has room. They can stay with Kathryn. Case closed," Samuel says, reaching for his hamburger as if there's no more need for discussion.

"I don't want to overstep," I start, but am cut off by Jensen's younger sister.

"You're not overstepping," she insists. "It's just that…Aunt Emma and Uncle Orval are…different."

Rhenn snorts. "Different, my ass. Those ol' birds are nuts—the good kind, of course."

Latham glances over at me with a serious face. "Let me ask you, Kathryn, do you own a sex swing?"

My eyes are as wide as the plate in front of me, and I'm pretty sure my blush is the color of a fuchsia crayon as the others hoot with laughter. "They bought one for Abby and Levi. You knew that right?" Harper asks her family.

I'm completely lost. I've offered up my home to a couple who uses a sex swing? What in the…

"Listen, Kathryn, that's very nice of you to offer. I'm sure they'd love to stay with you for a few days, if you really don't mind. Orval and Emma are good people, if not a little on the...eccentric side."

"They have sex all the time," Marissa whispers, her face blushing as badly as mine.

"All. The. Time," Rhenn insists.

"As long as you have earplugs, I think you'll be okay," Samuel assures.

"Just remember to always knock or make a lot of loud noise before you enter any room," Harper instructs.

"That includes the pantry or the broom closet," Freedom says with a giggle.

I glance over at Jensen with what is probably considered a horrified look. He gives me a big grin and takes my hand in his. "It'll be okay, I promise. They really are the best, but neither of them have a filter and can be a tad inappropriate at times."

"It's only for a few days. I mean, how much trouble could they be?" I ask.

I'm met with silence.

Something tells me I'm in for a little trouble.

Chapter Fifteen

Jensen

I've barely gotten my hands on Kate all week, and I don't like it. I've had Max during the evenings, so the only time I can steal a few minutes of alone time with Kate is during the workday. Not ideal, especially with a dozen or so workers finishing up around the house, but I've managed a quick make-out session in her newly finished kitchen pantry as well as a little teenage groping in the laundry room. The only thing that did was ensure I was jerking off late at night in bed to the image of her naked body.

It's Thursday, and I'm tired of seeing her in passing. She must feel the same way, because she invited Max and I over for pizza before she heads to my sister's shop for that Ladies' Night Out thing. The prospect of Kate doing a little shopping at the store has my cock so damn hard, I can barely think straight. In fact, I'm pretty sure Wes is wondering what the hell is wrong with me today, considering I started paving the back walkway with the wrong stone.

It's Kate.

She makes it so I can't even complete the simplest, most mundane tasks.

"Hey." I hear her sweet voice as I'm wrapping up the day. I've already sent Wes home a few minutes early so I can sneak out of here, grab Max from the sitter's house, jump in the shower, and get back here for pizza.

When I turn around, I'm awestruck at how fucking beautiful she is. "Hi," I reply, my tongue feeling a little heavy.

"So, I'll have the pizza delivered for six, if that's okay with you." She takes a step closer, her familiar scent wrapping around me and refusing to let go.

"Sounds good. I'm getting ready to head out. I'm grabbing Max and a shower, and we'll be back in about thirty minutes."

"Perfect," she says, a tentative smile on her face.

"What's up?" I ask, throwing my shovel to the side and giving her my full attention.

"Nothing," she insists quickly. "I was just thinking, since most of the updates are almost finished…"

I step forward again. Now my body is practically pressed against hers. "What?"

She exhales, her breath hitting me square in the face. "I think I'm ready to clean out the library and use it." Her words are a hushed whisper, but the impact is as if she screamed them.

"Yeah?" I ask, unable to hide my smile.

Kate nods.

"I think that's a wonderful idea," I confess. The thought of a woman as gifted as Kate not using her talent anymore made me a little crazy. Knowing she's thinking about painting again has me all sorts of excited for her.

"You do?" she asks, her brows furrowed together.

"I think it's the best fucking idea you've had all week."

"Even better than fondling my boobs in the laundry room?" she quips, grinning from ear to ear.

"Technically, that was my idea," I remind her, swiping at a piece of hair hanging down on her cheek. The only thing I manage to do though is streak that delicate skin with dirt.

"Ahh, yes, it was your idea. And what a brilliant idea it was," she says, running her hands up my very dirty T-shirt.

Lacey Black

I really should head out and shower, but I can't go without a kiss. I claim her lips with my own, hungry and full of days' worth of pent-up sexual frustration. Kate mewls against me, giving as good as I do. Unfortunately, this kiss can't lead anywhere, which is why it pains me to pull away. We're both breathing hard, her eyes glassy with desire.

"Fuck, I'd rather kiss you, but I really need to get Max."

She nods. "You'll be back shortly."

"Yeah," I confirm, placing another kiss on her forehead. "We're going to have to figure out a time where I can get you alone, fast."

"Your mom did mention she's ready for a slumber party," Kate reminds me, recalling the conversation my mom and I had at the Labor Day cookout this past Monday.

"She did. Maybe I'll give her a call on my way to get Max," I reply, already liking that idea. There are so many things I could do again with (and to) Kate with the entire day and night at our disposal.

"Go, before you're late to pick him up," she says, taking a step back and out of my reach. I miss her nearness already.

"See you soon," I holler as I grab my shovel and toss it in the job trailer. Then, I'm in the hot truck cab and heading toward the sitter's place for my son. It'll be a short night with Kate, but that's okay. She has plans and I'll need to get Max home, bathed, and in bed for school tomorrow. But at least I have something to look forward to this weekend.

Essentially, some much-needed alone time with my Kate.

* * *

"Do you want to check out the library before the pizza gets here?" Kate asks as I get Max situated with some cartoons in the family room.

184

"Yeah," he replies, glancing toward his son. "Hey, Max, Kate and I are going to be down the hallway in the library. Holler if you need us, okay?"

"'Kay!" he replies, not once taking his eyes off the cartoon dogs on the large screen.

As we exit the large, comfortable TV room, I reach for her hand, reveling in the feel of her skin against mine. We're down the hall in just a few seconds, and before she has the opportunity to open the closed door, I pull her against my body and press my lips to hers. This kiss is gentler than the one earlier in the backyard. With my son just a handful of feet away and the knowledge we can't do any more than just kiss, I don't want to get either one of us worked up in a frenzy. It's bad enough I can only indulge in stolen kisses and tender touches, so the last thing I need is to sport a hard-on the entire night because I can't keep my hands and my tongue to myself.

"Hi," she whispers, the feeling of her smile against my lips already doing things below the belt.

"Hi."

"Well, come on. We can't stand out here all night and make out like teenagers."

"Well, we could, but Max will eventually come looking for us when he gets hungry," I tell her, reaching for the doorknob.

Our hands are still locked as I slowly push open the door. The room is bathed in light, thanks to the floor-to-ceiling windows that face the backyard. They are a special glass that allows you to see out, but not in. It's dusty in here, thanks to more than a decade's worth of dormant house, and the first thing Kate does when she steps in is sneeze.

"I've got to get this room cleaned out. It's horrible in here," she says. "That's my plan for this weekend. I'm going to sort through my dad's desk and find out from the attorney what needs to be saved, if anything. Some of the old books I want to keep, but honestly, I have a ton of my own books I'd love to bring in here and fill the shelves with. I'll keep some of his favorites, but I've already talked to the used bookstore in town, and they've agreed to take them for me."

"Max and I can help, if you need it," I offer, hoping like hell she agrees. "He's going to Mom's in the afternoon on Saturday, but I'll have him back in the morning on Sunday."

"I'd love your help," she agrees, a warm smile on her lips. "Maybe instead of dinner out, we can just order in and hang out here," she offers.

"I think that can be arranged," I say, slowly making my way toward the easel by the window. I can already see the painting perched upon it, even though it's quite dirty from years of sitting. My heart starts to pound in my chest as I approach, my mind reeling at the image she created. I run my finger across it, knocking off a little dust and grime.

"That's us," she whispers beside me. I didn't even hear her approach.

"It's amazing," I tell her, taking in the gorgeous scenery of the ocean and the backyard before the recent re-landscape, as well as the young couple standing on the shore. "I remember that night," I whisper, taking in the way our arms are entwined and our bodies pressed together. It was the night I told her I was going to marry her. No, it wasn't a proposal, but it was a declaration.

A promise.

One I never got to fulfill.

Kate swipes at a bit of dust gathered along the top, her eyes pinned to the canvas. "I was planning to give it to you," she says with a shrug and it feels like my heart is starting to break open. "I started it that night after you left and worked until the wee hours in the morning. Your birthday was coming up. You'd always wanted one of my paintings," she adds.

"But you never thought they were good enough," I finish for her, remembering how she never saw the talent the way the rest of us did. I blamed her mother for that. She wasn't supportive of Kate's talents, always considering them a pesky hobby she'd grow out of. Annabelle Elliott was always more concerned with appearances than what could benefit her own daughter. She's a piece of work, that's for sure.

She gives me a sheepish grin and glances at the half complete painting in front of us.

"I still want this one," I tell her.

"But it's not finished."

"So finish it," I suggest, reaching around her hip and pulling her into my side.

"I haven't painted since that night," she reiterates, reminding me of an earlier conversation about why she stopped painting.

"Well, then I think it's time to grab a brush, Butterfly. Choose your own destiny," I add. I don't know why I said that last part, but it felt right, like it might be something she needed to hear.

Again, she grins up at me and then back to the artwork. "I'm not sure I'm any good anymore."

I blow an exasperated breath. "Are you kidding? I'm sure it's just like riding a bike."

That makes her laugh. "Sure it is." She exhales. "Do you know what? I do want to try. I don't know if it's being here in this room or everything that's led up to it, but I'd love to paint again. I've missed it."

Turning her in my arms, I interlock my fingers behind her lower back and hold her close. "It's time to rediscover you, Kate. Don't do it for your mom or because you think that's what you should do. Or even me. Do it for you. Do it because you have no other option but to paint."

Her eyes kinda glass over a bit, and I wonder if she's going to cry. "Can I ask you something?"

"Anything."

She hesitates for just a second before asking her question, and even though I knew this particular one would come up again soon, I wasn't it expecting tonight. "What's going on with us?"

It's amazing how right it feels to have her in my arms again, and for once, I'm not going to hold back when it comes to telling her how I feel. "Well, I'm enjoying the hell out of spending time with you, and I'd like to keep doing so. If that means you're my girlfriend again, then so be it, but life's too short not to just go after what you want, and Kate?" I ask, my hand moving up to cup her jaw, "I want you. I've always wanted you."

Then my lips are on hers. I have no idea how she feels about my blunt statement, but I don't give her the chance to reply. Instead, I slide my tongue along the seam of her lips, my body craving a taste, and she opens up for me. My tongue slides easily against hers as her hands reach around my back and grip my shirt. This kiss could very easily go from nice to holy-fuck in less than a second, but I won't let it. Not with Max in the other room.

The doorbell sounds, interrupting us. "That's probably the pizza," she says, resting her cheek against my chest and inhaling deeply.

"Probably. I'll go grab it," I tell her, kissing her forehead before letting her go. I miss having her near me already.

"Hey, Jensen?" she asks, stopping me as I reach the doorway. When I turn back to face her, she adds, "I want you too."

The ache in my chest that I've carried for the last dozen years suddenly starts to lift and a big smile breaks out on my face. "Good, because you're not getting rid of me this time," I tell her. The doorbell sounds a second time, which is why I find myself heading to the foyer, the biggest fucking smile ever on my face.

Pulling out my wallet, I reach the door and pull it open. I grab a few twenties to pay for dinner, but my hands stumble as I come face-to-face with who's on the other side of the door. Definitely not the pizza guy.

"Surprise!" my aunt Emma bellows from the doorway.

"Jesus," I say before I can stop it.

"No, just Aunt Emma, darling." She glances over to Uncle Orval, who's standing beside her. "I've been called God more times than I can count, but never Jesus, right, Orvie?"

"You got that right, Emmie," he coos, and I'm pretty sure he goosed her ass.

"Oh, stop it, you ol' goat. If you're a good boy, I'll let you call me God later tonight," she says in a sugary sweet voice that makes me want to vomit. "Well, don't just stand there, Jensen. The car is loaded with my things. Be a dear and bring them in for me?" Aunt Emma asks before pushing past me and just walking right into Kate's house. "Wow, what a magnificent home," she says, looking up at the chandelier.

"Thank you," Kate says, slowly entering the foyer. "I take it you're not the pizza delivery driver," she quips, going over to where my aunt stands.

"No, dear, I'm Aunt Emma, and the sexy older man at the doorway is my Orval. You must be Kathryn," she says, taking a few steps toward Kate.

"I am," she says, extending her hand.

Emma ignores it, instead pulling her into a fierce hug. When she finally releases her, Emma takes another look around the house.

"This place is beautiful. I bet there were lots of rooms to christen, weren't there?" she asks, catching Kate completely off guard.

In my defense, we did try to warn her at the cookout.

"Kathryn, this feisty old woman and her husband are going to be your houseguests for the next three nights," I say, holding the door open so my uncle can come in too.

"Four."

"Four?" Kate asks, glancing between the old woman and me.

"Yes, dear, four. We decided to head back home on Monday. I hope it's okay we are here that long. We could always head over a few towns to find one of those cheap hotels with bedbugs and hookers in and out all night long."

"Oh, no no no, that's not necessary. You're more than welcome to stay here with me," Kate says politely, but I can't help but shake my head. I feel like we were just played, or at least Kate was. I also have a feeling our quiet evening in on Saturday night will be anything but. Not with these two on the premises.

Let's just hope we can find a piece of privacy in this big house. I mean, it's eight thousand square feet.

Shouldn't be too hard, right?

Chapter Sixteen

Kathryn

As I head down Main Street in Rockland Falls, looking for a parking spot, I can't help but wonder, "So, Emma, I was certain we shut the gate. How did you and Orval get in?"

After Jensen went outside to get their four suitcases—apparently, Emma isn't a light traveler—the pizza deliveryman arrived and we all shared the pizza. It hit me that I had to buzz him in because the gate was closed, as it usually is.

Emma scoffs. "It takes a lot more than a little ol' security gate to keep Aunt Emma out, dear. My time with the FBI taught me a lot of valuable things."

I don't even know what that means, and I'm not sure I want to.

"I'm so excited to see what new things Harper has," she says, glancing around at the very busy streets, all lined with ladies taking advantage of the annual Ladies' Night Out shopping event.

"Have you shopped there before?" I ask, mentally slapping myself for asking such a stupid question. Obviously she has, if she's curious about her new stock.

"Oh, many times. Uncle Orval really likes the racy panties section," she tells me so casually I almost miss her statement.

I park in the first available spot I can find, just down the street from Harper's store Kiss Me Goodnight. As I climb out of the car, I realize this is basically the same spot where the Haunted House was set up, and suddenly, I'm blushing a bit at the memories.

When I glance back at Emma, I see she's already taking off toward the shop at a much faster pace than I would have expected from a woman her age. Jensen told me they're in their eighties, more than twenty years older than his mom, Mary Ann. The story is Mary Ann's dad remarried after his first wife passed away. Orval was a young adult then and didn't approve of his father's very rapid remarry and essentially cut them from his life. It wasn't until Orval and Emma's granddaughter's wedding that they reconnected after nearly forty years.

I have to practically run to catch up with her. She's a woman on a mission. "Thank you for inviting me to go with you, dear," she says, offering me a warm, grandmotherly smile.

I almost snort at her comment. There wasn't really an invitation. Once she heard I was coming up here after the pizza, she basically invited herself, insisting she come with me to buy some new goodies for the bedroom. I don't even want to think about what that means.

"You're most welcome," I end up saying as we approach the front door. "I'm happy to have someone to shop with." I'm not sure that's entirely true, but I've been enjoying my short time with Jensen's aunt nonetheless.

"I love shopping, dear. You'll see. Now that you and my Jensen are shacking up, I might have to buy you a housewarming gift." There's something in the gleam in her eye that makes me pause. I've heard all the stories of her *gifts* on Monday at the Labor Day cookout.

"Oh, uh, Jensen and I aren't shacking up. He and Max are still at their house," I tell her as we walk through the door of a bustling store.

Emma tsks. "Semantics, dear. As long as you're having *the sex*, then you're practically shacking up."

"Ummm…" I pause inside the door, realizing a few local ladies (one being my old fifth grade teacher) have overheard Emma's blunt statement. They stand there as wide-eyed and shocked as I do.

"Don't be bashful now. This place is perfect to outfit your bedroom escapades. Does my nephew enjoy crotchless panties? I know for a fact Harper carries them. Uncle Orval just loves them," she says as she reaches down and grabs my hand, pulling me through the throngs of people until we're standing in front of a display featuring the product she so vocally asked about. "These, dear. They're perfect for when you just need to unleash the one-eyed tube snake." She leans closer to me and yell-whispers, "That means his penis."

My face burns with mortification. Now, I can see exactly why Jensen's siblings weren't too thrilled at having Emma and Orval stay with them. If she acts like this all the time, and even after only knowing her about two hours, I'm pretty sure she does, I can see why they'd prefer her in smaller doses.

"Aunt Emma, are you harassing Kathryn?" Harper says, coming over to greet her aunt with a hug.

"There's no harassment, dear. I was just explaining how much my Orvie loves the crotchless panties I bought from here, and I'm sure Jensen would love them too. He seems like the type of man who likes to pound the paternal pistol."

I choke on the very air I breathe, while Harper just smiles down at the old lady. "Oh, Aunt Emma, I've missed you," she says with another hug. "But if we could refrain from talking about my brother's *pistol* and what he likes to do with it, I'd forever be grateful."

Emma blows out a hard breath. "Harper, your brother likes to pogo in the shrub as much as that sexy hunk of man-meat you're shacking up with does."

"Yes, but I'd prefer to never think about my brother's *anything* involving sex."

"Fine, dear. What do you have new for this evening? I'm in need of something to help accentuate my girls. One of my boobie tassels broke last week," she says, doing a full turn to check out the merchandise.

"Oh, uh, I'm very sorry to hear about the tassel," Harper replies, trying with all her might to keep a straight face. "I just got in a few new bustiers. One has fringe," she says, grabbing Emma's arm and gently leading her away.

"I do love fringe," Emma agrees.

Over her shoulder, Harper whispers, "Go, browse. I'll keep her entertained."

I offer her a grateful smile and turn away. It's not that I don't enjoy the little spitfire of a woman, but she's definitely a lot to handle in such a short amount of time. I find myself wandering through the busy store, checking out some of the beautiful pieces Harper carries. There are a few things I wouldn't mind trying on, but I'm just not sure I can with all these people milling about.

"You should try this one. It would look amazing against your skin tone," Harper says a bit later as she joins me in the corner of the shop. She's holding up a delicate nightgown in a soft blue. It looks like it hits mid-thigh and has a white lace trim around the bottom. It's definitely a gorgeous piece.

"Oh, it's beautiful," I tell her, watching as she reaches into the bin beneath the table and pulls out one that's my size.

"Here, go try it on," she insists, taking me by the shoulders and steering us toward the dressing rooms. Freedom is there and gives me a warm smile while still chatting with a woman about pajamas. Harper practically pushes me inside the dressing room. "I know it'll look amazing, but I want you to be comfortable," she says and then rips the curtain closed, leaving me alone in the small space. "I can't hear you changing," Harper yells through the curtain.

"All right, all right," I reply, setting the nightie down on the bench. "Hold your horses."

It only takes me a few minutes to change out of my casual jean shorts, fitted tee, and bra, but the moment I slide the nightie on, I know Harper is right. It's a perfect fit. And the color? Amazing. I can't help but stare at the reflection staring back at me. When was the last time I bought something so beautiful and sexy with the intention of someone else seeing it? A really long time, that's for sure. When Charles and I were together, I tried a few pieces of lingerie early in our relationship, but honestly, it never really felt right. Maybe that's because we were never really meant to be together. We were comfortable, that's it.

But this?

With the prospect of Jensen seeing me in it?

Liberating.

Sexy.

Feminine.

Suddenly, I can't wait to show him later tonight.

I get dressed once again in the clothes I arrived in and step out of the dressing room. "Well?" Harper asks, a knowing grin on her pretty face.

"It's perfect," I answer.

She does a little shimmy. "I knew it!"

I glance around at the displays, suddenly more excited to do a little shopping than I was before. "You know, I could really use a few new bra and panty sets."

Her eyes light up. "I have just the thing, come with me." And then she leads me off to shop her store.

An hour and three hundred dollars later, I'm standing off to the side with Marissa, enjoying some of the homemade sweet treats she baked and sipping a glass of wine as Harper helps the last of the evening shoppers. "I need to be careful or I won't be able to drive home," I tell Jensen's youngest sister.

"Don't worry about that, dear. Aunt Emma will drive," Jensen's aunt says as she approaches the goodies table. "Oh, these look divine." She picks a chocolaty brownie off the tray and eats it in two bites.

"Oh, I'm sure I'll be fine to drive. I've only had this one glass," I tell the older woman, who is picking up her second treat.

"Pssh! I can handle your sporty little car, Kathryn. If my stint in NASCAR taught me anything, it was how to handle an automobile."

I glance at Marissa, who vocalized the question I was thinking. "You drove in NASCAR?"

"Of course, dear. Those boys didn't know how to handle their sticks before Emma showed them how," she says casually, reaching for her third treat.

"I'm all finished," Harper says as she comes over to where we stand. "I'm exhausted."

"You had a great night," Marissa adds, starting to box up the remaining treats.

"Give me wine," Freedom bellows after locking the front door.

"Done," Harper replies, pouring two glasses of sweet red wine and topping off my glass.

"Oh, I shouldn't. I have to drive home," I reply, knowing I really shouldn't have a second glass.

"I'm driving her home," Emma insists.

"We should probably head that way, though. It's getting late," I add.

Emma glances at her watch. "It's still early, dear. Besides, Orvie isn't taking his pill until eleven. That means the love wand will be ready to play with by eleven thirty."

Marissa makes a choking noise and quickly chugs the rest of her wine. Harper giggles and leans my way. "She's staying with you, you know. I've heard they can be quite…vocal when the little blue pill takes effect," she teases, though I'm honestly not really sure she's teasing. I have a feeling she's speaking fact, not fiction.

"Thank God the guest room I have them in is on the opposite side of the house," I whisper to Harper, making her giggle.

It feels completely natural and comfortable to be with these women, hanging out, shopping, and drinking a little wine, and before I know it, my second glass is finished. Harper heads over (with her wine, of course) and closes out her register, seemingly very happy with tonight's profits. I don't know how much she sold, but I watched a lot of merchandise leave the store this evening.

Another hour later, after the lights are out and the wine is gone, we finally head out. I don't even care I'm letting Jensen's eighty-something year old aunt drive my fancy schmancy car (the one I really should just get rid of). Instead, I happily hand over my keys, grateful I don't have to drive home. Drinking wine and enjoying some of Marissa's homemade treats was great, but getting to know Jensen's sisters again, as well as his aunt, was the highlight of my evening. Not to mention a bag of goodies I can't wait to show Jensen.

Maybe even a little strip show…

We're pulling out of the parking lot, Emma talking a mile a minute as she almost takes the corner on two wheels, and I pull out my cell phone to keep myself from freaking out. I pull up his contact and send a text message.

Me: *I know it's late. I just wanted you to know I had fun with your sisters and aunt.*

A few seconds later, the bubbles appear on my phone screen, and I can't help but get a little giddy.

Jensen: *I'm still up working. I'm glad you had fun. Emma behaved?*

Me: *She gave me wine. Harper too. Hell, even Marissa gave me some.*

Jensen: *LOL Well, it sounds like you needed a night to cut loose. I'm happy for you.*

Me: *I bought things...*

Jensen: *Keep talking...*

Me: *I'd rather show you.*

Jensen: *I'm so hard right now.*

Me: *Show me.*

Jensen: *Jesus, Butterfly, you're killing me.*

I can't help it, I giggle as my fingers stumble across the screen to send another message.

"Are you sexting?" I hear the direct question echo in the darkened car.

"What? No!" I defend, probably a bit too insistently. I was totally getting ready to ask for a picture again.

"Liar. You're just like my granddaughters. They lie about dirty pictures too. I'm pretty sure my Lexi has a whole album of the goods on her phone, but will she share with her grandma? No! She keeps Linkin all to herself," Emma says as she nears my house.

"Umm, isn't that a little weird? They're your granddaughters."

Emma blows out a dramatic breath. "Of course, it's not weird. Those sexy men aren't my blood. Plus, I want to make sure all of my girls are taken care of, you know, sexually. They all picked well.

Maybe not Jaime and Lexi the first time around, but this last time? Totally hotties with a lot to offer a girl in the one-eyed trouser snake department, if you know what I mean," Emma says casually, as if she were discussing the weather.

"Yeah, I think I know what you mean," I reply as Emma pulls up to my gate and enters in the code before I can even tell her what it is.

I watch as the gate opens and we move forward, bringing the entire house into view. It's lit up with the lighting Rhenn installed, giving it a subtle, yet lovely appearance. The fountain is up and running in front, soft lighting illuminates the cascading water as it falls from the top. There's just enough light to see the gorgeous landscape around the fountain, as well as the front of the house.

It's the same place I grew up in, but I've made it mine.

I love it.

"...and you should always try the merchandise before you buy, dear. You never take home a new car without going for a little test drive, am I right?"

I startle, as Emma's words pull me from my own thoughts. "Oh, sorry, I was just admiring the landscape," I reply sheepishly, admitting I wasn't paying attention. But then again, I'm not sure I *want* to know what she was talking about.

"No matter," she says as she parks my car in the driveway with precision and expertise. "Anyway, let's get inside. Orvie is waiting for me, and I'm sure my nephew is sending those dick pics by now. If not, make sure you ask for the goods. It might help you later when you double click your mouse before falling asleep," she adds as she slips out of the driver's seat.

My face is red, I know. I was honestly about to tell him to really send one (you know, proof and all), but now I'm not sure I can.

Not with his aunt commenting like that. Instead, I'll just slip into bed and die of mortification. That sounds like a much better idea.

I follow behind, making sure the garage door is closed and everything is locked up. Orval left the light on over the sink so we can see as we make our way through the mudroom and into my new kitchen.

"Tomorrow I'll help you put away the rest of the stuff in those boxes," Emma says, nodding to the stack.

"I still have to go through some of them. I did a lot of it when I boxed it up before the construction, but I don't want to keep things just for the sake of keeping, you know?"

"Oh, don't I know it, dear," she says, shuffling with determination through the kitchen and dining room and toward the foyer where the grand staircase is. "Besides, I'm anxious to see those hottie construction workers before they're finished completely and close up shop," she adds.

I can't help but smile. I'm learning quickly that Emma is a hoot. My mother would die a thousand deaths if she were ever to meet this woman. She's blunt and talks about sex, something I was always told should never be discussed. Ever. *A lady never tells*, she's say.

We wave goodbye at the top of the stairs, and I can't help but notice the little extra bounce in her step as she approaches the doorway to the guest room they're using. A smile plays on my lips. I hope I'm half as spry as she is when I'm nearing her age.

Inside the master bedroom, I set my stuff down and reach for my phone. I notice a few messages from Jensen, but decide to get ready for bed before I answer him. I make quick work of washing my face and getting into my pajamas, the bag with my new items staring at me from the reading nook. Saturday night, I'll definitely wear one of them…

Climbing into bed, I finally unlock my phone and glance at his messages.

Jensen: *Are you there?*

Jensen: *Where'd you go?*

Jensen: *Seriously, Kate. Is everything OK?*

Jensen: *I'm starting to worry.*

Jensen: *I'm hoping you just passed out. Did you just pass out?*

Jensen: *Jesus, I think I'm coming out of my skin.*

Shit. It's been a solid twenty minutes since we were communicating. Knowing Jensen he could be halfway here by now to check on me.

Me: *I'm OK. I was talking to your aunt, who's quite the character. I'm in bed now.*

Jensen: *Fuck. Don't do that to me. I was ready to start calling the hospitals.*

Me: *I'm sorry!*

Jensen: *It's OK. *takes deep breath* Now I know you're not wrecked into a ditch somewhere, let's get back to discussing the fact you bought some lingerie tonight.*

Me: *I did. If you're good, maybe I'll show you Saturday night, if our date night is still on.*

I bite my lip and wait for his reply. I've never been forward, but with this man, I've always felt comfortable stepping out of the box.

Jensen: *Oh, I'm very fucking good, Butterfly. I can't wait to see what surprises you have beneath your clothes.*

My body is on fire. There's a slow burn creeping up my thighs and landing in the apex of my legs. I'm wet, anxious, and so very ready. If only he were here to help alleviate the ache. Before I realize what's happening, my hand is sliding beneath the elastic of my sleep shorts and into my panties. As expected, they're completely soaked.

Jensen: *Are you touching yourself, Kate?*

My fingers slide through my folds, my clit already hard. I should reply, but I can't seem to do it one-handed. My mind conjures up images of Jensen's hands, his mouth, and his cock. I slide a finger inside my body, followed quickly by a second. I feel the stretch, that glorious burn all the way down to my toes.

The ringing of the cell phone in my hand has me pausing. Jensen's name is at the bottom of the screen, letting me know it's a video call. My hand is a little shaky as I adjust the phone and click accept. His face instantly fills the screen, his head resting in the middle of his pillow.

"Butterfly, why didn't you answer me?"

I bite my lip again. "I was a little busy," I reply boldly.

His eyes flare with desire. "Show me."

It only takes about a half of a second to make the decision. The phone is moved downward, displaying my hand hidden beneath my shorts.

"Take them off. I want to see you," he instructs.

Setting the phone down on the comforter beside me, I shimmy out of my shorts and climb back on my bed. Picking my phone back up, I glance at the gorgeous man on the screen. "Done."

"Show me." I angle the camera downward so he can see my naked lower half. "Show me what you were doing when I called," he adds.

That constant blush is back. I try to hold the phone at the right angle and place my fingers between my legs. The moment they come into contact with my clit, I almost catapult from the bed. My body is wound so tight, it seems all of my blood is in one concentrated area. I slide my fingers through my folds, coating them in my wetness. "This is what I was doing," I tell him as I slide two fingers into my pussy.

A loud groan echoes in the room. "That's so fucking hot," he growls. "Keep going."

I move my fingers in and out, knowing this orgasm won't take long. Not with him watching and instructing me. "What are you doing?" I ask, turning the camera upward a bit so I can see. Jensen angles his downward until his very large, very hard erection fills the screen. His hand is wrapped around the base as he slowly slides it all the way up to the tip.

Now it's my groan that fills the room. Watching him pleasure himself while I do the same might be the biggest turn-on since the day Jensen walked down the hallway wearing Wrangler jeans and cowboy boots.

"Hold the phone down a little more so I can watch. I want to see you come, Kate. Show me how you do it when I'm not around," he says, his voice low and gravely.

"I want to watch too," I tell him. Jensen makes sure the phone is angled downward so I can see him stroke himself.

My fingers start to move on their own. He grips the root of his cock and gives it a squeeze. I can see the wetness ooze from the tip. If I were there, I'd put him in my mouth and lick it clean.

"Fuck," he groans, his hand moving faster and faster. "I'd do anything to have your mouth on me right now," he adds, confirming I must have said it aloud.

My muscles start to tense as my orgasm builds. I can feel the tightness in my legs, yet they spread as widely as possible. I pump my fingers in and out as my back arches off the bed and euphoria spreads through my veins. I vaguely hear the sound of Jensen's release as I ride the waves of my own.

It takes a solid minute before I'm able to move. My limbs are boneless and my breathing erratic as I force my eyes open. That's when I realize my phone is sitting on my stomach. Quickly grabbing

Lacey Black

it, I glance at the screen, his handsome, yet very sated face filling the device.

"Sorry, I dropped my phone."

"It's okay. I got to watch all of the good parts anyway," he tells me, a lopsided grin spreading across his face.

"I've never done that," I whisper, the blush already starting to creep up my neck.

"Me neither. It was fucking sexy as hell to watch."

"It kinda was," I agree, my own lips spreading wide into a smile. It's replaced quickly by a yawn, however.

"I'm going to let you go so you can go to sleep."

"Okay," I whisper, my eyes already starting to fall. The combination of wine and an amazing orgasm has just about lulled me into dreamland.

"Goodnight, Butterfly," he whispers.

"Night," I reply, giving him one last smile before clicking off the phone.

I set the device down on the nightstand, making sure it's charging, and snuggle into my pillow. I should definitely get up and clean myself up a bit, but I can't seem to make my legs work.

Images of Jensen and watching him stroke himself fill my mind once more. I'll definitely be filing those away for a later day. Turning on my side and curling around the spare pillow, I relax instantly and drift off to sleep, thoughts of the one man I've always loved filling my dreams.

Chapter Seventeen

Jensen

The carpenters are busy cleaning up their tools and inspecting their final product as I slip through the foyer and up the stairs. I've been here for about twenty minutes and haven't seen her. It's just after eight in the morning, and even though I need to get to work to finish up this project, seeing Kate is first on my list.

I reach the master bedroom and find the door closed. Without knocking, I slowly inch it open and peek inside. Even though the room is darkened from shades, there's enough light filtering around the edges to make out her sleeping form in the middle of the massive bed. My cock already springs to life in anticipation.

It takes me only a few seconds to slip off the old worn cowboy boots I occasionally wear for work and approach the bed as quietly as possible. She's tangled up in the comforter on her back with one leg sticking out, her hair a tangled mess against the gray pillowcase. A light snore slips from her open mouth, bringing a big grin to my face.

Very carefully, I lift the comforter and slide into bed. The moment my hand comes in contact with smooth skin, I realize she's not wearing any pajamas. My cock jumps for joy as I trail a finger down her hip and around to her pussy. I'm moving before I can talk myself out of it. I worm my way beneath the blankets, enveloping myself in warmth and her feminine scent. Her arousal from the night before still clings to the sheets, pretty much ensuring I'll be stone-hard for the rest of the day.

I position myself between her legs and run my hands along the silkiness of her thighs. She wiggles beneath my touch, but makes no other indication she's awake. I smile as I lower my head the last few inches down to where's she wet, my tongue sliding easily between the lips of her sweet, sweet pussy.

We both groan, hers in surrender and mine more primal. I go to work, licking, lapping, and sucking at her slick skin. Her hands dive into my hair, gripping my scalp, as she rides my tongue. I can tell she's close. Like a man possessed, I pierce my tongue inside her pussy repeatedly until she's rocking against my face, seeking the relief I'm promising. As much as I'd love to take my time, savor this moment, and taste every inch of her, I'm too addicted to feeling her come against me.

Pressing my finger against her clit is like the magic button. Kate detonates beautifully under me, my tongue buried deep inside her. I can feel her muscles contracting around me, and it's all-consuming even more.

"You're fucking beautiful when you come," I whisper, sitting back on my haunches. "I'd wake you up every day just like this if I could." I completely ignore the longevity suggested in my comment, not wanting to get into that topic right now, even though I already know how I want this to play out. I want her by my side for the rest of my life. I've always wanted her there.

Kate's eyes flutter open, a satisfied grin on her plump lips. I can't wait to kiss the hell out of them. Crawling up her body, I run my lips along her exposed skin, committing her sweet scent to memory. She squirms beneath my lips, but I keep going until they find hers. She tries to keep her mouth closed, mumbling something about morning breath, but I couldn't care less. I need to taste her everywhere, and that includes her lips.

Her hand on my crotch evokes another low groan from my lungs. Kate strokes me through my jeans, making my eyes cross. "You seem to be *up* bright and early this morning," she sasses, teasing my cock and my sanity.

I snort at her innuendo. "Funny girl. It's actually well after eight, so I'm not sure it's still considered bright and early."

"It is?" she asks, her eyes darting to the alarm clock on the table. "My word, I haven't slept that late in years."

"You deserve it," I tell her, running my nose along the side of her face. "Did you have fun last night?"

"Yeah. Your family is great. Plus, you know, after..." She strokes me with firm fingers as if to punctuate her statement.

"After," I groan, my lips finding hers once more. "This isn't what I came in here for." It's hard to peel my lips from hers.

"What did you come in here for then?" *Stroke, stroke.*

"I can't think when you do that..."

"This?" Again, she strokes, and I'm about to blow.

"Yes, that," I bite out with no venom in my words.

"I have an idea," she says, shimmying as she worms her way down my body beneath me.

"I can't wait to hear this idea."

"Yoo-hoo! Kathryn, are you awake?" The words slice through the room, dousing my body like a bucket of cold water just as the insistent knocking dances on the door.

"Crud, is that Emma?" Kate gasps, releasing my aching cock. "I'm not even dressed."

"Kathryn? I can't find Jensen. There's a problem," Emma hollers, her knocking becoming louder and more adamant.

"Shit," I mumble, jumping out of Kate's bed. My legs tangle in the comforter, almost causing me to fall.

"Are you okay?" Kate whispers, wrapping the sheet around her naked waist.

"Fine," I state, stumbling as I try to slip my feet into my boots.

By the time I get to the door, my jeans are bunched up around my calves and I'm pretty sure my boots are on the wrong feet. I open

Lacey Black

the door and slip out of the room, not wanting to give my aunt and uncle a peepshow of Kate half naked on her bed.

"Hey, Aunt Emma. Uncle Orval," I say, pulling the door closed behind me. "What's up?" I ask, glancing between their smiling, knowing faces.

"Orvie, it must be Take Your Erection to Work Day," Emma states bluntly, an ornery smirk on her wrinkled face.

"Those were always my favorite days at work too, my love," Orval replies to his wife, patting me on the back as if in accolade.

"Umm, yeah, so, problem? What's the issue?" I ask as I adjust my hips to try to mask my rapidly deflating erection, thanks to my elderly aunt drawing attention to it.

"Oh, there isn't an issue, not really. We just saw you sneaking into Kathryn's room and were worried that you didn't have enough protection." Emma gives me a look as if her comment was the most normal thing in the world.

"Protection?"

"Yes, you know, condom, love glove, rubber sock, raincoat. Do you have enough, Jensen?" she asks, watching and waiting (very eagerly, I might add) for my reply.

I can feel the mortification tinge my cheeks. So this is how Kate feels when she becomes embarrassed, huh? Fuck. I run my hand through my hair. "Uh, yeah, I think I'm covered."

"Oh, let's hope you suit up. It's a great way to avoid unwanted pregnancy. Or is she on the pill?" my aunt asks.

All I can do is stare at her in horror. "I don't know," I whisper, wishing the floor would open up and swallow me whole.

"Well, these are the things you should always ask on the first date, Jensen. If *the sex* is in the plans, you should ask about contraception. Maybe even stop by the local pharmacy beforehand, you know, just in case."

"Unless you're thinking with the little head, and you forget. That happened to me once," Orval says, staring off into space.

"That's how we got our Trish," Emma confirms.

"Wow, okay, look at the time," I say, glancing down at the wristwatch on my arm. "I really should be getting back to work."

"Well, we don't want to keep you," Emma replies, moving to the side so I can pass.

Of course I'm not out of earshot before I hear my uncle say, "You know, Emmie, all this talk about sex has my main sail ready to stand and salute."

That's something I'll never forget overhearing for the rest of my life.

* * *

By the time the workday draws to an end, I've had no less than four text messages, and not from the woman I'd prefer. No, these came from Ashley. Asking if she can call Max later (she knows she can). Asking how his school day was (he wasn't even out of school yet). Asking how work is going (she hated talking about my work when we were married). And my personal favorite, asking if we had any weekend plans.

I know exactly what she's doing and it pisses me the hell off.

She's fishing for information about any plans Max and I may have with Kate.

Ignoring the messages, I finish the job at hand. The plants are in the ground and doing well, the new paving and retaining walls are built, and the flowers blooming. My job here is done. Well, except for one thing…

With the job trailer loaded up, I send Wes home for the day. He'll pick up Monday morning, jumping right in to our growing list of landscape maintenance clients. With Brody back at school and participating in sports, Wes will pick up that slack in helping maintain clients. Between him and Jonas, I'm hoping I'll finally have a little more wiggle room to breathe. This business is still my life (and my livelihood), but there's no reason I need to work it twenty-four seven. Especially with Max.

And Kate.

This property, though...this property is the one I'll be maintaining, like my mom's property. And I won't be charging. I can't charge my mom, and there's no way I'll be able to invoice Kate either. Sure, she'll be billed for the initial job, materials, and labor, but from this point forward, I'm doing it because I want to. Because I love it. Because I love her.

Yeah, I said it.

I love her.

I've always fucking loved her, and having her back in town, back in my arms only reiterates that fact. I should be terrified. I should probably keep my distance, but I just can't. I don't want to. It's like the missing piece of my heart is finally back in place, back where it belongs.

That's why I'm taking a few of my hand tools to the pool house. The contractors put on the new roof and the plumbing was repaired, but the rest of it is mostly cosmetic, with a lot of cleaning. I knew Kate wanted to leave it as close to original as possible, just make sure it was secure. They did a great job on the updates, but there are a few things I wanted to do to the inside.

I step inside the building. The windows have been open these last few days, replacing that old, musty smell with fresh seaside air. I notice right away Rhenn updated the lighting, installing can lights in the ceiling and giving it an open, bright feel. The old chairs in the corner are gone, most of them damaged from years of being left out in the weather. The old curtains hang from the changing area, but I have an idea for that. The bathroom and shower stall are all new too, but there's a small touch I wanted to add to that room.

I know it'll take me a little time to complete the projects I have in mind, but I think the end result will be something to be proud of.

I head back to my truck and retrieve the pieces I've been working on in my garage late at night. After Max would go to sleep, I'd slip outside and work on the few touches I wanted to add to the pool house. Kate has no idea I've been working on them, which has me both excited and nervous. She may not like the changes I'm making at all, though I really believe she'll love them.

Glancing at my watch, I see it's just after four. I'll have to head out and grab Max at five, but this gives me a solid hour to get started. Beginning with the changing rooms, I rip down the old shower curtains from the wall and scrub the wooden doorframe. It's solid pine and still sealed well, so the dust and dirt from years of unuse clean off easily.

I take the new swinging doors and position them in the opening. My dad taught me carpentry when I was younger, one of the few things I took away from my childhood that I'm grateful for. Back when Harper and I were helping him build or refinish things in the garage was when our family was still happy. Before he tore it all apart for a few quick and easy lays.

The doors fit perfectly. I was always told to measure twice and cut once, so I was pretty sure I had the measurements right. The new doors fill about three quarters of the opening, leaving a foot of open space at the bottom, just in case. When you live along the ocean and the product you're building is for a pool house, you learn to prepare for anything.

When the new door is secured into place, I give it a few tests to make sure it swings easily. The new latch fits perfectly, ensuring whoever is changing inside the small room has privacy. I can't help but smile at myself, loving the way the pinewood matches the existing doorway. Latham helped me with that at his hardware store.

I glance at my watch, noting I still have thirty minutes. I run back out to my truck and grab the bench. My eyes dart to the house, but don't see the woman I'm searching for. She went with Emma and Orval this afternoon to my mom's house for a visit. Aunt Emma wouldn't take no for an answer, at least according to my uncle. She insisted the best hangover cure was my mom's home cooking, so off they went.

The bench is heavy, I'll admit. I spent a lot of extra time on the details on this thing. After Latham built my sister a bench for shoppers to rest for their shop, I decided to try my hand at one too. This one should fit perfectly between the tile shower and the sink. It'll give whoever is rinsing off the chlorine pool water the chance to set down their clean clothes or have a seat when changing. It's painted a beautiful sea blue color that matches some of the shower tile.

With the bench now in place, I get to work cleaning up the rest of the tiny bathroom area. It still needs a good scrubbing, but I figured I can do that this weekend when I'm watering the plants. All of the trash and debris is removed, leaving a fresh palate of space for Kate to finish the building. All in all, I'm happy with the few changes I've made.

By the time I make my way to my truck, I'm the last one here. I punch in the code on my way out, making sure the gate closes and is secured behind me, then head toward my old neighborhood to pick up Max. He's ready to go when I get to Mrs. Jergenson's place. Besides my family and Ashley's mom, Eileen Jergenson is the only person who has watched Max. She's like his third grandma, and I wouldn't want it any other way.

"Are we going to Kate's house?" Max asks as soon as I get him buckled into his seat.

"Not tonight, Buddy. It's just you and me," I tell him as I climb into the driver's seat.

"Awww, Daddy, I want to go see Kate!" Max bellows with disappointment.

My mind is whirling, because honestly, I want to see Kate too. I have nothing planned for Max and me, and since I'm spending tomorrow evening with Kate, I never got around to asking what her plans for tonight are either. I make my way to my house, driving past Ashley's as I go, and pull out my phone. As soon as I'm parked, I fire off a text to Kate.

Me: *Max wants to buy you chicken fingers from the café. Plans for dinner?*

I slip my phone into my shirt pocket and get ready to head inside. I grab Max's book bag and the kid himself, and before I have my key in the lock to open the house, my phone chimes with a response.

Kate: *How did he know I have a weakness for chicken fingers?*
Me: *Pick you up at six?*

I glance at my watch. That gives me just enough time to shower and pick her up.

Kate: *That's fine. I left your aunt and uncle at your mom's house. They were staying for dinner. Mary Ann will take them back to my place after.*

Me: *See you soon.*
Kate: *I'll be ready. :)*

"Hey, Max," I call as I enter the living room where he's already watching cartoons. "Wanna go have chicken fingers with Kate at the café?"

"Yay!" Max hollers, throwing his arms up in the air. "I love chicken fingers! And Kate! I'm sitting by Kate in the boof this time!" he says.

Lacey Black

"Booth, and I'm sure that can be arranged. I'm going to run through the shower, okay?" I ask before heading down the small hallway to the single bathroom we share.

I close the door and strip off my work clothes, recalling what Max said about Kate and loving her. It warms my heart that my son has fallen under the hypnotic spell that *is* Kathryn Elliott. The only thing that worries me is him getting in too deep. Max will be devastated if it doesn't work out between Kate and me, and being the reason my son is in pain is the last thing I want to do.

I guess I'll just have to make sure it all works out then, huh?

Max loving Kate?

It was bound to happen.

"That makes two of us, Buddy."

Chapter Eighteen

Kathryn

"I have news," I tell him as I lean over the table for four at the small café in the heart of downtown Rockland Falls.

"Tell me," he says, leaning forward and mirroring my position.

"I heard from my attorney a little bit ago. The papers were signed by the judge," I tell him, referring to the divorce papers, feeling victorious and free.

His smile spreading wide across his handsome face. "That's great news, Kate. I'm so happy you're rid of Charles Dunnington III." The way he says his name, with a rich, entitled accent, has me giggling.

"The fully executed papers are supposed to be delivered early next week, even though it's been official for a while now. I can't believe it. I'm finally free."

Jensen wraps his big, warm hands around mine and gives them a squeeze. "Thank God," he says with a wink.

"He's not contesting anything anymore, but I'm pretty sure he's making out like a bandit," I tell, taking a sip of my iced tea.

"What do you mean?" Jensen asks, glancing over to where his son sits in the booth next to me. Max is busy coloring a picture for my refrigerator on the back of the paper placemat.

I shrug. "He's getting a shit-ton of money in a one-time alimony payment," I confirm in a whisper. "Plus, I sold him my portion of my father's business."

"Wait, doesn't he come from money? With a stuffy name like Dunnington III, you'd think he has enough Benjamins to keep him warm and cozy."

"Oh, he does," I verify. "His family is old money in stock and bonds in New York. Their son went into real estate, though, and started at my dad's firm years ago, right out of college. He worked his way up the ladder, and while I don't want to take away from his achievements in closing many sales, he was Daddy's biggest suck-ass. He did anything and everything he could to get a leg up in the business."

"Including marry his boss's only daughter."

I shrug. I don't really want to get into the reasons why I married Charles. It's in my past, where I'd like it to stay. "I gave him whatever he wanted just to make him go away. I was ready to move on with my life, and frankly, the money means nothing to me. I have more than enough. Anyway, he owns fifty-one percent now and my mom owns the other forty-nine."

His eyes bore into me. "I bet that didn't make her very happy."

Again, I shrug. "No, it didn't. At the reading of the will, she became a tad bit distraught when she learned I was left majority percentage in his company and she was left only forty-nine. That meant she still was set for life, financially, but she didn't have the control over me. I think that's what upset her the most. Well, that and the fact I was left the Rockland Falls house. She was awarded all of his New York properties, minus the two-floor penthouse where the real estate company was housed. The moment I heard I received this place, I knew I was coming home."

Jensen smiles when I say the word home. In fact, it feels phenomenal. I haven't felt at home since I left Rockland Falls. "And I'm damn glad you did," he says, taking my hand from across the table.

"Kate, look! I made you a turtle playing baseball," Max joyfully exclaims, holding up his placemat so I can see his drawing.

"That's amazing, Maximiliano," I boost, which has the exact results I was hoping for. His young giggles bring a smile to my face, matching those worn by the four-year-old and his father.

"It's just Max, silly!"

"Well, Just Max, I'm going to hang this on my refrigerator when I get home, okay?"

"And I can come see it, right?"

"Of course you can," I confirm, ruffling the hair on top of his head.

"Mommy says I'm not supposed to go to your house, but I like going dare. Daddy, can I still go dare?" he asks, his big, innocent eyes full of hope and worry.

Jensen exhales. "Of course you can, Buddy. We're not going to stop visiting Kate, okay?"

Max seems pleased to hear that and quickly returns his attention back to his coloring. When I glance across the table, I can see the annoyance written all over Jensen's face. "Everything okay?"

He sighs and whispers, "Earlier this week, she gave me the song and dance about bringing women in and out of his life. I knew immediately what she was getting at, or who she was referring to."

"Me," I deduce.

Jensen barely nods his head. "Anyway, she thinks it's best not to introduce our 'dates' to our son, which I wholeheartedly agree. However, I don't look at you as just a date."

"No?"

Shaking his head, he answers, "No. You're more. Always have been."

I can feel the blush creep up my neck and the grin spread across my lips. "You're more too," I confirm as the waitress delivers our plates of food.

Max's plate is full of chicken fingers and curly fries, which he heartily dives into. Jensen leans over and squeezes a blob of ketchup on his son's fries and then squirts a little on his plate. Jensen ordered the meatloaf sandwich with fries, while I opted for the grilled chicken wrap and coleslaw.

The four-year-old at the table chats animatedly about his school day, complete with telling about every animal, color, and food that starts with the letter B. Of course, the moment he gets to baseball, his entire face lights up with joy. He tells me all about the game he watched earlier in the week, but quickly jumps into how he's going to spend the night with his grandma tomorrow night.

I can barely keep up.

Jensen gives me a private smile as his son shares all of the things he'll do with his grandma. I can't help but think of all the dirty things I'll be doing to his dad while he's away. I should feel horrible for letting those thoughts cross my mind in the middle of a family restaurant, while sharing a bench seat with the four-year-old, but I can't seem to find the nerve to care. That's just one more thing I love about the new Kathryn. Old Kathryn wouldn't have even entertained the idea of sex while at dinner.

"You're blushing," Jensen says from across the table, a knowing smile on his face. "Care to share whatever you were just thinking about?"

Leaning forward, I make sure little ears are occupied as I whisper, "I'd rather just show you."

His eyes flare and his little grin turns predatory. "I can't wait."

The rest of the dinner passes quickly. Max makes a decent dent in his chicken nuggets and fries, but ends up taking a handful of both home in a to-go container. Jensen pays the check, even though I offer to cover it, and before I know it, we're heading out the door.

"Well, I had a great time this evening, Just Max. I hope we can do this again," I tell him politely, his little hand tucked into mine as we walk down the street to where the truck is parked.

"Me too! Do you want ice cream? Daddy, can we get ice cream?"

Jensen laughs. "I thought you were too full to eat anymore," he says, setting Max's leftovers on the toolbox before unlocking the truck.

"I was, but now I'm hungry for ice cream!"

I can't help but chuckle. When Jensen's eyes meet mine, his brows raise together in question. "Oh, sorry," I reply, trying to wipe the smirk off my face. "You know, I could use some ice cream too."

"Yay!" Max hollers, jumping up and down before climbing into the back seat of the truck cab. "We can share duh white wiff sprinkles, Kate! It's my faborite."

"I have a feeling you're taking sides, Kathryn Ann Elliott," he says in a low, husky voice. It totally reminds me of sex.

Sex with Jensen.

Sign me up!

"I'm on the ice cream's side," I tell him as I climb inside the truck. "Besides, who can say no to vanilla with sprinkles?"

"Yay!" Max bellows from the back.

"I suppose we could stop for a scoop," Jensen concedes before shutting my passenger door and heading around to the driver's side. As he slips into the cab, he adds, "But let's get one thing straight. Neither of you get a bite of my chocolate ice cream with hot fudge."

* * *

Lacey Black

"This is a little weird, isn't it?" Jensen asks as he sets take-out containers in the picnic basket.

"Chinese food in my new seating area out back? Heck no," I assure him for the tenth time. I can tell he's a little nervous to have our first date in my backyard, especially knowing his aunt and uncle could make an appearance at any time. They're currently at the bed and breakfast with Mary Ann and Max, but that doesn't mean they won't pop in at the most inopportune time.

"I'm starting to rethink this. We should have gone out for dinner," he adds, giving me a worried look.

"No, we shouldn't. I'm a mess from unpacking the rest of the kitchen today. Plus, watering all the plants. I have dirt under my nails. That doesn't equal romantic dinner out. That equals romantic dinner in, as originally planned." I step forward and place my hands on his chest, feeling his strong heartbeat beneath my palm. "Plus, I wouldn't be able to do *this* in a fancy restaurant," I add just before my lips press against his.

"I do like this," he whispers, wrapping his arms around my waist and forgetting all about our makeshift backyard picnic. When I finally pull away, he says, "I told you I'd water the plants when I got here."

Shrugging, I grab two bottles of light beer from the fridge and follow him out the back door. "I wanted to do it. I kind of enjoyed taking care of them."

Together, we make our way through the patio area and around the pool. A big grin spreads across my face when we enter the private area, perfect for reading, painting, or just watching the waves crash along the shore. There are two chairs and a small round table along one side, and still the perfect clearing to bring out my easel and paints.

Jensen gets to work setting the table with the goodies from his basket. The scent of sweet and sour chicken fills the air, making my mouth water. "I'm starving," I announce as I set the bottles of beer on the table beside each plate.

We both dive in, the sound of the ocean singing in the background. "So how was your day?" he asks.

"Productive. The new paints I ordered arrived today," I tell him, taking my first bite of shrimp fried rice. I don't mention I cleaned up the unfinished painting and dipped my brush in some paint, just to see if I still had the desire.

"Great. Now you can get back to doing what you love." His blue eyes sparkle against the fading sunlight and the smile he gives makes my panties a useless pile of material in less than four seconds.

"After I finished organizing the kitchen, I unboxed all of the old movies in the entertainment room and put them on the shelves. I'm willing to bet the old VHS player doesn't work anymore, but I can't seem to part with the movies. There are so many Disney ones I watched a million times as a kid," I recall, remembering how my mom would turn on a movie to keep me entertained while I was young. It wasn't until I was approaching my teenage years that I was forced to put away the childish movies and attend all of their fancy dinners. They were horrible. Arrogant men and their uptight wives. Well, sometimes it was their wives. I do recall a few girlfriends in attendance every now and again, but no one ever talked about that, and questions were never asked, especially by a child.

"Tomorrow we'll tackle the library office. Together."

Finishing off a good portion of my plate, I reply, "I appreciate that. I'm afraid there are years' worth of unnecessary paperwork in there we can pitch or burn."

"I can light up the new stone firepit," he agrees. There's something about a man and fire that gets them all sorts of excited.

"That would be helpful, I'm sure."

Lacey Black

After dinner is finished, I stand up to gather our empty containers and dirty dishes. "I got it," Jensen says, taking the trash from my hands and tossing it in the basket.

"You don't have to clean up too. I'm more than capable of helping," I argue.

Jensen stops and comes around the table. He places his big hands on my upper arms, my body practically humming just with the slightest contact. "I have a better idea. Why don't you go inside and throw on a swimsuit. The water is perfect."

Excitement races through my blood. I used to love to swim in the pool when I was younger, but admittedly, haven't had much of a chance in my adult years. And even though the pool was just fixed and filled this week, I have yet to dip so much as a toe in the warm, crystal blue water. "Do you have a suit?"

His eyes dance with something on the naughty side. "I do," he says, low and husky, like lightning striking the apex of my legs. "I'll get this cleaned up while you change," he says, turning me toward the house. With a light slap on the ass, he sends me away to change into my bathing suit.

When I reach the house, I practically sprint up the stairs. My houseguests are gone, so I go straight for the suit that is sure to make Jensen's mouth water. Two years ago, Charles took me to Fiji for a week and I bought this suit on a whim. When I got there, I didn't have the guts to wear it, but now?

Now, I'd wear just about anything for Jensen. Or nothing at all.

I slip the lavender two-piece on, tying the two strings behind my neck. Opting to leave my swim wrap in the drawer, I head out of the bedroom, stop in the hall bathroom to grab two beach towels, and return to the backyard in under ten minutes. When I approach the pool, I find Jensen wearing swim trunks and skimming the top of the pool. The moment he looks up and sees me, I feel his appreciation as if it were a hand caressing my very bare skin. Usually, I'd feel completely exposed in such a skimpy little bikini, but not now.

Not with Jensen.

I feel liberated.

I feel sexy.

And if the way his eyes are devouring me are any indication, I'd say he definitely agrees on both.

"Jesus, Kate," he says, finishing the job before taking the skimmer over to the pool house and clipping it on the rack outside. "That suit should be illegal."

"This ol' thing?" I ask, running my hand along the small lavender triangles that barely cover my girls.

"Something tells me that isn't so old," he replies, heading my way with the approach of a jungle cat. I can see it in his eyes. He's about to devour.

Deciding to play a little hard to get, I dip my toes in the cool water. The pool is temperature controlled, and on a warm day like today, the cooler water definitely is refreshing. Before Jensen can get his hands on me, I throw an ornery grin over my shoulder and jump into the pool. The water envelops me, the force of my fall pulling me under, but I don't care. It feels amazing.

The moment I surface, I hear a splash. As I wipe water from my eyes, strong arms wrap around my waist and pull me into slick, warm flesh. My legs instantly snake around his hips, the hard erection between his legs pressing against where I want him most.

"This is the sexiest suit I've ever seen," he whispers, trailing a finger down my breastbone and between my cleavage.

"I've never worn it before," I admit, grateful to have taken the plunge, both figuratively and literally.

"I'm glad no other asshole has seen you in this but me, Butterfly. I'm not sure I'd be able to handle watching other guys drool all over you," he says, his finger toying with the string that connects one triangle to the other.

Rolling my eyes, I reply, "I don't think you'd have to worry about that." No one has ever looked at me that way. No one but Jensen.

"Bullshit. You've fucking gorgeous, Kate. The sexiest woman in the world."

"You're sweet, but even I know that's not true. There are many beautiful women in the world, Jensen."

"And I'm the fucking luckiest asshole ever because you're mine," he practically growls moments before his mouth descends onto mine.

This kiss is everything.

It's fierce and passionate.

A declaration and a promise.

His tongue glides easily against mine as my fingers slide through his wet hair. I dig my nails lightly into his scalp, loving the low hum that pulls from his throat. His hands move to my ass, gripping and holding me tightly against his very hard body. I rock my hips, reveling in the way he presses against my swollen clit. I realize I could very easily get off just by grinding against him.

"You're playing a dangerous game," he whispers.

"Not a game. I need you," I admit, wishing there were fewer clothes between us.

"Yeah?" Jensen slides a hand between us, cupping my pussy in his big hand. "Water's not exactly the best lubricant."

"Definitely not," I reply, remembering how we'd tried many times back when we were younger. It always seemed to make things a little more difficult.

"I have an idea," he announces, turning and swimming one armed toward the ladder. "Hang on."

He makes it to the side easily, even with me attached to his front like a spider monkey. I climb up the ladder, Jensen hot on my heels. When his feet hit concrete, he takes my hand in his and pulls me along beside him. I realize immediately where we're headed.

The pool house.

"It's probably not in the best shape," I start to say as he pushes open the door.

Inside, I'm stunned to find the majority of the space cleaned up, or at least, free of debris and dirt. My eyes fly around the room and take it in. I haven't been inside since I've returned home, and for the most part, it's exactly the same.

Except those doors.

As I walk over to check them out, Jensen releases my hand. They're beautiful doors that swing both directions. We used to have an old shower curtain that hung from the doorway, but these doors? So much better.

"You did this." It's not a question. I already know.

"I thought it was time to upgrade that nasty old curtain." His reply comes close, his hands slipping around my waist.

"They're gorgeous."

"*You're* gorgeous."

"Thank you," I tell him automatically, a warm feeling spreading through my chest.

"I made a few other changes," he adds, a tad on the reserved side.

"Show me."

Jensen moves me into the bathroom where I find a mostly-cleaned space and a new bench. "I thought I'd be a great place to set down clean clothes while you shower, you know? I always hated just setting them on the sink."

I turn to face him, my heart pounding with the force of a thousand drums. "You made them." Again, it's not a question. I can already tell he did.

A blush creeps up his neck. "Uh, yeah. I know they're not professional or anything, but I figured they'd get the job done."

He opens his mouth to say something else, but I cut him off with my lips. My hands grip his hair as I practically climb his body. "I love them. Thank you," I tell him between kisses.

"If this is the kind of thanks I get, I'll make you things whenever you want," he replies, holding onto my ass as my legs wrap around his waist.

"The only thing I want you to make right now is love to me," I whisper boldly, hoping he won't notice the way I slipped the L word in there. No, it's not a declaration, per se, but in a way it is.

Because if there's one thing I know, it's I'm one-hundred-percent in love with Jensen Grayson.

Always have been.

Chapter Nineteen

Jensen

My heart trips over itself in my chest when she says it.

The L word.

No, she didn't just declare her love for me, but still, to hear her ask me to make love to her was pretty much a damn close second. Her legs are around my waist and I'm wishing like hell I would have lost my swim trunks before I picked her up. I'm certain I could work around that tiny scrap of material between her legs, but my trunks will make it more difficult.

Her hands tug at my hair, an electrical shock zaps straight to my cock. I'm so hard and ready for her I'm not sure I can be gentle. But I need to be. Nothing says 'making love' like pounding the hell out of her against the wall.

Using the wall for leverage, I'm able to adjust one hand to move those little triangles that cover her glorious tits. Her nipples are hard and my mouth waters for a taste. I bend down and lick, a long moan of pleasure spilling from her lips. Her hips rock against me, my cock ready to burst in my shorts.

Focusing on her nipples, I lick and suck on one, then the other. The closer she gets to coming the faster her hips gyrate against me. "Reach between us and touch yourself," I instruct without removing her nipple from my mouth.

"What?" she asks, her eyes connecting with mine.

"Reach down and show me how badly you want to come, Butterfly. Show me what feels good," I tell her before nipping down with my teeth.

Kate gasps and then groans when I soothe the sting from my teeth with my tongue. "I'm going to suck on your tits, and I want you to come. Reach down, baby," I tell her, shifting her so her back is braced against the wall. She slowly reaches down, her hand disappearing behind the lavender suit. "Pull that to the side so I can watch."

She does as instructed, baring her beautiful, wet pussy for me. Kate leans back and tentatively slides her fingers through the wetness. I suck on one nipple, releasing it with a loud pop before turning and showering some attention to the other. I'm torn between watching her hand and wanting to watch her face as she comes. Her eyes close as she moves her fingers over her clit, gently massaging it.

"Your mouth on me feels amazing." She gasps as I suck hard, her hand moving even faster against her clit.

"Show me how you come, Butterfly."

My words are like the match, her body the flame. She detonates powerfully, her hips rocking in the rhythm of her release. As soon as she starts to come down from her high, I release her nipple from my mouth and adjust her body so she's a little higher on my hips. Using one hand, I magically get my wet shorts down past my hips, not caring for a second they're stuck to my thighs. All I can think about right now is feeling the results of her orgasm around my cock.

"I don't have a condom," I tell her, hating I didn't think to grab one from my shorts back at the house.

"We don't need one, and I'm clean."

"Me too, but maybe I should go grab my shorts," I tell her, hating the idea of stopping this, but knowing it's probably the right thing to do.

"Don't you dare. I trust you," she confesses, her eyes boring into mine with a thousand truths.

"I trust you too," I state, on the verge of confessing something else too.

"Then make love to me without anything between us, Jensen," she demands, shimmying a little lower until her wet pussy is against my cock.

There's no way I can think right now. Not with her warmth and wetness against me. Not with her hands grabbing my shoulders and her nails biting my skin. Not with her eyes on me, full of trust and honesty. Not with the unspoken truth that lies between us.

I'm so in love with her.

Without much of a shift, I'm able to slide right into her warm body. Her muscles are still tight from her orgasm, which only drives me closer to the edge of insanity. I rock up, burying myself to the root before slowly pulling back out and doing it again. It only takes a few seconds before my body starts to move on its own. My legs and arms burn, but there's no way I'm stopping. With Kate positioned against the wall, I pound into her sweet body, over and over until I can feel her muscles starting to tighten around me.

"You gonna come again, Butterfly?" I pant, not letting up on my swift pace. My strokes are long and fluid, her nipples brush against my chest.

"Oh God, don't stop," she begs, resting her elbows on my shoulders and riding me hard and fast.

"I never want to stop this. I could make love to you all day long," I gasp, trying to hold off my own release that's barreling down on me. I won't come until she does.

"Yes, all day," she groans, her head falling back against the wall.

"Every day."

Her eyes meet mine in a moment of pure euphoria and verity. She explodes beautifully, her pussy milking my cock for everything it has. My release follows, my hips pumping automatically as I come harder than ever before. Kate's head falls forward, nestling between my neck and shoulder, and I feel the slight twinge of her teeth on my skin. My hips buck up, burying myself even deeper inside of her and causing her internal muscles to grip even tighter.

"Do that again," I grunt, ignoring the numbness in my arms and legs.

Her teeth scrape against my flesh once more, causing my cock to jump and her pussy to tighten. "Fuck, that feels amazing," I whisper, unable to catch my breath. "I can feel everything, Kate."

"Me too," she murmurs, resting her head against my throbbing shoulder.

As much as I hate to move, my body is no longer able to hold us both upright. With shaky arms, I start to lower her to the ground, my cock slipping from its warm home inside her body, very happy and *very* sated.

"I don't recall you being strong enough to hold me up like that the last time we were in here," she pants, a fond smile tickling her lips.

"It wasn't that I couldn't hold you, it's the fact I didn't have the patience to wait even thirty seconds longer before needing to be buried deep inside you," I tell her, kissing her bare shoulder.

"Hmmm," she purrs, trying to stand on her own two legs. "My feet are numb."

I step around her, grab a washcloth off the shelf in the bathroom, and place the dry piece of material between her legs. The moisture is already running down her thighs, and a primal feeling roars in my chest. With a gentle hand, I wipe at her legs, not even caring that I'm covered too.

Instead, I find myself pressing her against the wall and devouring her mouth with my own. She opens instantly, her tongue slipping out and sliding against my own. My hands dive into her soft hair as I hold her still. Her hands grip my shoulder blades, her fingers dancing along my flushed skin. Suddenly, I'm growing hard and thinking about round two.

Until…

"Yoo-hoo!"

Kate and I both go statue-still. There's no noise inside the pool house with both of us holding our breath. I know who the owner of that holler was, and I'm praying with everything I have that she doesn't open the door.

For the love of God, please don't let her open the fucking door.

You know, considering my ass will be on full display the moment someone walks in.

"I know they're out here, Orvie. I can smell it," I hear Aunt Emma say just outside the door.

That's all it takes.

Kate and I are both moving as the knob on the door turns. I can't even find a second to enjoy watching her adjust those little triangle bikini pieces, while grabbing at the wet shorts molded to my thighs. Have you ever tried to pull up your pants when they're wet?

"Oh, here they are!" I hear over my shoulder just as I'm wrestling the pants over my ass cheeks. "It appears as though we missed a game of pool, Orvie," my inappropriate aunt announces, cell phone poised in her hand.

"Pool?" Orval asks just over his wife's shoulder.

"Two ball, middle pocket," Emma hollers, making sure we all hear her.

"Christ," I mumble so only Kate can hear.

"Well, we just wanted to let you know we're going for a swim. You know, in case you need to cool off," Aunt Emma says before turning and leaving us alone once again in the pool house. "I hear the water's an aphrodisiac," she adds, stepping out the door. "But you two already know that, right?" With a wink, she's gone.

"I'm pretty sure my aunt just saw my ass."

Kate giggle-snorts, covering her mouth with her hand. "But it's such a cute ass," she replies, batting her eyelashes.

"That may be true, but that doesn't mean I want my eighty-whatever-year-old aunt seeing it. Knowing her, she snapped a picture and will post on Twitter. You saw her phone, right?"

"Snaptalk!" Emma hollers from the other side of the door, letting us know she isn't outside earshot.

"Fuck, my ass was just sent to everyone in my family, wasn't it?" Realization sets in. I'm never going to hear the end of this.

* * *

We're elbow deep in dust and dirt, but making progress. Slowly.

After waking up and making omelets, I joined her in the shower, where I helped wash her from head to toe (concentrating on her clit...with my tongue). Then, we made our way to the library and office and started cleaning. I started with the heavy lifting, moving all of the furniture pieces she's keeping along the wall and taking those she wasn't keeping to the garage for donation. By late morning, we had help. Emma and Orval both joined us, assisting Kate by moving and cleaning books, while she concentrated on going through the piles of files and papers in the desk.

I kept my focus on the job at hand and *not* on the fact Kate was painting again. She didn't say anything, but I could tell right away the piece she had started so many years ago had some fresh paint on it. She had been working on the landscape detail, and every time I glanced out the wall of windows at the backyard, I felt a familiar pang of longing where she was concerned. I didn't voice my thoughts, just stole kisses every chance I got, making sure she knew exactly how badly I want her.

"Lunch is served," Mom says as she joins us in the office, Max hot on her heels.

"Kate!" he hollers as he runs into the room carrying his baseball.

"Maxim, my little buddy! How are you?" Kate asks, dropping to her knees in front of the desk and hugging my son. My heart slams into my rib cage, and I almost say it. I almost tell her right then I'm in love with her.

Max starts to giggle. "I'm not Maxim, silly pants! It's just Max!" he exclaims, resting his head against her shoulder.

"Well, Just Max, I'm happy you're here. I have the perfect job for you," she says, slowly standing up and taking his hand in hers.

"I can help?" he asks, his eyes wide with excitement and disbelief.

"You sure can. Do you want to help?"

"Yep!"

"Then, I have something I need you to do for me. It's a very important job, and when you finish it, I've got a surprise for you."

He stops walking and glances up at her, smiling. "A surprise?"

"Yep," she says, stopping when she reaches her easel and a crate in the corner. "See this bookshelf here?" she asks, pointing to the wall right behind the crate. "I want to put all of my paints and brushes on these shelves. Do you think you can manage to help me with that?"

Max nods furiously. "I can help! I'm good at helping!"

"Perfect. I would love to put all of the paints on these two shelves, and the brushes and palettes on the bottom shelf. Do you think you can manage that?" she asks, pulling the crate closer to where Max stands.

"Yep!" he hollers, reaching down and grabbing two bottles of paint. I watch as he gently sets them down on the top shelf before grabbing two more. Then, when he gets all of the bottles out, he arranges them by color before starting on the tubes of colorful paint.

"She's amazing with him," Mom whispers beside me, standing and watching in awe as Kate sits back and allows Max to arrange her painting area. And the best part is she does it with a smile on her face.

"She is," I reply, not taking my eyes off either of them.

"He couldn't stop talking about her last night, you know," she adds, the smile very evident in her words.

"Max does like hanging out with Kate," I confirm, wiping my dirty hands on my jeans.

I can feel Mom's eyes on me. "He's not the only one," she quips, bringing a smile to my own face.

"True. We're having fun, getting to know each other again."

Mom wraps her arm around my waist, my arm immediately going around her shoulder and pulling her into a hug. "I'm happy for you," she whispers into the side of my chest.

Warmth spreads up my chest as I watch Kate with Max. He's concentrating on his organizing, moving things around until he has it just right. She doesn't say a word as he adjusts and readjusts for the tenth time, his little tongue sticking out of his mouth as he focuses. She has him tell her the colors as he moves them, helping him get the similar ones all together. He's having a ball, and most importantly, feels like he's a part of the process.

"Come on," Mom says, pulling my arm toward the kitchen. "I brought some pulled pork for sandwiches and Marissa made Amish pasta salad."

My stomach growls on cue. Everyone in the room hears the call for lunch and makes their way out of the library and to the kitchen.

I watch as the two people I love most in this world join hands and follow the elders. Before they round the corner, Kate glances over her shoulder, a big smile on her face. She throws me a wink, and I practically throw my heart at her feet.

It's hers anyway.

It's always been hers.

Chapter Twenty

Kathryn

After Mary Ann takes off to return to the bed and breakfast, I get Max set up with paint and an easel. Jensen helps place the drop cloth down on the floor, knowing the four-year-old won't be as careful about keeping the paint on the canvas as I am, but do you know what? I couldn't care less. I hope he gets paint on the floor. My mother always frowned upon paint splatter, insisting she get the floors professionally cleaned every six months. Me? I say let there be paint!

"I can paint this whole big thing?" Max asks of the eleven by seventeen canvas I set in front of him.

"The whole thing. Whatever you want," I tell him, getting a palette and paint ready on the small table beside him.

"I'm painting a baseball field," he states decisively.

"What colors do you need?" I ask as his dad adjusts one of my old T-shirts with rubber bands on the excited child. We found a small bag in the desk, which Jensen decided was perfect to tie the paint shirt on the little boy.

"Green for grass. And brown for the dirt. And white for the lines. And some red too for the ball." Max's eyes are dancing with excitement as I pull all of his specified colors out and squirt them one-by-one on the pallet. "Oh, and purple."

"Purple?" I ask, glancing over at the smiling boy.

"Yeah, for the flowers."

"Flowers?"

"I'm putting them at the back. This way, it can be a girl's painting *and* a boy's. Baseball for me. Flowers for you."

My eyes fill with tears. "That sounds like a wonderful painting." This little one has very quickly wormed his way into my heart. The thought of not having him (and yes, his dad) be a part of my life brings an ache to my chest. Losing Jensen all over again would be difficult, but add in Max? I'm not sure I would survive the loss.

"You okay?" Jensen whispers against my ear, pulling me into his chest.

The tears spill over, but I'm able to mask my emotions with the hug. "I'm okay."

"Look, Daddy! I'm making Kate a painting," Max states. We both glance over at painting to find lots of green grass already coming to life on the canvas.

"Do you want me to draw it out for you with pencil?" I ask, keeping my cheek against the soft cotton of Jensen's shirt. The scent of his deodorant, mixed with the soap from my shower is intoxicating.

Max seems to think over my question before nodding his head.

"Okay, I'll just make a general outline of the ball field and then you can add the details that you want. Does that sound okay?"

He nods feverishly.

While I make a quick outline of a ball field, Jensen presses his lips to my forehead and heads over to where his aunt and uncle are reorganizing the books. We went through them, making a pile of those I wanted to keep and one for those I'll donate to the used bookstore in town.

"I'm going to run outside and turn on the sprinkler system. The yard is shaded enough to give it some water. Plus, I want to check on the purple wisteria trees out by the gate," he says before throwing me a wink and slipping out the door.

As soon as I'm finished with Max's outline, I head back over to the pile of paperwork needing my attention. I've gotten through most of it, but there are still two drawers from the filing cabinets left.

Most of the papers can be shredded, but I've found a few things I'd like to keep. A couple of letters from my dad's first few house sales, as well as old deeds to properties he's owned and sold. I don't know why I'm keeping them, really, but it makes me feel closer to him nonetheless.

"Oh no," Emma says, the sound of papers hitting the floor pulling my attention to where she stands. "These pages fell out of this old book." I get up and head to where she's by the bookshelf. Emma bends over and quickly starts to gather the fallen pages. "Wait, these aren't from the book. I think they were stuck inside it," she says, opening up a handful of old, handwritten pages.

I glance over her shoulder to see what they are. "They look like letters." Taking the disarray pile in my hands, I look at the one on top, finding a scratchy handwriting in black ink filling the page. Reading the first line, I have a startling realization. "It's a love letter."

"Really?" Emma asks, grabbing my hand and pulling the letters closer to inspect. "Are they dirty?"

I move my hands so she can't grab the pages and skim over the words. "No, I don't think so. At least, not this one. I think it's to my mother," I realize as the writer talks about taking a dip later in the pool. The handwriting doesn't exactly look like my dad's, though there are similarities. I'll have to pull a few of his old contracts and compare the writing.

But then again, who else could they be from?

My heart starts to pound in my chest. When we moved, Mom insinuated a few times that there was infidelity on my dad's part. I never saw it, but you never know what really goes on behind closed doors. Dad was always the sweetest, most caring man I'd ever met. He was known as a shark in the business world, yet always had a softer side when it came to Mom and me.

I read over the letters, noting they're all addressed to and end the same way.

To my dearest Pookie.

From your ravishing Honey Bear.

I think I throw up a little in my mouth.

After five or six letters, I realize that these aren't from my dad, at least not to my mother. They can't be. They talk about slipping away unknown and about passing each other in town, yet unable to show any sign of knowing the other person. It's an affair.

My dad's affair.

It has to be, right?

Why else would these letters be kept in one of my dad's books in his office? No one ever used this room except me to paint and him to work. My mom wasn't a reader, so why would she come in here? It's the perfect place to hide correspondences you don't want anyone else to find.

I think I'm going to be sick.

"The sunlight reflects off your skin like a beacon of home, radiating love and joy wherever you go." I realize Emma is standing beside me, reading over my arm. "That's a tad on the cheesy side, if you ask me," she adds, adjusting the book the letters fell out of. "But I'm sure he still got some. Ladies always eat that sweet stuff up."

"What book was it in?" I ask, my hands shaky.

"The Scarlet Letter. Huh, that's sort of poetic, right? The proverbial homewrecker who cheats on her presumably-dead husband and has an illegitimate love child."

My eyes must be as wide as saucers when I look at the older woman. Emma must be able to sense my duress and grabs the chair behind the desk. As if on autopilot, I take a seat, the familiar panic attack rearing its ugly head. I hear Emma speaking, but I can't make out her words. All I can do is stare down at the unfamiliar handwriting and the blurring words.

Suddenly, Jensen is there, crouching down in front of me. His eyes are full of concern and his mouth is moving, but I can't hear him. My blood is roaring in my ears and the sound of my labored breathing is echoing off the walls. He reaches up and cups my cheek with his warm, calloused hand. The sensation instantly soothes me and I can't help but close my eyes.

"That's it, Kate. Deep breaths," I finally hear, his voice firm, yet so soft and approving.

I focus on my breathing, in through my nose and out through my mouth. When I open my eyes, he's there, a tentative smile on his lips and eyes so full of relief. "There you are," he says gently, running his finger up and down my cheek. "You scared us for a second."

"I'm sorry," I croak through my dry throat.

"I'll grab some water," Emma says, disappearing from the room.

I glance to the right and find Max, tears marring his small face. "Oh," I choke, reaching for the little boy and pulling him into my arms. "I'm so sorry I scared you."

"You couldn't breathedid. I didn't like it," he whispers, his small arms hanging on to my shoulders for dear life.

"I'm so sorry, Max." I pull back to look at him in the eyes. "Sometimes, I have what are called panic attacks. They hit me fast and make it so I have a hard time breathing, but it always passes within a few minutes." His eyes bore into me as he listens, trying hard to understand what I'm saying.

"Are you sick?"

I give him a small smile. "No, sweetheart, I'm not sick. It's just something that happens every once in a while."

"I don't like it," he confesses, pulling me into another hug.

"Me either," I reply softly, engulfing him in my own hug.

"Here you go," Emma interrupts, handing Jensen a glass of water.

"Take a drink," he instructs, handing me the glass. I slowly pull back from the little boy and reach a shaky hand for the glass. "Max, Kate is going to be okay. Do you want to go over and finish your painting while she relaxes for a few minutes?"

Max seems hesitant to leave me, and if I weren't totally in love with this little boy before, I'd be all the way there now. But I do love him. Him and his dad.

"It's okay, Just Max. I'm going to be fine. You go finish your painting, and when it's finished drying, we'll hang it on the wall."

"We will? Where?" he asks, his baby blues wide with surprise and elation.

"Well, after it's dry, we can walk around the house and find the perfect spot for it. How about that?" I ask, giving him a warm grin.

"Yay! I'll go finish it now," he hollers before taking off to the easel, earlier panic and fear all but forgotten.

"You okay?" Jensen asks, pulling my attention back to him.

I nod, taking a small sip of cold liquid in my mouth.

"What brought that on?" he asks, his warm fingers lightly caressing my upper thighs.

"We found these letters," I tell him, glancing around for the papers I had in my hand before the attack. Orval gathered them up. They're a little wrinkled from my death-grip on them, but they're still legible and intact.

"What kind of letters?" he asks, taking the stack from his uncle.

"Love letters. I think my dad was having an affair," I whisper, hating saying the words aloud. In all honesty, I'm surprised, yet I'm not. My father worshipped his family, but my mother was a tad on the…frigid side. If he had an affair, while I don't condone it in any way, shape, or form, I can sort of see why he might have gone looking for affection elsewhere.

God, this is hard.

Jensen reads the letter on top. His eyes fly to mine, as if seeking confirmation, before flipping the page and reading the next. And the next. Redness tinges his cheeks and his ears as he takes in the words spoken between my father and his mysterious lover.

"Where did you find these?" he chokes out, his blue eyes wide with disbelief.

"They fell out of one of the books your aunt was putting away. The Scarlet Letter. Can you believe that?"

Jensen's entire demeanor changes. He looks…angry. His handsome face is tight and his blush more pronounced. His entire body is rigid, and not in that sexy way I've come to know and love.

"Are you okay?" I ask, reaching my hand forward and resting it on his.

His face softens, but only a little. He looks so forlorn, so upset. "I'm fine, Butterfly, don't you worry about me. I'm the one who should be worried," he says.

"I'm fine. The attack has passed," I insist.

As soon as my words are out of my mouth, he stands up and starts to pace. Three steps to my left before turning and making half a dozen in the opposite direction. Then, he turns and does it over again. I open my mouth, but no words come out. I have no idea what has happened to change his entire demeanor, but I definitely don't like it.

Finally, he stops directly in front of me, tosses the letters on the desk, and takes my face in his hands. "Listen, I have something I need to go do. Can I leave Max here for a little bit?"

"Of course, but what—" I start, but am cut off.

"I promise to explain when I get back. I just need to run and talk to someone real fast, okay?"

His eyes are pleading, and even though I want to ask more questions, I'm not sure I'd get the answers right now. There's something clearly going on, and Jensen needs to figure it out. Alone. So as hard as it is to not demand he stay and talk to me, I simply nod my head. "Okay, we'll be here when you get back."

Jensen gives me a smile that melts my heart and pulls me to his lips. They're urgent, hungry even, but don't stay nearly as long as I'd like them to. "Thank you," he urges, placing a second kiss on my forehead. "I'll be back shortly and then I'll explain."

I feel the loss of his skin as he lets me go and heads over to his son. "I have to run an errand, okay, Buddy? You're going to stay here with Kate and finish your painting," he says to Max.

"Okay!" Max agrees easily, barely taking his eyes off his work of art.

Jensen ruffles his son's hair before turning and heading to the doorway. When he reaches it, he stops and glances my way. "I love you."

The shock of his words causes my mouth to fall open and my heart to try to pound its way out of my chest. Before I can even think about replying (and heaven knows I want to say it back), he disappears, the sound of the front door closing heard a few seconds later.

"Well, there's nothing like a love declaration to get the ol' vagina juices pumping."

The words shock me out of my stupor. I glance over at the elderly woman, who wears a mischievous grin on her wrinkled face. "You probably shouldn't say vagina in front of the four-year-old," I whisper, turning to head back to my pile of papers.

I grab what's left of the stack and start flipping through it. Most of the records are old and don't need to be kept, and I end up just tossing them in the shred pile. *I love you.* His words repeat over and over in my mind, and I can't help but grin widely.

"That's the smile of a woman in love," Emma says, shuffling over to stand beside me.

Glancing her way, I reply, "I love him too."

"Of course you do, dear. I knew that the moment I met you. I'm just glad our boy finally said it."

I turn to check on Max, who's happily swiping brown paint across the canvas. When I move to face Emma, I finally whisper, "We haven't said it yet."

She gives me one of those knowing, gentle pats on the arm before replying, "You may not have both said the words, but it has been felt for a while. In fact, it probably never left. Not really. Sure, you both moved on for a short period of time, but the love you two carry runs deep and true. It was bound to pull you back together again."

My eyes burn with unshed tears as I hold her gaze. She's absolutely right. Did I love Charles? Yes. Was it the same kind of love I feel with Jensen? No. This love is all-consuming and powerful. It's as if I can't fathom waking up in the morning without him by my side. It's crazy, really. We've only reconnected for a handful of weeks, but here we are, in love and anxious to see what comes next.

"Where do you think he went?" Orval asks, taking his wife's hand in his own and bringing it to his lips.

"I don't know," I confess.

An uneasy feeling sweeps through me as I try to imagine whatever it was that pulled Jensen away so quickly. If I had to guess, I'd say it had something to do with my dad's letters, and that part scares me most of all.

Why?

Chapter Twenty-One

Jensen

I drive my truck down the street and pull into the driveway. I feel like I've just run a race, my heart is pounding and my breathing labored. Can this really be happening? There's only one way to find out. Taking my keys from the ignition, I climb out of my truck and head for the front door.

My knock is loud and insistent, and it only takes a few seconds for the door to open.

"Jensen?"

My dad stands there, his hair almost completely gray and with his faded T-shirt stretched tightly over his paunch belly. "I need to talk to you," I reply in way of greeting, not even waiting for him to open the screen door for me. I pull it open and slip inside.

"Uh, okay," he says as he closes the door behind me. "Can I get you something to drink? Water? Soda? I think Baylee has some of that fancy flavored tea crap that tastes like garbage," he replies, rubbing the back of his neck in a nervous manner.

"Did you have an affair with Kate's mom?" I blurt out, unable to hold it in any longer.

Dad's eyes widen, almost comically, before he takes a seat on the couch. "Sit down," he says, sounding defeated.

"I'd rather stand," I bite.

He exhales. "Please, Jensen. If we're going to have this conversation, I'd rather you sit."

Not wanting to give in, I go ahead and take a seat. Something tells me I won't like what he has to say anyway. "Fine. I'm sitting. Now, did you have an affair with Annabelle Elliott?"

"Yes."

I close my eyes, hating the confirmation. Hating the man for putting me in this situation. Hating the carnage he always seems to leave in his wake. "Why? When?" I reply, my voice barely audible.

"It was after I left your mother, if that's what you're asking." It was what I was asking, but that only makes me feel marginally better. "I met Annabelle when I did some custom building work at their house."

"When?" I demand, needing to piece together the timeline.

He seems to think about it for just a moment before answering, "Your senior year of high school."

I shake my head, my heart dropping into my boots. "My senior year? While I was dating Kate?"

Dad nods his head once to confirm. "These things just happen," he says with the wave of his hand, like there's no big deal.

"Just happen? Buying the wrong spaghetti sauce *just happens*. Forgetting to stop for milk after work *just happens*. Your dick falling into my girlfriend's mother *doesn't* just happen!" I realize I'm standing up, pacing in front of the worn couch.

"Jensen, settle down. It's not like I was looking for an affair. I was happy with Tasha," he says, referring to the much younger woman he cheated on my mom with.

"Obviously," I retort, sarcasm very evident in my bite.

Dad exhales and sits forward, resting his hands on his knees. "Listen, I don't have to explain my personal life to you, but I'm going to in this case."

"This case? This case? You were screwing my girlfriend's very married mother, Dad."

"I know, Jensen. We met when she hired me to build a desk for her husband's office," he says, and my stomach falls to the floor. The desk in the office was built by my dad? Seriously? Can this shit get any worse? "I went over to meet with her and one thing led to another."

Not wanting to hear any of the details, I interrupt. "Letters. You wrote her letters."

Dad seems surprised by my statement. "How did you know that?"

"Kate found them about an hour ago."

"Oh," was his only reply. Clearing his throat, he continues. "Well, yes, we wrote each other letters. We couldn't exactly call each other or risk Tasha and Hans finding out about our times together."

"How long? How long did you screw a married woman behind everyone's back?" I demand.

Dad sighs. "About six months. The entire time it took me to build the desk. When the job was complete, I ended things."

I blink repeatedly at my dad. "*You* ended things?"

He nods. "Yes. You had just graduated from high school and were planning to go to school. Kathryn was going with you, right?" he asks. When I give a single head nod, he goes on. "Well, when I knew you were serious about the girl, I told Annabelle we had to stop."

"You ended it for me?"

"Well," he starts, adjusting in his seat. "Well, that and because Hans had found out."

I close my eyes and shake my head. "That's why they left," I whisper, mostly to myself.

"Yeah. She wanted to keep seeing me on the side, but I wasn't so sure. Tasha had left when she found out about the affair. Hans came over and confronted me. Tasha was here. She took off immediately. I told Hans I was done, but he was still pissed as hell."

"You don't say," I growl, unable to hold back the sarcasm.

"Anyway, she showed up on my doorstep later that night, distraught. Hans was leaving and going to New York. She wanted to stay with me, but was accustomed to a lifestyle I couldn't give her. I told her it was fun while it lasted, but it wasn't long term."

I stand there, staring in shock at the man I really don't know. He's so blasé about having an affair, about ending it, about the fact he was wrecking lives and didn't have a care in the world.

"Don't look at me like that. She knew going into it I didn't want forever. I wanted a good time, but that was it."

I shake my head in disgust. "I can't even believe I'm related to you."

He seems shocked by my statement. "Listen, son, I know I've made my share of mistakes, but don't ever doubt my love for you and your siblings your entire lives. Yes, I cheated on your mother. Yes, I cheated on Tasha with Annabelle. Yes, I've regretted it each and every time, but I've been trying to be a better man."

"You're a coward," I whisper, hating the fact sadness is mixing with my anger, but at the end of the day, he's still my dad.

He hangs his head. "I am."

"I'm going home to tell Kate about this. I won't keep it from her, especially after she found the letters," I tell him.

He seems conflicted. "It was a long time ago, son."

"Yeah, but she needs to know why she was moved in the middle of the night without warning or reason. She needs to know it wasn't her father having the affair, as her mother had stated. She needs to know why her life was ripped apart all those years ago."

Dad just slowly nods his head. "Okay."

As I turn to head toward the front door, he stops me. "Jensen?" I don't look over my shoulder to where he still sits. "How did you know the letters were from me?"

I close my eyes and exhale. "I stopped by for a visit my senior year, helped you work on something in the garage. You had a phone call and tried to step outside for privacy. The garage door was open and some of your words carried. It was clear who you were talking to was female and probably someone you shouldn't have been speaking to. You called her Pookie."

"I'm sorry, son. I never meant to hurt you. Back then," he stops and shakes his head. "I just wasn't in a good place. I was selfish, and that's on me. There are a lot of things I regret. Hurting your mother and you kids is at the top of the list." I barely hear the words they're so quiet, but the one thing is evident: his remorse.

Before I completely slip out the door, I turn his way. "I just hope you treat Baylee better. She doesn't deserve you lying and cheating."

"I'm not, I swear. I haven't done…that since Annabelle."

I look him in the eye and nod. "Good."

"Hey, Jensen?" he asks, stopping me once more. "If you ever want to…you know, talk or have dinner or something, let me know."

Torn between wanting it and wanting to walk away, I give him the only answer I can right now. "I'll think about it."

Dad nods and doesn't stop me again.

I make my way to my truck, the weight of his confession heavy on my shoulders. I know I need to talk to Kate, but I just need a minute. I need time to process. Time to come to grips with the road paved with our parents' mistakes and the impact they've had on our lives.

Instead of driving out to the Elliott mansion as planned, I head in another direction, one that's just as familiar as any other path. The familiar landscape comes into view as I slow to make the turn. I head up the driveway and park in front of the garage, next to my sister's car and Rhenn's truck. Before my feet hit the steps, the screened door opens and my mom walks out, a bright smile on her face.

"Well, if this isn't a pleasant surprise. Twice in one day."

"Hey, Mom." I shove my hands into my pockets.

"Is everything all right? Max?" she asks, coming toward me across the porch.

"No, no. Everyone's fine. Max is fine," I reassure her.

Mom covers her heart with her hand, as if trying to compose herself. "Oh, okay. Well, good. Come have a seat," she offers, going to the porch swing and taking a seat.

My feet are leaded, my legs wooden, as I make my way over to the where she sits. We're both quiet for a few minutes, both lost in our own thoughts. Finally, I speak. "I saw him today."

Mom doesn't reply for a few long seconds before asking, "Oh?"

"It was a mess. After you left Kate's, we went back to cleaning the library and office. Aunt Emma dropped a book and a few papers spilled out. They were letters." I tell her everything that happened afterwards, from calming Kate to going and confronting Dad.

"Are you okay?" she asks, after a few moments of silence.

"Am I okay? What about you? Are you okay?" I ask, completely flabbergasted Mom seems so calm about the entire situation.

"Oh, Jensen, I'm fine. I've come to peace with what happened in our marriage and how it ended."

"But…he cheated on you. You forgave him for that?"

Mom sighs. "It took a while, Jensen, I'm not going to lie. I was angry for a long time, but do you know what? He left me with the best part of him. You. Your brother and sisters. Was it hard? Most days I didn't want to get out of bed, but I did because of you. You all needed me. I picked my heart up off the floor and put it into this place and into raising you all. Do I hate he left us? Absolutely. Am I saddened you all barely have a relationship with him because of his actions? More than anything. But am I still upset and crying over him leaving? No. We can't change our path in life, only adapt to the twists and turns. I adapted, and in the process, forgave him. I was able to move on."

I glance her way, hearing her words and seeing the smile on her face.

"Besides, it's his loss, Jensen. He doesn't get to play catch with Max or see the smiles on his daughters' faces when they talk about their loves."

I clear my throat. "He asked if he could call me or visit sometime."

"And what did you say?"

"I told him I'd think about it."

She looks me square in the eye. "And I hope you do. For you *and* for Max. No one is perfect, Jensen. He's made mistakes. If he's finally ready to own up to them, I think you owe it to yourself to consider forgiving him. For you, not for him. It's gotta be for you."

Moving my arm so it's resting on her shoulder, I pull her into my side. "You're pretty smart, you know that?" I tease, loving I can still make my mom laugh after such a serious conversation.

"I do know," she assures me, drawing my own laugh from my gut.

"I'll think about calling him," I tell her, knowing I honestly will. I do miss my dad, more than anything. Knowing my mom has moved on and forgiven him for his affairs is a step toward mending our severed relationship. "I can't say we'll be best buds or anything, but I do want to let go of the hostility I've been carrying for all these years. And I want Max to know his grandpa."

Mom squeezes my leg in support. "You'll get there. Go at your own pace."

I pull her head toward mine and kiss the side of her forehead. We sit there and swing for a few more minutes, both of us lost in our own thoughts. For me, I think about my dad and the years we've lost following his infidelity. I was an angry teenager, directing all of my rage toward him for tearing apart our family. And while those feelings were completely valid, it's been many years. I'm tired of carrying the baggage on my shoulders. I'm ready to let it go. Will I forgive him? Maybe. Maybe not. Only time will tell.

"Any chance you have any of that chocolate zucchini bread left?"

Chapter Twenty-Two

Kathryn

"This is the perfect spot," I tell Max as we admire his painting hanging prominently over the couch in the entertainment room.

"Do you like it?" the young boy asks, his baby blues full of hope and excitement.

"It's the best baseball field with flowers I've ever seen," I assure him, crouching down and giving him a hug. "I love that you gave it to me. Thank you."

"In here, I can come see it all the time when I play games." His smile radiates like a lighthouse in the night sky.

"You sure can. You're welcome to come over and play games and watch television in here anytime, Max."

"You called me Max," he giggles, catching the fact I didn't go with one of the alternative versions of his name this time.

"I'm sorry, my mistake, Maxarena."

His contagious laughter fills the room and my heart. "That's not a real name," he insists through his happy giggles.

I can't help but chuckle too. "No, it's not, Just Max." He yawns. "You've had a long day, my friend."

"Am I spending the night here?" he asks, innocently.

Glancing at my watch, I realize Jensen has been gone several hours. It's early evening and probably a bit past the appropriate time to feed Max dinner. I know we have some leftovers in the kitchen I can heat up, but I wish Jensen would call or text. I have no clue what's going on or how long he'll be. Emma and Orval went up a while ago to rest and I expect them to come down soon for dinner.

"I'm not sure," I answer honestly. "Why don't we go see if we can find a snack?"

"Okay," he replies, sticking his little hand inside of mine and allowing me to lead him from the entertainment room and to the kitchen.

I help him sit on a stool at the island and head over to the fridge. "How about a peanut butter and jelly sandwich?" I ask, knowing all kids like those, right?

"I wove them!"

"One PB and J coming up!" I state, pulling the ingredients out of the fridge and pantry. It only takes me a minute to whip up a sandwich for him, cut into fourths the way I remember Rosie, my childhood nanny, used to do. I retrieve the gallon of milk from the fridge next. It's skim milk, but I think I can find a bottle of chocolate to help mask the different taste.

"Thank you," Max says as he takes a drink of the chocolate milk. He has jelly smeared on his cheek, but he seems happy and enjoying his sandwich.

It's when I'm contemplating making myself a sandwich that I hear the front door open and close. Before I can head in that direction, Jensen comes into view, a hesitant smile on his gorgeous face. "Hey."

"Hi," I reply, standing up straight and giving him my own grin. "Everything okay?"

He nods. "It will be."

"Hi, Daddy! Kate maked me a sandwich," Max says, taking another big bite.

"Made you a sandwich, and that's very nice of Kate. Were you a good boy while I was gone?" Jensen asks, coming over and kissing his son on the forehead.

Max nods insistently. "I finished my painting! We hungded it where the big TV is!"

"Hung it," his dad corrects. "And I can't wait to see it."

"Finish your sandwich and we'll show him," I insist, cleaning up the crumbs I left on the counter from cutting the sandwich.

Jensen comes up behind me, his warm arms caging me to the countertop. "Thank you," he whispers, his hot breath tickling my neck.

"It was no problem. He's a wonderful little boy," I tell him, turning my neck ever so slightly as his lips skim over my sensitive skin.

"He is," Jensen practically grunts. He wraps his arms around me and holds me to his chest, my back to his front.

"Is everything okay? Really?"

Jensen exhales loudly. "I have some things I need to tell you, but not tonight. I need to get Max home and in the bathtub. He has school tomorrow and it's Ashley's turn to pick him up. Can I come by after work tomorrow night?" he asks, sitting his chin to rest on my shoulder.

"Sure. I can make dinner," I offer, trying to mask my nervousness.

"No, I'll bring something. I don't want you to have to worry about cooking," he suggests, making me worry a little more.

"Okay," I reply, cautiously.

After Max shows his dad the painting, they gather up his few belongs and get ready to head out. I don't want them to but don't invite them to stay. If Ashley is giving them a hard time about me, finding out they both spent the night would probably cause even more problems. Instead, I walk them to his truck and tell them goodbye.

"Bye, Just Max," I say as the little boy wraps his still-sticky hands around my waist and hugs me tightly.

"Bye, Kate! I'll see you soon," he says. His happy-go-lucky demeanor brings unshed tears to my eyes and a fond smile to my face.

When Jensen has him buckled into the seat, he pulls me into his arms and kisses me soundly. "I can tell there are a lot of things going through your head right now. Yes, I have some things to tell you, but it doesn't change us. It doesn't change who I am or who you are, and it definitely doesn't impact what we are together."

"Okay," I whisper, gripping the back of his T-shirt as he pulls me tightly against his taut chest.

"See you tomorrow," he assures me, placing his lips on my forehead and turning and heading to get in his truck. I feel the loss of his body heat immediately.

I wave goodbye as they head down the long driveway, until I can no longer see the truck. A deep sadness sweeps in, a longing to spend more time in their presence. I love Jensen, and I love Max. The thought of being separated from them, even for the night causes my chest to tighten with sorrow.

Back inside, I make a sandwich, enjoying a quick peanut butter and jelly, just like I had as a child. There's a smile on my face the entire time. After the dishes are cleaned up, I head back to the library. The piles of paperwork are gone, except for the box that will need to be shredded. Emma and Orval both pop in for a second, but they're on their way to enjoy their last evening with Mary Ann.

That's another thing I'll miss. The sounds of having guests with me.

I decide to paint. While I spent a little time yesterday cleaning the canvas and adding a few simple touches, I have this deep-rooted desire to finish Jensen's painting. It's more than twelve years overdue. So I pull out a handful of shades of blue and green and set out to work on the ocean landscape.

For the next hour, I watch the reflection of the sun setting off the ocean and the waves crash on the beach. I pull in the darker, more mysterious waters toward the edges of the painting, opting to see a moonlight reflection like I'm witnessing tonight. I'm just completing the waterscape when the doorbell rings. Realizing I must have locked the front door, I hop off my stool and make a mad dash for the entryway. When I reach the door, I turn the lock and pull it open, presuming to find Emma and Orval. Instead, I find the one woman I never expect.

My mother.

"Well, I see your manners haven't improved any," she says, sweeping her perfectly styled hair off her forehead. "Are you going to invite me in?"

With a quick shake of my head, I step back, pulling the door open farther to allow her to enter. "Of course, my apologies."

Mom strolls past me, a cloud of expensive perfume trailing in her wake as she glances around the freshly painted and decorated foyer. "Well, this is…different."

I shake out of my surprised stupor and shut the door. "It is different, yes. What are you doing here, Mother?" I ask trying to head her off before she continues on to the rest of the house.

She stops and gives me a look. It's one I'm very familiar with. Part disappointment, part exasperation. "What I'm doing here, *Kathryn*, is saving you from making a mistake."

"Excuse me?"

She places her hands on her hips and just stares at me. "Did you think I wouldn't find out?"

Her question startles me, mostly because I have no clue what she's talking about. I've been here for a while now, happily cocooned in my Jensen-filled bubble. There's no way she could have known we've rekindled our relationship if she just arrived in Rockland Falls.

Mother sighs dramatically and reaches into her bag. She pulls out an envelope and hands it to me. The word confidential is written across the top, but it's the other name that draws my attention. My attorney. "Did you think you could just divorce Charles and I wouldn't find out about it?"

Slipping the papers out of the envelope, I flip through the familiar papers until I get to the end. My entire body relaxes when I see Charles's scrawl across the line. "Well, Mother, considering I was the one married to him and not you, I figured the divorce didn't require your approval."

She throws her hands in the air. "Of course it requires my approval. You can't divorce a man like Charles Dunnington III. What are you thinking?"

"I'm thinking I'm happier without him," I answer honestly.

"Oh, you don't know what you're feeling. It's probably because of this place. It's toxic. Too many ghosts and bad memories," she argues, glancing around as if one of those ghosts may jump out and get her.

"This place is my home."

"New York is your home, with Charles. This place is nothing, Kathryn. Small town people with their small minds. Their biggest decision is whether to wear the blue jeans or the shorts to the town festival."

"I love this town. Father knew it. That's why he left me this place," I insist, digging my heels in the ground.

"Your father left you this place because he knew I didn't want it. You need to put it on the market and come back with me. We can still fix this mess you've created with Charles," she says, grabbing me by the arm and starting to pull me toward the doorway.

"Stop!" I yell, pulling my arm from her grip. "I don't want to fix anything with Charles. I'm not going back to New York, Mother. I'm sorry, but I'm staying. I'm happy here." My heart starts to pound in my chest and I can feel the sweat breaking out on my brow.

She stares at me with lifeless eyes. "This better not be about that boy."

"That boy? You mean Jensen?" I gasp, glaring at her as if she's someone I don't recognize. And maybe that's just it. Maybe I've never really seen the real Annabelle Elliott.

"Yes, *him*. His entire family is trash, Kathryn. You're so far above them it's not funny," she says, crossing her arms over her expensive, designer top.

"But I'm not, don't you see? I don't want to be above him. I want to be *with* him," I insist.

"You're talking nonsense, just like his father did all those years ago," Mother retorts, an angry bite of the tongue.

That stops me in my tracks. "What do you mean?"

As if realizing what she said, she waves a dismissive hand. "Never mind, darling. It's enough of this game you're playing now and time to come home to New York."

"I won't. I'm staying."

"You are so much your father's daughter."

Her words strike me as an intended insult, but honestly, I feel honor. My father was a good man, despite whatever affair he had when I was younger. "I'm not leaving, and the papers are signed. I'm not married to Charles anymore, Mother, and if you value any sort of relationship with me, you'll respect that."

Her eyes flare with anger. "You want the trailer trash? You want a man who can't provide for you the way you're accustomed to?"

"Don't you see, Mother? I'm not accustomed to anything. You are. You're the one with the impossibly high standards, not me. I love him. I don't care if he runs his own business or if he were a trash collector. It doesn't matter to me. It's the way he makes me feel. That's why I'm with him."

She just stands there, staring at me as if I were a stranger she barely knows. "You've always been so noncompliant."

"That's because I'm my own person with her own wants and needs."

Mother rolls her eyes dramatically. "Fine. You want to slum it with the town lawnboy, then you've made your bed. Don't come crying to me when he takes all of your money and leaves you with nothing."

"Clearly you don't know Jensen Grayson," I state.

"If he's anything like his father, I'm sure I can figure it out," she responds, though I'm not sure she intended for me to hear it.

Unsure why Jensen's father has now been brought into this a second time, I decide to try to salvage any relationship I have with my mother. "It's getting late. Do you have a place to stay?"

She looks at me with wide eyes. "I thought I'd be able to stay with my only daughter."

I exhale. "Of course you can stay. I can get one of the other guest bedrooms made up," I tell her.

"My bags are in the car," she replies, walking around me and entering the main living room. "You've made a lot of changes."

I noticed she didn't compliment those changes, so I opt to just say, "Yep. I'll grab your bags."

Outside, the evening air is cool against my skin as I make my way to my mother's BMW. Three large suitcases are in the popped trunk, and it's hard to get them out and up the stairs. Did she pack for a month's visit? Oh God, she's staying a month, isn't she?

After the third bag is brought inside, I set them beside the staircase, deciding to give myself a little break before trekking them up to one of the rooms.

"You've updated the kitchen, I see," she says, walking through the formal dining room I have yet to use.

Lacey Black

"I did."

She simply nods again and turns my way. Before either of us can speak, the door behind me opens. Emma and Orval enter, laughing, and stop when they see me standing before them. "Oh, good evening, dear. I didn't know you had another guest," Emma says, a warm, grandmotherly smile on her face.

"I'm Annabelle Elliott, Kathryn's mother," Mother replies formally. She walks over, extending her hand rigidly.

"Oh, well, good to meet you, dear. I'm Emma, Jensen's aunt, and this hunk of burning love is my Orval."

"Pleasure," Mother replies, though I can hear the disdain dripping in her words.

"Well, we better get on to bed and leave you two to catch up," Orval replies, taking his wife by the hand and gently leading her to the staircase.

I watch as the man escorts his wife carefully up the stairs and then disappears around the corner. "I can't believe you're taking in people like that, Kathryn. Haven't I taught you anything? People like that could rob you blind and you wouldn't even notice."

"Emma and Orval? Rob me? They're in their eighties, Mother. What do you think they're going to do, load up their Buick with the good china?"

"Well, you never know, darling."

Rolling my eyes dramatically, I head for one of her bags. "Come on, let's get you settled in one of the rooms."

"The master suite, I'm assuming? Can you pull my car into the garage?" Mother asks, not even bothering to stop and grab one of the two remaining bags left in the entryway.

"Fine," I grumble, hating I've giving in to her so easily. But if it's one thing I've learned about Annabelle, its that it's always better to just agree.

Except where Charles is concerned.

There's no way I'll agree with her on that.

When her sports car is secured into one of the garage bays and I have the third bag carried up to my bedroom, Mother comes out of the bathroom dressed formally in her nightgown. I grab a sleep shirt from my drawer and retreat from the room, hating how she's just taken over my personal space. In the small bathroom off of my old childhood bedroom, I wash my face and get ready for bed. However, it's not the bed that calls to me.

It's the painting.

Instead of crawling under the covers, I slip down the hallway and descend the stairs. I silently close the door and flip the switch, bathing the library in soft light. My painting sits perched upon the easel as I make my way toward it. I grab a clean brush and squirt a glob of paint on the palette, diving right into the breathtaking scene before me.

I work into the night, not stopping to take a break, until it's done. My eyes fill with tears as I gaze at the image of Jensen and myself, a younger version of love and adoration so very evident in the work. I set it aside to finish drying and grab a clean canvas. My brush dips into new color and my hand starts to move, spreading the paint and bringing the image to life. It isn't until the sun starts to peek over the ocean that my eyelids start to droop. As wired as I was to create this piece, now that it's also complete, the exhaustion of working through the night settles in. I feel the fatigue clear down to my bones.

I drop my brushes in the solution and turn off the small light I used to help keep the space illuminated during the dark of night. My legs are heavy as I move through the room. Instead of carrying me up the stairs, I find myself heading to the couch in the entertainment room. A tired smile crests my face as I gaze up at the handmade painting adorning my wall. The ball field with purple and yellow flowers.

Max's painting.

It's the last image I see before exhaustion carries me off to sleep.

Chapter Twenty-Three

Jensen

My lips press against her forehead, rousing Sleeping Beauty from a deep, heavy sleep. When her eyes crack open, I can't help smile down at her tired, yet stunning face. "Hey," she whispers, rubbing the sleep from her eyes.

"Why are you in here? Did you sleep here?" I ask, my voice carrying the slight concern I felt the moment I saw her lying on the old, leather couch.

"Yeah, I did. I was painting until the sun came up and this is where I fell when the exhaustion settled in. What time is it?"

"Almost noon," I answer, running a large, calloused thumb along her jawline.

"Shit, I should get up. Emma and Orval," she starts, but I stop her in my tracks.

"They just left. They wanted me to thank you for the hospitality. Emma says she left you a housewarming gift on the guest bed, but I have to be honest, I've heard about some of her gifts, and I don't think we want to know what it is."

I can't help smile at her giggle, thinking about my elderly aunt and the naughty little gifts she likes to give her granddaughters. "I'm sure it's completely inappropriate," she replies, smiling widely.

"I see you finished my painting," I say, nodding my head toward where the finished pieces were set to dry.

"And I did another. I want to put it in the master bedroom, above the bed," she tells me, glancing to where the beautiful bird spreading its wings flies free. It's soaring high above the ocean.

"It's stunning. I can't wait to see it there. Do you want me to go hang it now? I have a little time while the sprinklers are running."

"Oh, uh, no. Someone is in there." My heart taps violently in my chest at her words.

"You have someone in your bedroom?" I quip, but I'm sure she can see the question evident in my baby blues.

"Well, not *someone*. It's… Mother."

I blink several times in disbelief before finally opening my mouth. "Your mother is here? In Rockland Falls."

"Well, it's good to see you too, Jensen," my mother says at the library doorway.

"Surprise," she whispers, trying to give me a reassuring smile, but knowing that it falls short.

"Mrs. Elliott, so lovely to see you again." I'm polite, sure, but she can tell my words are clipped and body tense.

"Yes, you too," Annabelle replies with the flippant wave of her manicured hand. "I'm going shopping. I'll be back later."

Suddenly, she's gone, the scent of her familiar perfume left floating in the air. Kate sighs, closes her eyes, and flops back down on the couch. "How long is she here?" I ask.

"Who knows. She didn't even tell me she was coming. She just showed up with my final divorce papers in hand."

"Really?" I ask, a smile playing on my lips.

"Yeah, but only because she wanted me to reconsider, not because she was being polite and delivering them."

"Fuck," I grumble. "So we get rid of one set of houseguests and replace with another? Am I ever going to get you alone again?" Bending down, I run my lips along her smooth, soft cheek.

"Yes, definitely. I was thinking…tonight," she says, gripping the back of my shirt and pulling me the rest of the way down to her lips. She's hesitant, probably because she's just waking up, but I don't care. I just want to feel her against me any way I can, morning breath be damned.

"I'm almost finished here and then I have to run to check out a new job. I'll be back after six with dinner," I tell her, hating I have to go.

"Okay," she replies, stretching and yawning once more.

"Go shower, grab something to eat, and maybe take another nap. After our talk, I plan to keep you up half the night." I throw a wink her way and then kiss her forehead before forcing myself to exit the room. Having her mom underfoot doesn't exactly bode well with my plans for later, but maybe having her here to answer any questions Kate may have will be beneficial.

And I'm sure Kate is going to have a lot of questions.

* * *

Typing the code into the security gate, I make my way up the familiar drive, the scent of Chinese food filling my truck cab. A fancy silver BMW is parked in front of the house, which tells me Kate's houseguest still isn't gone. I don't like her being here, not when she has a habit of making Kate feel inadequate at times, but what can I say? She's not my mother and this isn't my house. All I can do is be there for Kate when everything explodes and the dust starts to settle.

And something tells me it'll definitely explode.

But not us.

We're stronger than that.

I'm not letting go this time without a damn good fight.

With food bags in my hand and a duffel flung over my shoulder, I head for the front door. I'm just about to ring the bell when I hear the arguing. Kate is clearly upset. It's evident by the muffled sobs. Without giving it a second thought, I throw open the door and come face to face with Kate and her mother. The look on Kate's face guts me. Tears stream down her stunning, makeup-less face, a look of pure anguish marring her soft features.

"What the hell?" I ask, dropping my duffel on the floor and setting the food on the entry table.

"Jensen, this doesn't concern you. Why don't you head home and Kathryn can call you tomorrow," Annabelle demands, not even bothering to glance my way.

"Uh, actually, I think I'll be staying right here," I reply to her without so much as a look her way. My eyes are glued to the woman I love. "Kate, what's wrong? Why are you upset?"

"She just learned the hard truth about her father, Jensen. She needs time to accept the fact he wasn't who she thought he was," Annabelle states on Kate's behalf.

"I'm talking to Kate," I snarl, placing my hands on her shoulders and gently turning her to face me. "Hi," I whisper when her eyes connect with mine. They're full of sadness, and fuck, if I don't want to kill whoever put it there.

But something tells me it was her mother, and killing her mother probably isn't the best course of action right now.

"Talk to me," I say softly, watching helplessly as the light dims from her hazel eyes.

"His affairs." She whimpers softly in the Kleenex crumpled in her hand.

My blood starts to pump. I'm going to put an end to this right now. "He wasn't having any affairs, Kate. Your mother was."

A gasp is heard behind me, but I keep my eyes focused on the one I love. "Excuse me, young man, how dare you!"

"Don't listen to your mother, Kate. Those letters you found weren't from a mysterious lover to your father. They were to your mother," I state.

"What? How do you know?" she asks, her eyes pleading for some ounce of the truth.

"Because the letters were from my dad." I hate saying the words aloud, admitting my father played such a huge part in Kate's departure from town.

"That's a lie!" Annabelle insists behind me. "Kathryn, don't you listen to a word of filth this man is spewing! I would never—"

Kate's eyes are wide with shock. "She did. I went and talked to my dad, Butterfly. I recognized the nicknames. I overheard my dad on the phone once and he kept calling the person he was speaking to Pookie. Since I'm pretty sure my dad and your dad weren't having the affair, I deduced it had to have been your mom."

Kate looks past me toward her mother. When I turn, I see the defiance mixed with her guilt. "Mother?"

Annabelle is silent for several long seconds, and I start to think she's not going to say anything. But eventually, she does. "Fine. It was me." She shrugs her shoulder as if it was no big deal.

"What? Why?" Kate gasps, wiping away the remnants of tears on her cheeks.

"Why? Your father was always working or spending time with you. I came in third in my own marriage."

"But… Daddy was always trying to get you to go away with him. I heard him ask you."

"To the mountains? On some fishing expedition in Canada? What kind of trips are those? I wanted Tahiti or Bali. Paris for a month, not just a week here and there."

"Do you even hear yourself right now?" Kate gasps, looking at her mother as if she doesn't even know her.

Annabelle rolls her eyes. "Stop acting so high and mighty."

"You had an affair…and blamed it on him! *You* were the reason I was whisked away in the middle of the night and kept away

Lacey Black

from Jensen. *You*, not him!" Kate bellows, the tears streaming down her face once more.

"Affairs are a part of marriage, Kathryn. The sooner you realize that the better. Did you think Charles was faithful to you the entire time? With your forlorn eyes and your solitary disposition?" She laughs humorlessly. "He was probably screwing his secretary before the ink was even dry on the prenup."

"It wasn't Daddy who forced me to work for him, it was you." It wasn't a question. She already knew the answer.

"Of course, I did. You needed something to do besides sit around and cry over the boy you left behind. Real estate gave you something to focus on until you were a wife. Then you could sit at home and spend Charles' money," Annabelle says, matter-of-factly.

"I didn't want to be a housewife," Kate insists.

Again, Annabelle rolls her eyes. "This I know. You always wanted to mess around with that art stuff that was never going to take you anywhere. Marrying Charles was the only way for you to make something of your life."

Now I've had enough.

"That's where you're wrong. Kate has always been the most beautiful, most courageous, most fascinating girl I've ever known. Even with paint speckles on her skin, there was a light in her eyes that shone brighter than the sun. You dimmed that light by denying her the chance to live her life as she saw fit. All I've ever wanted to do was bring out the sparkle in her eyes and the smile on her face," I say to Annabelle, but turn to face Kate. "She's amazing, and I want to spend the rest of my life with her."

"Oh, for heaven's sake. You can't provide her with any sort of life."

"I can provide her with everything," I state, holding her gaze. "Because I love her."

Kate smiles the warmest smile I've ever seen. "I love you too."

Then she's in my arms and her lips are pressed to mine. It's a kiss that begins the rest of our lives, one that bridges the gap between our past and our future. This kiss is everything, because *she* is everything.

"Fuck, I can't believe you're really mine," I tell her, tracing her lips with my own.

"As long as you want me," she answers, a smile on her delectable lips.

"Well, that works out pretty fucking great for me, considering I'm thinking forever."

Her eyes light up like fireworks in July. "Forever it is."

My lips descend once more, my tongue sliding easily against hers. She's pressed against my body, which is already very well aware of the fact I can feel every dip and every curve. My cock is hard, aching with need, and ready to show her just how much I fucking love her.

"You two are actually perfect for each other. You're both dreamers." Annabelle's words pull us out of the happy little bubble we've found ourselves in.

Kate stands up straight and turns. "Mother, I think it's time for you to leave."

"You're kicking me out?" she bawls, dramatically. Her eyes fill with tears and her hands cover her mouth.

And the Oscar goes to...

Before I can give her a piece of my mind, Kate says, "Yes, I am. If you can't support me and the decisions I'm making with my life, then I think it's time you went back to New York. Besides, you've been lying to me about Daddy, and I'm not ready to move past that yet."

Lacey Black

As if flipping a switch, the tears dry up and her hands rest on her hips. "Fine, Kathryn, have it your way. Don't call me, crying, when you realize you've made a mistake."

"The only mistake I've made is letting you control my life for as long as you have. That stops now. I'm where I want to be, with those I want to be with. Those who love me."

"Love is a mirage, Kathryn. You'll learn that sooner or later," she says, glancing up at the second floor. "My bags are upstairs."

"I'll get them," I answer, practically sprinting up the stairs two at a time. The moment I step inside the room, I can feel the change. Annabelle's things are strewn all over the place, taking over as if she were moving back in.

Ain't happening.

I grab the three pieces of luggage that probably cost more than my truck and toss them onto the bed. I start shoving clothes, personal toiletries, and whatever else I see that doesn't belong to Kate in the bag, not even caring they'll wrinkle. I hit the bathroom and closet, making sure I have everything that looks out of place. Once I've completed my task, I head back downstairs, a bag in each hand.

"That was fast," Kate quips, a secret smile on her face.

"Just doing my duty and helping," I reply, throwing her a wink before flying back up the stairs for the third and final bag.

When I reach the entryway, I find the front door open and Kate already loading the first bag in the fancy trunk. Grabbing the last bag on my way by, I take the final two pieces of luggage and toss them in the back. "There."

"I'm going to head back upstairs and make sure you got everything," Annabelle announces from the doorway.

"No need. We'll ship you anything I may have overlooked," I state, offering a friendly smile.

She just glares back at me. "Fine. I suppose I'll be heading out now." She stops as if waiting for one of us to object, which of course, we don't. I'd rather have monkeys fly out of my ass than spend another minute in her presence. She sighs and slowly heads toward the driver's side. "I suppose I could find a hotel or something this evening, though it seems a little extreme."

"I'm sure you'll be fine, Mother. Finding expensive hotels with spas seems to be one of your many talents," Kate retorts, coming over to stand beside me. I throw my arm around her waist and pull her comfortably into my side. She fits like a puzzle piece.

"I wish I could say it was a pleasant visit, but that would be a lie," Annabelle bites, always having to get in the last word.

"Well, you do know all about lying, don't you?" Kate says, making me beam with pride.

"Goodbye, Kathryn. I'm sure I'll be hearing from you soon," Kate's mom says as she climbs behind the wheel of her car and shuts the door.

"I'm pretty sure you won't," Kate replies, snuggling deeper into my chest.

After the car exits the drive and the gate closes, I turn her so she's against my chest. "You might want to update the code."

"Yeah, I definitely need to do that. I kept it the same during the construction phase, with the intention of changing it after. I'll call the security company and get a new code programmed in the morning."

"Good idea," I tell her, placing my lips on the top of her head.

"I still can't believe it was her having the affair. I mean, actually I can. It makes way more sense than my father as the adulterer. But your dad? Jensen, I'm so sorry," she says, gazing up at me without an ounce of accusation.

"I'm the one who's sorry, Butterfly."

Lacey Black

"Why? You didn't do it, right?"

"Uh, no. But I guess I feel…"

"Stop it. You did nothing wrong. You're as innocent in this mess as I am. Our parents made the choices, not us. All we can do now is move past their mistakes. We're here—together—and that's all that matters."

Smiling down at the woman I love, I hang on to her words like a life raft. "You're right."

"Of course I am," she giggles, burying her nose against the place in my chest where my heart beats only for her. "So, what was this about keeping me up half the night?" she asks, looking up at me under heavily lidded eyes.

"We didn't get to eat dinner." My cock doesn't care. He's hard and raring to go in my jeans.

"True, but maybe we can throw it in the fridge. I hear Chinese food makes a great midnight snack," she replies, batting her eyelashes my way.

"You drive a hard bargain, Butterfly, but I think I can get on board with this plan."

She slowly pulls away, but doesn't release my hand until the last possible second. Kate glances over her shoulder, her eyes full of love and adoration that's only for me. I smile like an idiot because, fuck, I know I'm a lucky son of a bitch, and can't wait to spend the rest of my life showing her how grateful I am for the chance to return her love.

We may not have everything all sorted out, but we're headed in the right direction.

And speaking of direction, I give her a wolfish grin and say, "Race you upstairs."

Chapter Twenty-Four

Kathryn

Jensen definitely made good on his up-half-the-night proposition.

After making love, we talked more about the mess our parents made the first time we were together. The fact my father knew about it, confronted by Jensen's dad, and took his wife and daughter away spoke volumes for the family man he was. He loved his wife enough to stay married or at least try to fix it, but the only way to get past it was to move on.

To move away.

I understand that now.

Jensen told me about his conversation with his dad, how sorry he was for making such a mess out of everything. He told me the apology his dad sent back with him seemed sincere, and for that, I'm thankful. Jensen also mentioned his dad wants to get together with him sometime. I can understand Jensen's hesitancy, but could see the hope reflecting in his baby blue eyes. He wants a relationship with his dad, even if he's not ready to say it or know to what extent.

Some of my mother's words keep coming back to me. Her blasé attitude towards marriage vows and monogamy speaks volumes for the type of woman she is. I'm almost certain she probably didn't remain faithful to my dad, even after they moved us to New York. In fact, being in a much bigger city was probably easier for her to cover her transgressions.

But that's not for me to worry about now.

Right now, I have to figure out how to use this fancy new outdoor grill my landscaper designed into the back patio area. It's huge and has burners on one side. I've been staring at it for the last few minutes, trying to figure out if pushing the buttons will result in lighting it or preparing it for take-off.

"Problems?" Jensen asks, coming around the corner from watering the front.

"I don't know how to use this," I answer, waving my hand toward the appliance dramatically. He snickers, bringing a frown to my face. "Are you making fun of me?" I ask, crossing my arms. His eyes immediately drop to my cleavage.

"I'm not," he smirks, those blue orbs lazily drawing up to mine. "I swear."

"I was trying to do a nice thing and grill us those steaks, but now I'm thinking differently."

"You're doing a very nice thing," he says, pulling me into his arms and wiping the frown off my face with his lips. The kiss is full of urgency and passion, and I instantly start to melt into his embrace.

"You're distracting me," I mumble against his lips.

"Is it working?"

"Maybe. You did that last night too."

"That's because you were trying to hide the generous gift my aunt and uncle left you," he replies with a chuckle.

"Yes, that's because I don't think that…thing was appropriate to leave out for anyone to see," I huff, feeling the burn in my cheeks as I recall discovering the *gift* Emma and Orval left me.

"Say it."

I adamantly shake my head.

Jensen places a tender kiss on my neck. "Say it…"

Closing my eyes, I can't stop the smile from spreading across my face. "Vibrating clitoral stimulating cock ring."

His lips nip at my sensitive skin. "I love it when you say cock."

Swatting at his arm, I can't help but giggle. "That's the weirdest gift anyone has ever left me."

"They are definitely a little different. Thank you for trying to cook dinner," he says, pulling me in closer to his chest.

"I would have succeeded if not for this stupid contraption," I retort, kicking the grill for good measure.

"Don't hurt it. This baby can cook enough food to feed the entire western hemisphere," he adds, rubbing a gentle hand along the shiny stainless steel handle.

"Planning on grilling for this half of the country, are we?" I quip.

"You never know who might stop by for dinner, Butterfly. You still haven't met the extended family."

"I'll have my chance next weekend, right? Are we still going to Jupiter Bay for a visit?" I ask, excited to meet the rest of the family, including Emma and Orval's son-in-law and his new bride, and their six granddaughters.

"We are. I've already talked to Ryan and Jaime. I was going to book us a hotel room, but they insisted we stay in their guest room. They're getting ready to turn it into a nursery, and I'm pretty sure he's wanting help moving everything out before we leave," he says with a smile.

"I can't believe almost all of your cousins are pregnant at the same time. How crazy is that?"

"They're a crazy family, and I mean that in the best way possible. I enjoy spending time with them. Plus, Max is pumped to see Sawyer again," he says, referring to the former pro-ball player married to his cousin, AJ, and Max's biggest hero.

"Speaking of, when do you get Max?" I ask as Jensen opens the cabinet below the grill, turns the propane valve, and pushes the circular button on the bottom left of the massive grill. It fires to life. "Jerk."

"Don't be a sour sport, Kate," he laughs, pulling me against his chest once more. It's warm and firm and right where I want to be. "To answer your question, he comes back Thursday after school."

"That's so far away," I grumble into his shirt. It smells like his deodorant and dirt—my favorite combination.

"It's hard when he's with his mom," he agrees.

I grind my hips against his. "Yes, very hard."

"Minx, that's not what I meant."

"No, but I kinda like my version better. It keeps my mind off your adorable son and how much I miss him when he's not here."

"I have an idea," he says, grabbing me by my arms and leading me around the grill. We walk down the cobblestone walkway until we're standing alongside the pool.

"What are we doing?" I ask.

He doesn't reply, just smirks. I know I'm in trouble. He places his shoulder into my stomach and lifts. I have just enough time to close my eyes and hold my breath before we hit the refreshing water in a giant splash. I come up sputtering and wiping water from my face. "What the hell was that?"

"You were looking a little hot. I thought I'd help cool you down," he says, pulling me back into his arms. My legs wrap around his waist as his mouth devours mine. The firmness of his erection presses hard against my clit. All sorts of dirty images parade through my mind.

"Do you want kids, Butterfly?" he asks, kissing down the column of my neck.

His question doesn't even faze me. "I want to fill all of those rooms upstairs."

"That's a lot of rooms," he growls, rocking himself against my body.

"So many rooms. There's one for Max and one for every child God blesses us with," I whisper, not quite sure how I'm still able to form complete sentences with him teasing me the way he is.

"I want that too, Kate. With you." His electric blue eyes lock on mine and I can see his conviction as clear as the vibrant sky.

I reach down, grazing my hand along where his erection strains within their blue jean confines. "We should probably start, though. They say it doesn't always happen on the first try."

His hands grip my ass, holding me firmly against him. A moan of pleasure spills from my lips as my head falls back in ecstasy. "Practice makes perfect," he growls, licking my neck before his lips land on mine once more.

This kiss is everything.

Our future.

"I'm not a patient man, Butterfly, not when it comes to you. I've waited for you for years, but I don't want to wait anymore. I want to marry you and get you pregnant more than I want my next breath," he confesses, his fingers trying to get through the wet material plastered to our bodies.

"I want it."

"Then maybe you need to join me in the pool house, Butterfly. We can get a jump," he says, flexing his hips upward, "on that practicing."

Jensen swims us to the stairs, and with me still wrapped around his waist, steps out of the pool. His jeans are rough against my bare thighs, but I don't complain. Instead, I pull myself closer and press my lips to his. He carries me to the pool house, the screened door slamming behind us.

He presses me into the wall, deepening the kiss. Everything I've ever wanted is wrapped up in this one man and his son. Everything I see for my future is right before me, waiting. "I love you," he tells me, running his lips along the shell of my ear.

"I love you too. Now let's get to practicing."

Epilogue

Jensen

"Happy birthday to Just Max. Happy birthday to you," Kate sings beside me. I can't help but smile at her slightly off-key rendition of "Happy Birthday."

We're celebrating Max's fifth birthday at Kate's place. Well, soon to be our place. I've tried to take it slow, but it's not working. I want to be where she is, and since she's here, well, that's where I am as much as humanly possible. I still have my house, but not for too much longer. We may be moving fast, but neither of us cares. We've missed so much over the last twelve years, so in my opinion, we're not moving fast, we're slightly behind.

Max loves her. I had to have an awkward conversation with Ashley last week, because I knew the next step for Kate and me was right around the corner. She cried, but swore she'd make an attempt to get along with Kate for Max. That's all I can ask. I promised not to replace her and she promised to try to be cordial. At the end of the day, it's all I can ask for.

Kate made a trip to New York City this past week to finalize the sale of her portion of the company. She said it was as amicable as expected, leaving the city the moment all documents were signed. She didn't even complain about electively signing over a portion of her inheritance to her ex. Since she received it during their marriage, he was entitled to part of it, but she just wanted it to all go away so she could move on so she didn't fight it. While I couldn't say I agree completely with her choice to write him a check with more zeroes than digits in my phone number, I respect her decision, especially now that it means she's all mine to take the next step in our lives.

This place looks great, and I'm not just talking about the completed landscape my family keeps ooh'ing and ahh'ing over. Kate went all out with the decorations, from a baseball piñata hanging from the tree to the blue and red plates and napkins to represent Max's favorite team's colors.

"How about you open presents while I cut the cake?" Kate asks while my mom delivers heaps of presents to where Max is sitting.

I head over with the cake to where Kate gets everything lined up. We watch as Mom and my family help Max open his presents. After each one, he hollers, "Daddy, Kate, look!" and shows us whatever new gem he received.

Kate slices the funfetti cake with strawberries in the middle, which is in the shape of a baseball bat. Max and Kate worked on it until bedtime last night, and then I licked icing off Kate's naked body after bedtime. "I know what you're thinking about," she says, setting a piece of cake on one of the small plates.

"You mean about how much you moaned when I licked the icing off your clit?" I whisper, realizing all this replaying of last night isn't helping keep me cool below the belt.

"Stop," she gasps, hip-checking me as she laughs.

"I will not stop," I tell her, pulling her into my arms and touching the tip of her nose with my frosting-covered finger. Then, I lick it off before locking my lips with her sweet ones once more.

"Kate, it's your present!" Max yells from across the patio.

Kate startles back, wiping her lips, and turning her attention to my son. She looks dazed, which is just the way I like her—drunk from my kisses. "Oh," Kate says, wiping her hands on the towel and heading toward Max, grabbing my hand as she goes.

My girl vibrates with excitement as we watch Max open the box. First, he finds the painting, the one she completed just the other day of Wrigley Field. It's one of the oldest, most beautiful parks in the country, and even though Sawyer played for the Nationals, Max has always loved the Cubs the best.

"Daddy, look! It's Wrigley Field!" Max exclaims, holding onto the massive painting that's as big as he is. Samuel's there, helping make sure it doesn't tumble to the ground.

"It is, Buddy. Didn't Kate do a great job?" I ask, smiling over at my little man.

He looks at the art in awe and then back to Kate. "There's something else in the box," she says, nodding toward the big tissue-filled box in front of him.

My brother takes the painting and sets it aside while Max dives back in for more. When he comes up with the envelope, Kate and I move in closer. I kneel beside his chair and help him hold what's inside. Kate squats on the other side of the chair and waits with bated breath for him to figure out what he's holding.

"What's this?" he asks, his eyes searching the tickets in his hands.

I nod for Kate to tell him the news. "Those are tickets to see the Cubs play the Rangers this coming Tuesday night at Wrigley Field," she says, barely able to contain her excitement.

"It's the playoffs!" Max hollers, his eyes wide with shock.

"It is, game five. We're going to fly out that morning, go to the game, and then stay in a hotel that night. We'll go to the Shedd Aquarium and Navy Pier too," I tell my five-year-old.

"An airplane?"

"Yep," I reply, ruffling his hair with my hand.

Max throws his arms around Kate and hangs on tight. "Thank you, Kate!"

"You're welcome, Just Max," she says, smiling with her eyes closed as she holds on tight.

"I love you," he whispers.

Her eyes open and lock with mine. They fill with unshed tears as she gazes over Max's head at me. "I love you too," she whispers, placing a kiss on top of his head.

"Let's eat cake!" Mom hollers, drawing everyone's attention over to the cut up baseball bat cake.

Marissa, Rhenn, Samuel, Harper, and Latham all make their way to eat dessert, but I halt Kate from joining them. "Hey, Buddy, we have one more present, right?"

"Oh, yeah, for Kate!" my little guy replies and reaches behind his back.

My eyes remain on her while she watches my son pull the small jewelry box out and hold it up. She gasps in shock, her wide eyes fly to meet mine. "Kate," I start, taking her hand in mine as I drop down to one knee. "I knew you were the one I'd spend the rest of my life with when I met you. Our life took a little detour, but eventually, our roads crossed paths once more."

Her hand is trembling as she crouches in front of me, Max right where he belongs—between us. "I can't wait to spend more birthdays and Christmases and every day with you by my side. You're amazing with my son, and that means everything to me. I want to wake beside you every morning and fall asleep with you in my arms every night. I want to create more babies with you and watch them all grow up together. I want you by my side as we grow old. Kate, my Butterfly, will you marry me?"

She's a sobbing mess now. I hate the tears, but know they're happy ones.

Max puts his arm around Kate's shoulder and hugs her close. "You're supposed to say yes," he instructs softly, making both Kate and me laugh.

She grins over at my son and sniffles. "You're right, I'm supposed to say yes. Thank you for the reminder," she says, giving Max a kiss on the cheek.

Then, she turns those hypnotic hazel eyes my way and whispers, "Yes." My heart pounds and my blood swooshes in my ears. "Yes!" she exclaims loudly before throwing her arms around my neck and kissing my lips.

Cheers echo around us as I kiss my fiancée for the first time, and definitely not the last. There will be a whole hell of a lot more kissing and celebrating later.

Naked celebrating.

"I love you," she whispers, her grin pressed firmly to my lips.

"I love you more," I tell her.

Max chimes in. "And I love you too! Let's eat cake!"

And just like that, he's gone, the proposal now a distant second to eating a slice of his birthday cake.

"I can't believe you did that now," she says, placing her hands on my cheeks.

"It was Max's idea," he confesses, shrugging. "We were talking the other day about me asking you to marry me, and he said I should do it in front of Grandma and his aunts and uncles. We decided his birthday party was the perfect place to officially ask you to join our family."

She just smiles and glances down at the ring I slipped on her finger. "It's beautiful."

"You're beautiful," I reply, stealing one last kiss. "What do you say we join everyone and have some celebratory cake?"

"I say lead the way, handsome," she says.

Standing up, I take my fiancée's hand in my own, and slowly lead her to where my family is gathered to give hugs and congratulations. Max takes the biggest piece he can find over to the patio table and digs in. While Kate hugs my mom, I head over to where my big five-year-old is sitting, shoveling sprinkle-filled cake into his mouth.

"Did you have a happy birthday?" I ask, even though his birthday was technically the day before. Ashley and I split the weekend, with her taking him all day Saturday and Kate and I having him all day Sunday.

"Yep! And now Kate is my mommy too!" he says between bites.

My heart hammers in my chest. I love the way he calls her mommy but know Ashley wouldn't find it too funny.

"Daddy? Do I call Kate mommy or Mommy mommy?" he asks, his blue eyes wide with concern.

"Well, Max, your mommy will always be your mom. She loves you more than anyone else in the whole world. And Kate? Well, Kate loves you too, and she'll have a special place in your life."

"So I'm not losing Mommy?"

I ache at his young questions. "No, Buddy, you're not losing your mommy. You know, I bet we could come up with a name that's just for Kate. You know, something only you call her? It'll mean she's as special as your mommy but won't ever replace her. How does that sound?" I ask, hoping I'm doing the right thing here.

"How about Mama Kate? Can I call her that?" he asks, his trusting eyes boring into me with anticipation.

"I think that's the perfect name for Kate. Mama Kate. Then you can keep calling Mommy by that name, and you'll have something different for Kate."

Max seems to consider it for a second before nodding. "Mama Kate. I like it. Mama Kate, come have cake with me!" he hollers, drawing the attention from everyone in attendance.

I glance at Kate and see fresh tears swimming in her eyes. She gives Max a grin, grabs a small slice of cake, and heads in our direction.

She slides onto the bench beside me. "Mama Kate?" she whispers, a hitch very evident when she says those words.

I shrug. "It was Max's idea."

"Do you like it, Mama Kate? Can I call you that? Then I can keep calling my mommy Mommy," he says as he scoops another bite of cake in his mouth.

"I love it. I'd be honored to be called Mama Kate. As long as I can keep calling you Maxalificent," she insists, taking a small bite of her own cake.

Max throws his head back and giggles. "It's just Max!" he declares.

"Oh, you're right. I'm sorry, Just Max."

His laugher floats all around us as he dives back into his birthday cake.

I reach over and touch her bottom lip, leaving a trail of icing in its wake. "You missed some…here," I mutter, moving my fingertip to the seam of her lips.

Kate opens her mouth and playfully bites the pad before licking off the remaining icing. "Tastes better when I'm eating it off you."

A wide smile breaks out on my face. "Funny, I was thinking the same thing." I kiss her lips once more, savoring the mixture of pure Kate with sugary icing. "I love you, future Mrs. Grayson."

"And I love you. Always."

The End

Don't miss a new release, reveal, or sale! Sign up for my newsletter at www.laceyblackbooks.com/newsletter

Acknowledgments

There are so many that help in the production of a book, and I'm going to try to not forget anyone!

Sara Eirew – Thank you for another amazing cover photo.

Melissa Gill – Thank you for bringing the photo to life with this phenomenal cover.

Give Me Books – Thank you for your tireless work organizing the cover reveal and release.

Kara Hildebrand – Thank you for your editing expertise.

Sandra Shipman, Jo Thompson, and Karen Hrdlicka – Thank you for beta and alpha reading, and for your help in making the storyline consistent.

Kaylee Ryan – Thank you for always being just a text or phone call away.

Holly Collins – Thank you for always believing in me.

Brenda Wright, Formatting Done Wright – Thank you for another amazing format.

My ARC team – Thank you for the early reviews and for sharing the book with the world.

Lacey's Ladies – Thank you for your continual support and for making me laugh every day.

My family, husband, and kids – Thank you for always standing by my side.

Bloggers and Readers – Thank you, thank you, thank you!

About the Author

Lacey Black is a Midwestern girl with a passion for reading, writing, and shopping. She carries her e-reader with her everywhere she goes so she never misses an opportunity to read a few pages. Always looking for a happily ever after, Lacey is passionate about contemporary romance novels and enjoys it further when you mix in a little suspense. She resides in a small town in Illinois with her husband, two children, and a chocolate lab. Lacey loves watching NASCAR races, shooting guns, and should only consume one mixed drink because she's a lightweight.

Email: laceyblackwrites@gmail.com
Facebook: https://www.facebook.com/authorlaceyblack
Twitter: https://twitter.com/AuthLaceyBlack
Website: www.laceyblackbooks.com

Made in the USA
Middletown, DE
28 March 2020